Sea, Sand and, Katrina …

by

Sam Grant

Foreword

Author's first novel *"Atlantic Hijack,"* draws on author's professional seafaring experiences, in its narrative description of life aboard a cargo liner, in the nineteen-sixties.

Latest novel, **Sea, Sand and Katrina,** is set in contemporary time. Ben Sharpe, a former merchant navy officer, buys paddle steamer **Princess Katrina**, with an inheritance left to him by his Aunt Rose. He is married to Felicity, and they have three children. Caroline the eldest; then Patrick and Justin. Erica, Ben's mother joins the family aboard for Christmas, while her apartment is being re- decorated.

Author's merchant navy shipboard journey:

Relates to maritime novels – **Atlantic Hijack, River Escape** and **Chilling Encounter by Sam Grant**

Amazon.com/author/grantsam

M/V Shaftesbury, was a five-cargo hold, general cargo passenger liner*, which would carry a full cargo, to discharge at Montevideo and Buenos Aires. Return to UK, with a full cargo. Mainly, wool, cotton, grain, but also cases of corn beef, and tinned fruit; bulk quantities of sorghum, linseed and sunflower seed, onions, and cattle animal product, which supplied British industry. A few passengers aboard, for the three-week voyage, outward and homeward trip. This variety of vessel features in action, mystery novel **Atlantic Hijack** by Sam Grant

A four-year, deck apprenticeship (less, sea school remission) led to sea service, for author, aboard firstly, cargo liner, **M/V Shaftesbury** * *(general passenger, cargo liner);* **M/V Joya McCance;** *(ore carrier);* **M/V Imperial Transport** *(formerly, refined oil carrier); and* **S/V Royston Grange** *(refrigerated passenger cargo liner).*

Latterly, in deck officer role – **S/V Beauval** *(bulk oil tanker – chartered to Shell);* **M/V St Merriel** *(general passenger cargo liner) and* **M/V Mabel Warwick** *(ore carrier)*

Aboard, **M/V Shaftesbury,** on departure, the ship's carpenter (Chippy), was responsible for battening down and wedging, the five cargo holds. We two apprentices, assigned by First Mate H Anstis, assisted to secure, each hold, to resist Atlantic rollers, that would break, mainly on the foredeck, before the ship reached quieter tropical seas.

Each hold was covered with wooden hatches, supported by metal beams; covered with two light weight tarpaulins (tarps) and a final heavy duty outer tarpaulin. Tarpaulins, tucked into cleats, at edges, with metal battens between tarpaulin and cleats.

Wooden wedges, hammered in to cleats, by we apprentices, and Chippy. Aligned, so that the wide wedge end would meet wave break on deck, and to force wedges, further into cleats.

Metal locking bars, reached across tops of holds, clamping down these fabric canvas tarps, to prevent crash of waves and howling wind, from ripping away the canvas.

Robbie, a ship's carpenter character, in this novel, *Sea, Sand and Katrina,* is partly created from author's sea-going experiences and memory. Also, recall of a skilled carpenter friend, of author's father. Childhood experiences, recalled from young life into teenager years, of crewing aboard, National Redwings, twelve-foot dinghies, catamarans, and cruisers.

Paddle Steamer *Princess Elizabeth,* was moored in Torquay's outer harbour, before author was accepted for pre- sea training (1960-62) and captivated, author's imagination at the time. After following the restoration of Paddle Steamer *Waverly,* author conceived idea, for *Sea, Sand and Katrina*. A novel about a family who live aboard a paddle steamer.

Three brothers, students at author's second school, did live aboard an old-fashioned motor yacht. A bow sprit. Varnished panelled cabin accommodation, and a grey/green funnel midships, gave out a vision of sea adventure.

After service aboard ore carrier *M/V Joya McCance,* author, attended, a mid- apprenticeship release course, which followed with, a six-month trip on American coast, aboard *M/V Imperial Transport.*

River Escape, (action, novel mystery) Authors, second maritime novel, draws for professional shipboard description, from author's service aboard *M/V Imperial Transport.*

Similarly, third maritime novel *Chilling Encounter,* takes from sea service experience aboard refrigerated passenger cargo liner *S/V Royston Grange,* and trips to Lagos and west Africa ports, aboard other vessels.

Latest novel, *Sea, Sand and Katrina,* incorporates author's sailing and yacht club background from young life with professional sea- going life experience, which followed on. This latest novel followed a screen script writing, in 2023, by author for *Chilling Encounter* by Sam Grant (Sam Grant, a pseudonym adopted by author while writing commentary on articles in the New York Times)

Bayonne New Jersey became, authors adopted home port when *M/V Imperial Transport* was on contract to the Metropolitan Oil Company of New York, to deliver oil from Venezuela and Mexico for six months.

Author, regularly travelled on a Greyhound bus, which stopped in Times Square, New York, whenever leave was available. Aged eighteen, at the time, author was impressed at how welcoming and friendly the American people were to a British youngster from a British seaside town.

Chapter 1

A carousel's melody filled the air, above generator noise, that emphasised a fun fair was in town. Specifically, it straddled the water front. Brightly, coloured stalls, and attractions, pitched along a harbour road to the car park.

High mounted, two-tiered accommodation, twin funnelled, Princess Katrina, was visible in the outer harbour. Moored, to black buoys at bow and stern. Yellow, gold, paint streaks, radiated from paddle boxes that described the vessels propulsion mode.

Rescued from the scrappers by Benjamin Sharpe. Tiny flags, mainly red, white, and blue, interspersed, with an occasional union jack, left from a jubilee celebration, ranged from forward mast, to an enclosed upper wheelhouse. Absent from both funnels, but continued across, to the after mast and down to meet a red ensign, which flew at the stern. Flags, flown to recommend the regatta season as much as the fair's arrival in town.

It was well past midday and Benjamin, having completed a postal delivery, was sat in the wheelhouse, after he'd sculled the steamers second-dinghy, from slipway to paddle steamer. He ate cheese and pickle sandwiches and waited for a kettle, powered by Calor gas to boil. Sandwiches, intended for a mid-morning break, which he abandoned, to visit council offices to pay a mooring fee. Felicity, his wife was at work, a supply teacher. There were three children, at school. Caroline, would arrive back before Felicity collected Justin and Patrick, for the return to Princess Katrina.

Importantly, an up-to-date boiler inspection, with safety pass was needed, before Princess Katrina could move toward being operationally seaworthy and not just another interesting vessel, moored in the harbour.

Yes, Ben, did have reservations about a house sale, which was part of a bequest to him from Aunt Rose. After all, he had a family to support and was no longer attached to a ship as Second Mate. Free, from shipboard attendance and now independent in his life plans. It was still touch and go, the process of making Princess Katrina seaworthy once more. Previously, to the boiler inspection she had been dry docked and to meet safety requirements, metal plates were welded across the stern.

A solitary tug, towed the paddle steamer around the coast. Ben, viewed the situation, from the bridge, while he checked any extreme course deviation, with the ship's wheel. Part of work needed to get Princess Katrina properly seaworthy could be seen from the wheelhouse. Stove in deck timbers were tarpaulined.

'Where are you daddy?' The voice of his eldest daughter penetrated his slumber. Ben, used to claim that he never slept in the afternoon. Intention was to work, on maintenance, to bring Princess Katrina back to her former glory. But fell asleep, after he downed a second mug of tea. Within seconds he was up from the wheelhouse chair and on the bridge.

He gave a wave, to Caroline who was sat, on the jetty wall, holding her school bag. With both oars, in the rowlocks of the dinghy, he was soon skimming toward the slipway.

Caroline, the eldest at twelve, smiled, and grabbed the painter flung from the bow as the dinghy slid alongside the slipway. The tide was out, which exposed rubber fenders around the slipway end. This allowed Caroline to bring the pram dinghy alongside.

'I won't tell mother, that you were asleep.'

'I wasn't.'

'You were. I can see into the wheelhouse, from the top tier.' Caroline pointed behind at a railing, which circled the car parks highest tier.

'Dad, you were slumped in the chair.'

'Just forty winks. Your mother doesn't have to get up at four in the morning.'

'I know, but I need to get back on board, and the only way is in the dinghy.' Sensible and practical, and at an age where she found that, although her parents talked about doing things correctly, they didn't always follow through with their own actions.

'You said that we could go to the fun fair at the weekend.' Caroline coiled the painter and threw it back into the bow, once her father had taken hold of a rubber fender. She deftly stepped from slipway, into the pram dinghy and on to the stern floorboards. No mean feat, itself. Six months of living aboard paddle steamer Princess Katrina had given all three children "sea legs," with regard, to boating activities. Caroline, aged twelve, was a strong swimmer.

'I'll need to pass it by your mother,' replied her father as he prodded the slipway with an oar, to swing the dinghy away, for the row back.

'Won't we go as a family?'

'Caroline, your mother's been at school and might want a rest.' Ben was feathering the oars as he made the dinghy skim across the harbour.

'I've been at school, all week, as well'. Ben didn't pick up on this. o keep control of children in a class, where several might be, both energetic and vocal like his daughter, he appreciated, could be a demanding and exhausting experience for wife Felicity or any teacher, for that matter.

'We'll see when your mother's back with Justin and Patrick. How was school?'

'Not good it's Thursday.'

'You don't like Thursdays?' A honking came from the harbour master's launch. Ben stopped rowing and waved in acknowledgement, before Caroline replied.

'Only, the first Thursday of the month. We've to attend and listen to the school end of term show rehearsal. It's the same people, in everything at that school.'

'Did you want to be in the show.'

'No, you know I didn't.'

'Well, it doesn't matter, does it?' Caroline didn't respond to this, but said, 'Mother said that, you'll need to start the generator to charge up batteries on devices.'

'Yes, I'm on to it,' Ben replied. Caroline was twelve and at an age when she gave support to her mother's mission in life to get domestic situations, resolved with a father prod, when Felicity was absent. After Ben shipped oars and Caroline had hold of the paddle steamers gangway his phone buzzed.

'Ben, don't forget there's a grocery delivery due, about four thirty.'

'Yes, on to it. Just getting Caroline aboard, from school.' Ben was in hen pecked territory, but wouldn't have it any other way.

'Won't be back before five. There's an after-school meeting.'

'Okay, no problem,' said Ben. We'll look out for you. What about Justin and Patrick?'

'They're staying with Ann. I'll pick them up on my way back.' Ann being Felicity's friend, who was also a parent at the same school.

'Okay, bye for now,' said Ben. Caroline was now at the top of the gangway and called back,

'Generator dad.'

Chapter 2

An intention was to get Princess Katrina sea-worthy and able to take passengers on trips. Very much a dream scenario, where a window of opportunity ran from about April, through to mid or late September. Ben was not an engineer, but hoped to enlist help from friends with qualifications and skills to overhaul parts of the engine and replace where necessary.

The tide had risen on to the slipway by the time Felicity arrived with their other children, Justin, and Patrick, who were spaced at two-year intervals, after Caroline. Two trips from steamer to shore were required, because their online grocery delivery arrived, as Ben came alongside for the remainder of his family to embark. It was fortunate that Felicity was there to reassure a slightly bemused driver that the delivery was for them and he was not left, to face an empty slipway, with no actual house.

It wasn't a regular event, but with both working, it made sense to manage domestic activities, and make time available to be with Caroline, Justin, and Patrick. Although all three children could swim it was compulsory to wear lifejackets if they wanted to play outside on the decks, around the accommodation housing. On arrival back onboard Patrick the elder of the two boys, said,

'We want to build a race track along the deck.'

'Well, you'll need to wear your lifejackets,' his mother, replied.

'Everyone at school says they want to swap places and live on a paddle steamer, but I tell them they wouldn't if they had to wear lifejackets.'

'I don't mind,' said Justin. 'It's better than being in the class room. I like my cabin better than the small bedroom at the house with no cars going by at night.'

'I'm glad one of you approves,' said Felicity. 'Where's Caroline?' Ben, was about to get back aboard the dinghy to fetch the groceries.

'In the wheelhouse. Receptions much improved up there, I've been informed.'

'She needs to get ready to join her sailing class, at five thirty.' It was convenient that the paddle steamer was moored five minutes away from the clubhouse, which jutted out from the main pier. Five cadet boats were provided by the club and another three were bought for the children by their parents. It was the intention that they should form a cadet boat group, for competitive races. First basic skills needed to be learnt about handling craft and rules like those who are sailing on a port tack, give way to those on starboard. Today, each helmsman and crew were being taught how to right a capsized boat. This would require a deliberate capsize of a cadet boat. Once in the water, crew and helmsman would keep hold of the capsized boat and attempt to pull on the drop board, to refloat it. In actual race conditions, the race would likely be over. Time taken baling, would allow other contestants to be too far in front, to catch. A rescue guard boat near, to offer, assistance. After minutes in the relatively cold water both crew and helmsman taken aboard and their cadet towed back to harbour. With proficient helmsman and crew, a speedy, bale out of surplus water could lead to being under sail again. Speed, gathered under sail, allowing a self-draining mechanism to clear water. Experts, agile in art of capsize retrieval, known to continue in the race.

In the circumstances those aboard Princess Katrina had a good view of the cadet capsize training, which took place inside the harbour wall, not far from the mooring. Television reception was quite good, in that an aerial was attached to the top of the funnel but all three children had phones and activity on these for Patrick and Justin was of more interest. Felicity kept a close watch on Caroline and her friend Abigail, who agreed to crew for the practice capsize. She need not have worried since they were first to right Caroline's cadet.

Felicity, wanted to catch up on lesson planning for the month ahead and the deal was that provided, the grocery delivery was stashed away in lockers, the children fed and the two boys were settled in bed then Ben could visit the yacht club that Thursday evening. With a tide advanced to nearly the top of the jetty, there was further to row the dinghy, but less distance to wheel it to the stand at the top, away from the water. Once Justin and Patrick were settled, and Caroline brought back aboard, from her cadet training Ben was able to finally get ashore and padlock dinghy and oars in the galvanized stand at the top of the slipway before he walked across to mount the railed concrete steps, which led into the yacht club. Darkness, allowed Berry Head lighthouse to mark its presence with bleeps of light. Ben counted, one, and, two, and, three, and, four, before a second light bleeped Fifteen seconds elapsed before the sequence would start again. He did not as frequently watch and check lighthouse signals as before. Years of bridge watch keeping, had instilled, you might say, a reflex action to count time light spaces, to match, in his mind, a chart registered lighthouse.

A cheer came from the clubhouse, where a darts match was in progress. A last bastion of pub-like atmosphere held together by members who shared a love of sailing. Yes, there were arm chair sailors, like football supporters, forever analysing what went wrong for participants in individual races, but members were there, to escape a work treadmill, in most cases, in one shape or form.

'Ben's ashore folks.' It was Ollie. These two went back. A call Ollie would have made to Ben when he returned from south America or other distant part years ago. Living aboard Princess Katrina was not deep sea, but Ollie did have it right in that he was ashore, albeit from the steamer moored in the harbour.

'When are we going on a booze cruise? Me and the lads, that is?'

'Never replied Ben.'

'Marriage has made you meaner. Not that we're blaming Flick. Warned her about you, back in the day, didn't we? He turned to seek affirmation from the group.

'Come on Ollie. You're not like marriage counsellor extraordinaire? Leave Ben alone,' said Liz Bowers. The group were both sat and stood near a main window, which showed outside a liquid black bay, with occasional lights. Four persons, which included Liz and Emily, were sat around the table.

'How's the restoration work going? Harry Sturges, cheer leader, for Ben and his off-grid like way off life, returned with a drinks tray.

'Progressing,' said Ben. Glad, to receive a more positive reception from Harry.

'We've started a kitty,' said Liz. It's fifteen pounds, on the app, but we'll let you off with ten. You only drink halves of lager.

'What's that supposed to mean?' Questioned Ollie, who held a half full pint mug.

'If the cap fits,' said Liz. 'Ben can only stay until nine- thirty, isn't that right Ben?'

'Can't really stay any later. Got a four a clock start.'

'Don't know how you do it,' said Leo.

'Well work is a foreign country to you Leo. Let's be honest,' said Emily.

Leo worked in his father's business and did seem to have an inordinate amount of free time.

'Untrue, I have to man counters, with staff shortages.' Leo's father owned a sea front business which sold beach equipment, of the bucket, spade, and lido category, but a major part of the business was the sale fish and chips, ice cream, coffees, cake, soft and fizzy drinks, plus takeaway sandwiches. An amusement arcade also contributed to the coffers.

'Poor little you,' replied Emily.

'Break it up you two,' said Liz and turned to Ben,

'How's Flick and family?'

'Fine. Felicity's up to her ears in school marking at present. Kids hope are asleep.' Ben removed his phone and transferred ten pounds stipulated by Liz to the kitty app.

'It's through Liz,' he said.

'What are you having then Ben? Asked Harry, who seemed to have taken charge of ordering and fetching from the bar.

'The usual half of Stella, Harry.' Although Emily made comments about Leo's employment status, it was more to get his attention than annoy. It did seem to work, since they were sat together chatting on the best of terms.

'Won't be a mo. Ben, I've met a guy who knows about boilers and steam and all that jazz,' said Harry.

'Oh right,' said Ben. There was a "positive," coming out of this yachtie group. No longer focused so much, in Ben and Felicity's social life.

'Good to know that Harry,' said Ben. He had never been, you might say a main stay of the group, since they all stayed in the town and he went away to sea. Now, more an outsider with responsibilities for family life, as were others, but this group remained much the same, from days gone by. It was for Ben, at any rate, a form of networking, where others knew about yachts and had connections.

'You said that you'd invite us aboard,' said Emily. That was a difficult question for Ben to answer. He wasn't averse to having you might say a boat warming party, but Felicity valued privacy and didn't want personal space invaded by anyone, at that point. She made clear to Ben that was the case, when he suggested the idea.

'Too much of a mess Emily.'

'Didn't know that you were house proud or should I say paddle steamer proud.'

Liz saved the discussion by saying,

'Don't expect Ben makes those sorts of domestic decisions, if I know Flick.'

'No, no.' Ben tried to rescue the situation,

'It really is about the state of things aboard. Some of the planking on the main deck needs replacing and well, there are health and safety issues. Hope to get things sorted next season, Emily.' At which point Harry returned from the bar.

'One half of Stella for paddle boat Bennie. Didn't know that I was a sea poet, did you?' He said as he placed the glass on the table in front of Ben.

'We still don't,' said Freddie who had re-joined the group. Freddie was

13

the one, who Ben felt he could trust to be there for him, in time of trouble. They met up when he returned from sea and Freddie had been to sea school, although he later joined his father's accountancy firm and did have a willingness to understand and emphasise about the life of a former seafarer. The others were very much embedded, in a culture that embodied being a member of a yacht club. Light hearted banter, with no ill intent, from a group who stuck together under the banner of membership. No denial in that they were a privileged section of society, but social groups form around activities and for all the privilege associated with yacht club membership it was a sporting activity. Prowess and achievement, in yacht racing, came from sports men and women in all walks of life. Fancy racing yacht ownership, was no prediction of race or sailing mastery, in its owner.

'We'll have to leave you,' said Liz, who was part owner of a cruiser and tended to carry sway over the group.

'There's a gig at the Burlington. You can have what remains in the pot. Liz and Emily were single and the Burlington offered opportunity to meet like-minded souls, who enjoyed rock bands and associated buzz.

'Have to go Leo,' said Emily. There was no denying Leo was besotted with Emily. No one else would be able to question his work status and get away with it. Emily kept him hanging on. The group understood that it was a will they? won't they? situation which played out between the two. Children following from any relationship, not a given. Both valued their social life, but it was a relationship that might make a step change into marriage. Provided that Leo, in his besotted capacity accepted that Emily's falling in love moment arrived when she first saw her reflection in the mirror.

Freddie and Ben walked across to the bar to chat away from the group.

'Is it still ten-thirty closing, Jock?'

'You'll be kidding me, if you're not knowing that, sir.' Jock wore a double-breasted gold buttoned stewards coat and gold epaulettes. He towered over Freddie, who received an amused, reprimanding smile. Jock picked out a wine glass from a bowl out of view behind the bar.

Chapter 3

'Never saw you settling ashore Ben. Don't you miss getting away?' Asked Freddie. Excitement of new places? Meeting new people? It's the same old crew here.'

'You could say there's something reassuring about that. I mean being with the same group. Although in the past it never troubled me moving from ship to ship.' Ben and Freddie, after glass refills, walked to sit in a pair of easy chairs.

'Cannot for the life of me see how you won Flick around to life on a paddle steamer that you rescued. Looks like a bottomless pit to me.'

'Why are you throwing negatives at me Freddie? Jealousy, is it?'

'You've gotta be joking. I'm here for you Ben. I mean there could be a story in this for Devon Daily, after all.' Freddie had recently moved from roving journalist to deputy editor. Like certain promotions in business, it was not unrelated to family connections. The fact, that his Uncle Sam Bradstone owned a printing group.

'That makes me newsworthy and worthy of consideration, then.'

'You know I don't mean that. We go back. I mean you're going through a phase, Ben. Like you're still sleeping aboard a ship while in due course you'll come to your senses and want to live in a place with bricks and mortars. Like normal everyday people.'

'Is that what you call yourself?'

'And when are you going to find something more in tune with your background?' 'My background being?' Asked Ben.

'Well middle class and with a career future. You could do more than...'

'Work in the delivery business? Is that what you mean? It puts bread on the table and that is a priority. Isn't it? Ben didn't follow up by saying that it was alright for Freddie with family connections, although there was a factual difference from Freddie, who went from sea school to working ashore. Dispute over what Ben should do with his working life ended with a mobile call. It was Felicity.

'I'm on my way.' He replied to Felicity's enquiry of,

'Do you know what time it is?' Ben was under orders after that call.

'Got to go Freddie.'

'Just need a word with Harry.' Harry was in a queue at the bar. The clubhouse had filled up with older members who congregated around the bar area, which kept Jock busy. Ben, walked across.

'Harry, that guy you said knows about boilers,' Ben called out to be heard above the chatter around the bar area.

'Sure Ben, he's at the yacht chandler. You know, up from the second slipway, and under the car park. Ask for Jamie. He's there most days. You on your way?'

'I have had the call.'

'Say, hello to Flick for me. If she wants to get back into racing, I could do with an extra crew for Wednesday evenings?'

'Unlikely Harry, but I'll mention it. See you about.'

Harbour light, caught on the red leaded dinghy's underside, dampened by drizzle, as Ben approached the slipway, after leaving the club room bar. Seaweed stench, accentuated from rain on sun warmed concrete, drifted up from mussel and weed encrusted pillars. Pillars which supported two reinforced concrete slips, adjacent to each other. Constructed, during World War Two, when manoeuvres with naval landing craft took place. Today, they housed dinghy tenders for harbour pleasure craft and for the wheeled launch of both motor and sail boats into and out of the harbour. Savvy yachtsman kept their boats on launch trolleys. Whereas, visitors dipped road trailers, which carried speed boats into the water, and floated them away, which invited salt and rust damage to bearings.

After release of the chain which secured dinghy and oars to a slipway cradle, Ben wheeled his dinghy down to the waters' edge before deftly stepping aboard. Stood, with legs astride the middle thwart he held an oar by its blade to push the pram dinghy into deeper water.

Harbour lights, danced across, inky black water around the dinghy as Ben rowed back to Princess Katrina. Worn paintwork, hull rust and overall neglect, no longer so prominent under canopy of night. In the dark, imagination, could envisage for Ben a re-vitalized appearance. An auxiliary generator hum could be heard as he approached the paddle steamer. A light was on in the wheelhouse, which had become de facto – dual lounge and bedroom, while renovation work progressed, in the vessel's cabin and restaurant space. Felicity's face appeared, and disappeared, at a window, with recognition of his approach.

Apart from the sound of water licking, on the sides of fibre glass yachts, and occasional rigging rattle, it was still. Once alongside, he attached twin wires with hooks from a main one. Winched the dinghy aboard and turned it face down on deck. Raised the gangway, with minimum noise to avoid wakening Caroline, Justin, and Patrick. All cabins had yale locks on their doors save for the wheelhouse sliding doors, which required opening with a silver key. It was ten fifteen, when Felicity called out to Ben.

'You don't have to make out your being quiet I'm still awake.' Floodlights on deck shone in and the bedside light gave light to read by. On a shelf, under the wheelhouse windows, an array of battery lights were kept charged for emergencies. Felicity insisted that venetian blinds were fitted above the five windows that ran across the wheelhouse. These were lowered. For the generator to run efficiently, at least eight lights needed to be lit. Twin deck floodlights, fore and aft, more than matched this quota.

'I worry about you getting enough sleep,' Felicity removed a bookmark. Placed it to where she was, and put the book on a twin stack of crates that served as a bedside table.

'I didn't know you cared that much,' said Ben.

'Do not be so bloody crass. I don't want you ill!' Felicity, was never slow to make her opinion known, when she felt her husband failed to face reality.

'It's not that late,' and Harry's found a boiler and steam expert. 'It was worth a visit.'

'There's so much that needs putting right Ben. It's not just about the engine and boiler. I'm wondering how the children will react as they get older.'

'Have they been complaining?'

'Caroline, will be getting to an age where she identifies with her peer group and well, won't want to be different. I can understand that.'

'Wouldn't that happen anyway? Parents can just be seen as wanting, alongside their perfect parent model.'

One of two public toilets, on the upper deck had been converted to a family bathroom. Felicity insisted that this alteration was made, together with other modifications before she agreed on the move from a rented chalet. Ben departed to brush his teeth and prepare for sleep. Felicity had turned off the bedside light and when Ben switched the flood lights off, the generator switched itself off.

When he returned to the wheelhouse, come bedroom, Felicity's book had slipped to the floor and she was asleep. He picked the book up. It was three men on a boat by Jerome K Jerome. Felicity was maybe researching information about a boating life. He placed the book on the top of the crate. Kissed Felicity gently on the cheek, so as not to wake her. Set the alarm on his phone, and placed it on the floor by his side of the bed and was asleep in minutes.

Chapter 4

Ben's mother was due a visit. Well, she deemed it necessary to give moral support to daughter-in-law, Felicity and, of course to see her grandchildren. Erica, a name inherited from a Norwegian grandmother. A family, that were not keen for her to exchange their Nordic surname Larsen for Sharpe. It was felt the name Sharpe did not match the prestige of that of Larsen. John Sharpe, Ben's father, now passed on, first met Erica when engine failure delayed his ship in Oslo. A relationship developed after he met Erica while she assisted her shipping agent father.

That Saturday, following on from Ben's visit to the yacht club, he brought his family ashore in a boat dinghy. Launched, from forward davits on the port side of Princess Katrina. An altogether more substantial ferry boat than the pram dinghy, with forward housing and outboard motor. Forward housing, offered shelter, should it rain and it more comfortably accommodated the family. It was unlikely, that his mother would board Princess Katrina today, but it was made clear that she would only travel in the ferry boat and not the pram. Erica, was amazed, at the time, of Ben and Felicity getting together. That a woman existed on the planet who would partner her son. Sympathies rested with Felicity. Ben's enthusiasm for Princess Katrina meant that there was more than a possibility that the paddle steamer could make demands on his time, that overlapped those of wife and family. Erica was concerned that Felicity should be supported wherever possible and not allowed to be restricted. It was that mother and daughter in law shared an empathy and understanding, which was effectively a management role, regarding, the handling of Ben by mother and wife.

Erica, was not sure that being seen aboard a paddle steamer would add any value to her social standing and made pre-conditions that facilities aboard were improved. One, was the conversion of the woman's public toilet into a bathroom facility. Also, that a section of the forward decking was repaired. The bathroom facility was achieved but the decking area was still cordoned off and tarpaulined, much in the same way as road workings necessitate barriers, to protect passing motorists. Ben was not in a hurry to repair the decking and have his mother aboard. Or give priority toward accommodation improvement over that of first making Katrina seaworthy.

The Sharpe family met, as planned with Erica on Saturday, for ten thirty, at Macari's, an Italian Gelateria ice cream café, in the street, occupied with fairground stalls and rides.

Erica, greeted the family as Ben, Felicity and children arrived. Background noise from the fair outside, penetrated through the café window. A deal was agreed with the children that a visit would follow afterwards. Patrick and Justin, were keen on a meet up with their gran. Caroline less so. Ben was keen to contact Jamie, the boiler expert, recommended to him, by Harry, at the yacht club.

Erica, found that her grandsons were more attentive to her. She came from a family of three sisters and found grandsons to be less critical and respectful toward her than members of her own sex. She would, however vehemently disown any idea that she favoured her grandsons over Caroline. Justin and Patrick studied a list of ice cream delights listed on the board behind the counter, after a table was found.

'I do like your pinafore dress,' said Erica.

'It's nothing special. How are you managing with your new apartment Erica?'

Caroline, meanwhile had steered her father to where Justin and Patrick were stood. The family group had the café mainly to themselves, save for a few visitors seated near to the serving bar.

'It's perfect, and overlooks the bay, but it will have to be redecorated. The wall paper in the lounge is a disgusting orange and red. I have an appointment with a decorator later.' Unexpectedly she asked,

'You do have your own account?' Erica, was elegantly dressed, in a blue trouser suit, and reached down to remove a green leather handbag from within a floral raffia shopping basket.

'Yes,' replied Felicity, wondering where this was going.

'Here,' Erica said, while Ben was with the children. She took a cheque from her handbag and handed it to Felicity,

'A little something to help.'

'That's very kind of you Erica.' Felicity placed it in her handbag, noticing it was for fifty pounds.

'I know my son and he'll likely prioritize his obsession with that clapped out old paddle steamer rather than his family.' Felicity smiled. They never asked for help, but unlike Erica she was a keen yachtswoman. Sailing, for her, was on hold to an extent, and was enthusiastic for Caroline to be part of a local sailing community. To share in her successes. Patrick and Justin were more in the mould of their father, who sailed, but saw sail racing as one of several interests. Most recently, the acquisition of Princess Katrina, more than an interest, for Ben. There were plenty of outgoings, like a recent purchase of school uniforms, although they no longer had to find monthly rent. Caroline walked over to the window table where her mother and granny were sat.

'Granny, would you like anything with your coffee?' Caroline, sent over, with instruction from her father, which was,

"Keep granny sweet Caroline. See if she'd like anything more than a coffee.

'No, I'm perfectly alright Caroline,' said Erica.

'Tell, your father I'll have a latte Caroline,' said her mother.

'I think he's already ordered one for you"

'Looks like I don't have a choice,' Felicity said, smiling at Erica.

'That's what you usually have isn't it?' Caroline, unwilling to let blame lie with her father.

'And anyway, we don't want to be in here all morning.' Caroline, returned to the counter. Erica smiled.

'You have competition in the organizational stakes, Felicity.'

'She's a daddy's girl,' you mean said Felicity.

'It's to be expected, with you having the boys, Justin and Patrick,' said Erica, who could cause friction, when she felt her son was not giving her the right kind of attention.

After crucial decisions were made, over flavours of ice cream; namely, mint chocolate chip for Caroline, and chocolate fudge for Justin and Patrick, Ben, carried a coffee tray over to where Felicity and Erica were sat.

'Granny, are you going on the dodgems?' Asked Patrick.

'You said they're your favourite,' Justin joined in. To which Felicity replied,

'Your Granny will probably be quite happy to watch you two, I expect.' Erica, returned her coffee cup to its saucer.

'Felicity, my dear you just complained about my son making decisions for you.

I might just be tempted you never know.'

'Can I be in your car if we do?' asked Justin.

'That, you will live to regret,' said Ben.

'Passed first time. My driving test that is. Your father needed two goes.'

'First time he nearly knocked a cyclist over didn't you dear?'

'Moving quickly on. I've got to see a man about the boiler.'

'Did you really father?' Asked Caroline who had returned from the front window, where she got a better view of the fairground.

'Your father passed. That's all that matters,' said Felicity, keen not to let Erica rile Ben. They were sat around the table when Erica asked,

'How's school?' A question directed at her daughter-in-law.

'School's off limits,' said Ben, who was sat next to Felicity. The children looked up from eating ice creams, but returned on realization that the question wasn't directed at them.

'It's much the same granny.' It works well now that we're all together,' said Felicity. Caroline was less satisfied with her mother's explanation.

'It's alright for you,' but we're the only children in the school that has their mother as a teacher.' Justin and Patrick were too engrossed in their ice creams to give the idea much consideration. Erica, did not agree with her grand-daughter's observation.

'I would think it might have advantages educationally.'

'I get far more feedback from other teachers than most parents do, if that's what you mean?' Can we move on to the here and now.' She turned to Ben.'

'Are we having the pleasure of your company at the fair?'

'Yes,' said Caroline, before Ben could answer either way.

'Oh, you have a spokesperson,' she said with a smile.

'For a while, but would like to pop over to see the Yacht Chandlers, later on,' said Ben.

'Can I come father?' Asked Patrick.

'Your father wants to talk to a man about boiler maintenance, isn't that, right?'

'That's true. Not that interesting Patrick. Granny will probably want a partner on the dodgems.'

'Hold your horses,' said Erica. I've yet to make that decision.'

'There's a ride called the Energizer, granny' Caroline, joined in. 'You just have to sit down.'

'And no doubt get thrown everywhere when it starts,' said Erica.

'Not sure I'd feel energized after that.'

The fair, beckoned, it seemed, when a group of youngsters opened the café door, and the cry of "pay on the ride,' could be heard above a music song mix, and fairground hubbub. Other family groups walked in and within minutes a customer queue developed by the café's counter.

'This coffee's not overly hot,' Felicity said, after she'd investigated Ben's empty cup. Resolved that a start on the fairground experience should be made, she continued,

'You three can take your ice creams with you.' If you're ready to go that is Erica?'

'Be with you in a minute,' just need to powder my nose,' replied Erica.

Chapter 5

'Watch out,' Felicity reached out to pull Justin back when a seagull swooped down toward his ice cream. They'd stepped out beyond the canopy of the coffee shop on to the road, and Justin was occupied in navigating covered, fairground cables that ran into the road to power ride attractions. He was also the smallest of the three children with an ice cream. To avoid the incident developing into a scary place, Ben distracted from the shock with,

'Chocolate fudge must be the seagulls favourite.'

'They don't have favourite ice creams,' said Justin.

'No, perhaps not but yours might have been the best, because there's more left,' said Felicity, who luckily was immediately at her youngest son's side to forestall the attack. Caroline who felt a need to contribute to seagull understanding, said,

'There's a video clip of a seagull that walks into a shop to snatch a bag of Doritos and it always takes the same flavour. Perhaps Chocolate Fudge was that seagull's favourite flavour?' Erica, who was walking on the other side of Felicity, and came over, in part to calm the situation, was unexpectedly confronted by Justin with,

'Will you go on the dodgems with me granny?'

'I'm not sure granny is dressed for the part,' said Felicity. Erica's smart trouser suit, suggested that there were no plans to go on fairground rides.

'I'll be the smartest dressed dodgem rider then,' she said and put her arm around Justin, who was fast forgetting the seagull incident.

'Father's going in my dodgem, but I'm driving,' said Caroline.

'You will won't you daddy?'

'Don't you trust me in the driver's seat?' replied Ben.

'No, it's not that. But I'm older than Justin and I want to drive. That's all.' Not to upset her father, she said,

'You can be like the instructor though.'

'Thanks, Caroline,' said her father. Perhaps not that keen for participation, in the upcoming ride.

'That just leaves you and me Patrick.' Felicity turned to Patrick, who was at her side.

'You can drive mum. Caroline will drive like a maniac and you're a good driver.'

'And so is granny,' said Justin, who joined in. Not to be left out. Erica smiled benignly.

The dodgems, were in the main car park area. Upper floors were still open for cars but a wider space, which ran near to the slipways, held most of the mechanical rides.

A Ferris wheel dominated the harbourside venue. Persistent, hot dog aroma from a nearby stand wafted across and intermingled with seaweed exposed to air from a low tide. Next to a pong, from green threaded slipway seaweed. Diesel fumes from generators, could waft over. Competition was strong to be the dominant stench in the fairground.

A seasonal fair, competed with attraction of beach and sand on sunny days. This day was no exception. Rides were not that busy. A fairground that didn't become alive until about five in the evening. A carousel was whirling around, with half a dozen riders, when the family made their way to the dodgems, in the centre of the ride area. Two pairs of youngsters ahead of them made the ride feasible, with five cars in action. Soon sparks were flying from the connector rods as each car attempted a circuit.

Caroline turned her car and collided with Patrick, which was expected by Patrick. While Erica in the main successfully steered Justin away from collision situations. The youngsters, ahead of them in the queue, were mainly concerned with colliding with one another and were warned by the dodgem minder, who grabbed on to passing cars, to tell them not to attempt head on smacks.

In what seemed all too short a time a high-pitched whine from the speaker signalled the end. Power was cut and car occupants lost steerage. Riders extricated themselves from cars dotted around the dodgem arena.

Next, the three adults were made to experience a ride on the Tea Cups. Large tea cups, as the name suggests, with interior seating. A sign signalled that they should not be twirled while in motion, but this did not prevent two elder children Caroline and Patrick doing just this with their parents. Afterwards it was only the children and Erica who ventured on to the carousel. Ben and Felicity watched from a distance as they revolved past.

'How near are we to making Katrina sea worthy, if you have the boiler tested and certified as fit Ben?' Asked Felicity. It was late September and they had to survive, is probably the word, a winter aboard Princess Katrina. It was, at that moment not as cold as expected and life was relatively peaceful with much less harbour activity during the season's end.

'Can't go anywhere until the forward decking is repaired?'

'And the public toilet facility is improved,' said Felicity, 'And then, there's the restaurant bar café, which means getting a licence and stocking up with drink.'

'You're placing obstacles in the way,' said Ben.

'No Ben, I'm being realistic.'

'We don't need to have a licence. I'm not sure that we should advertise any indication that we're running booze cruises.'

'What do you suggest then. Advertise that we serve cream teas?'

'No seriously Flick, that could be the draw. More family and pensioner orientated.'

'Not too many older passengers,' said Felicity, 'Or we might need a doctor on hand.'

'Okay, forward planning is alright, but the decking has to be repaired.' 'Your mother's said, she's not coming aboard until it's fixed.'

'I don't see that as a problem,' said Ben.'

'That's very unfair,' she's on her own and the children love having her around.'

'Okay, I've met up with a retired ships carpenter and he says he'll have a look at it.'

'Why haven't you told me before? That, sounds positive.'

'Didn't want to build up hopes. It's one thing having a look. Another, to doing the job.'

The carousel was near to a fairground burger bar, where sausages sizzled on a grill. In anticipation of the children, in particular Justin and Patrick, asking whether they could eat one of the delicacies on offer Felicity was ready with a diversionary tactic, when Patrick claimed, that he was famished.

'We can walk into town, if that's alright Erica, for some food?'

'Perfectly Felicity. I need to do some shopping. Perhaps, we could have lunch at the small bakery.'

'The one that smells of coffee beans. do you mean granny?' Asked Caroline.

'That's right, Caroline. It entices you in, don't you think? That roast coffee smell and seeing the coffee machine in the window.'

'Not straightaway, though, it's only ten-thirty.' said Felicity.

'Your father needs to see a man about the boilers on Princess Katrina. You won't be more than an hour, will you?' she turned to Ben.

'No, no, shouldn't think so. How about we all meet up at what's its name?'

'Tonkins,' said Caroline.

'Yes,'

'No later than twelve thirty,' said Felicity. Ben turned to Patrick.

'You can join me, if you like Patrick?' Patrick's face lit up at this. Justin and Caroline did not rate a visit to a yacht chandler, alongside that of going into town with their grandmother.

Chapter 6

The yacht chandler's, was tucked-in, beneath the upper deck of the tiered car park. A visitor aquarium occupied most of the remaining space plus a fishing trip and cruise vessel ticket office. There, Princess Katrina's cruise tickets would be available, next year, if everything went according to plan.

A window display featured, a red fibre glassed dinghy, with outboard motor, in one window and a sailing dinghy in full rig, in the other. A selection of yacht anchors and coiled drums of mooring ropes were dotted around both pram and dinghy. A strong stench of tarred rope hung around the store's entrance, but was less apparent once inside.

Galvanized and stainless, steel shackles of various sizes, rigging wires and connections were separated into waist level boxed display. Boat hooks were bracketed on to a stand near the entrance. On the right-hand side, a section, at the back was given over to sea anglers needs, which included rods, reels, floats, complete fishing sets, and clothing. Most of the floor space near the front racked with sea-going clothes like heavy grade sweaters, tee shirts, men's, and women's sail cloth trousers. Yellow waterproof tops and trousers, which gave off a strong, fresh plastic like, smell.

Patrick remained at the front of the store to look at a range of outboard motors set on stands. Ben, meanwhile walked over to the stores long wooden counter. Behind which, was a floor to ceiling file like display of small and larger labelled drawers. Storage for fishing lines, hooks, various nuts bolts and fitments especial to the needs of yachtsmen.

A bearded assistant in his mid-forties, was engrossed online, making entries. He gave Ben the curtesy of calling out.

'Be with you in a sec.' Ben, a not infrequent visitor to the chandlers was given good attention. A moment later he said,

'Yes, can I help you.' Fingers over keyboard, in readiness to tap in a code or search for a stock item.

'Oh hi, is Jamie in today. I mean could I speak with him? The assistant left his work station and walked across to the entrance, which led into the warehouse.

'Jamie,' there's a customer to see you.' A voice called back

'Right, right Alistair, I'll be out.' Alistair returned to his station and before he sat down said,

'Jamie will be with you in a moment, sir.'

'Thanks for that,' said Ben, who was browsing a catalogue from a stand on the desk.

Minutes later, Jamie walked out from within the stock room.

'And so, you're wanting to see me are you, then.' Jamie's blue overall coat was partly buttoned, with red shoulder length hair, and more progressive beard than the counter assistant. He placed a clipboard and pen on the desk.

'Yes, said Ben. He paused, due probably to an appreciation that he was meeting with a formidable character, through his direct manner of address.

'Harry informed me that you know about boilers.'

'I'm a qualified boiler engineer, if that's the person you're looking for. And what would be the vessel that needs attention then?'

'Princess Katrina.'

'Really? Would this paddle steamer be your beauty?'

'Yes. You like her?'

'Ah, when I saw her arrive, in the outer harbour, I said that's as fine example, as ever I've seen. And she'll be in want of as much attention below decks as above. Am I right about that?'

I need to get both boilers up to Lloyd's certification standard,' said Ben.

'A labour of love, for the both of us. I will need to inspect the boilers and give you a realistic assessment of the condition and we can go from there. It depends whether the boilers are sound. The pipes can be replaced. It does depend on the condition of the boilers, though. A large lottery win would be needed to cover their replacement. There you are, you fell in love, and nothing else matters. I can understand that. And you have funds?'

'I'm glad you see it that way. Funding is very much work in progress. I guess you wouldn't buy a car without seeing that the engine's in working order.

'But Princess Katrina's no car, she's a sea princess that needs to be given care and attention.' Patrick, returned to stand by his father.

'And how do you feel about living aboard Princess Katrina? Asked Jamie.

'I get teased at school, but they're jealous, I think.' Patrick paused.' Dad, can we have a Swiss Army knife? Patrick gave inclusiveness to the idea of owning one of these multi-purpose pocket knives, uncertain whether his father would run with buying one just for him.

'There, you see, your son is already looking toward the needs of Princess Katrina.'

'I'm not sure about that,' said Ben. When might you be able to have a look?'

'You do realize that should boilers need replacement; the funnels will need taking out and it will be a shipyard visit?'

'I'm hoping for less damage than that.'

'I'll certainly do an inspection to see how the integrity of the boiler stands up. I can do an inspection and we'll go from there. Let's see, I've a week off, next Monday. Tuesday morning. Any good?'

'Yes, yes, that's fine.

'I'm not sure a Swiss army knife will fix things though.' He smiled, at Patrick.

'But it's a useful piece of equipment.' This led Ben to walk across with Patrick to the angling display, where there was a cabinet of knives.

'You'll need for the cabinet to be unlocked,' said Jamie who followed them across. It was one of those ambiguous situations which worked to Patrick's advantage. Ben felt that he should make a purchase after the attention given to his enquiry by Jamie. A knife was bought, but with instructions from Ben, that it would be kept in a drawer in the wheelhouse, available for whenever it might be needed. Ben arranged to meet Jamie outside the

Chandlers for next Tuesday, at ten o'clock

'We'd better get a move on to meet up with everyone,' said Ben to Patrick. It was a twenty-minute walk from the harbour, up to the top end of town, where the café type restaurant was situated.

They walked on the pavement next to the funfair past the Burlington, now partly a venue for hire for Bingo or social events, and occasional rock band disco type venues. Once a popular ball room and dance hall. Days of glory remembered by a canopy across the front to shelter those queuing. Two globes, with clustered bulbs either side of a double doored entrance. Reached by steps, with ornate black wrought iron railings either side. Now with boards to advertise the visit of pop or rock groups, and a prominent notice to declare "Bingo on Wednesday." And a flea market for the first Saturday of every month.

A once vibrant holiday resort that retained memory of former glory with its now empty department shops, awaiting development. Ben and Patrick crossed over from the harbour to the Strand, which led up past a more recent shopping centre and central car park, at the upper area of the town and to the restaurant set within a bakery. An area, where when not occupied by estate agent's financial advisors and charity shops, supported bijoux gift, craft, and delicatessen retail outlets.

'It's like, Caroline said, I can smell coffee beans,' Patrick remarked to his father as they approached the restaurant or more aptly described bakery with café

'In Buenos Aires it was the smell of chocolate that was strongest in the main street I used to walk along,' replied his father.

'Did they have a fun fair? Asked Patrick.

'Not that I remember but there was a football ground which was surrounded by big rolls of barbed wire.'

'Why was that?'

'Excitable bunch. It was to prevent fights spilling out into the city if there was disagreement over the result.'

'There can be fights between supporters here,' said Patrick.

'The authorities were afraid of riots on a different scale near to the city. I think it was the Latin temperament. In the cinemas there was feet stamping and shouts if the film did not start on time or when there was a projector failure. A plus was that smoking was banned and most films were British or American with Spanish sub titles. One street had cinemas on both sides. There were always plenty of films to choose from.'

'But there is now dad. You can download any film you like with a subscription.' A realistic, bordering on adult observation of the situation.

'It's not the same as going to a theatre with a big screen. In the interval popular national singing groups performed for the cinema audience.'

'Do you think they still have cinemas like that?'

'Possibly not. They're probably getting films streamed just like here.' Patrick called out,

'There they are dad.' He pointed toward the bakery window, as they approached. There was a large table a little way in from the entrance with the family sat around it.

Chapter 7

Whether, the coffee roasting machine played a part in the actual running of the café side of things might have been a fiction. An aroma of roast coffee beans in the street outside was certainly a draw, for those who enjoyed coffee. Awninged space allowed for a few outside tables and chairs. A border collie was tied around the leg of one table and gave an occasional yelp to inform its owner of where it was. Inside meanwhile, the dog's owner stepped occasionally from out of the queue and waved to the dog, which responded with a whimpering sound and tail wag. This intrigued others, but probably annoyed occupants of a table next to the dog. Ben and Patrick walked through the door and over to where the family group were sat.

'You took your time,' said Felicity.' It was twelve thirty-five, which in the scheme of things a not bad approximation for twelve thirty, but Felicity considered the weekend, family time, and expected Ben to be with them. It was felt that Princess Katrina was on her moorings and they were ashore and needed to act like a normal family at the weekend. Erica, was after all Ben's mother and Felicity expected him to answer any off-field remarks Erica made with regard, to the feasibility of Katrina as a family home? Erica's daughter, Fredrika, three years younger than Ben was married to a bank manager and to Erica's way of thinking led an altogether more respectable life, with Fredrika and Bernard respected in the community. Bernard, her husband, a member of Rotary and a brother in the Masonic order, which, in Erica's estimation established their credentials, even further. Her father's role as shipping agent to prosperous Norwegian companies was perhaps a template, for her proclivity toward preferment for secure and dependable employment situations. Ben, her son, had diverted from a programme of career behaviour she admired in other family members. But this was attributed to rogue genes in her mother's antecedents, who related back to Viking ancestry. Not that she considered pillaging and looting to be excusable, but more that outlier behaviour in her son she felt more likely to have arrived through that female line.

'We've all decided what we're having,' Caroline said.

'Meals seem to revolve around chips as a main background,' interjected Erica. Ben was reserved a seat next to Felicity with Patrick sat on her left.

'Any success? Asked Felicity, once Ben had sat down and picked up the menu.

'He has the week off from Monday and is coming aboard on Tuesday, to do an inspection.'

'Does that mean we'll be able to go out into the bay. We could do some mackerel fishing, said Justin, who was a keen rod fisherman and teamed up with a school friend to fish off the harbour wall.

'It won't be as speedy as that, I'm afraid Justin,' said Ben.

'It's progress though,' said Felicity and gave a reassuring smile, as her husband leant forward to study a straightforward menu.

'Pasty chips and peas fits the bill for me and a coffee.' Said Ben.

'Can I have the same but with baked beans,' said Patrick. This visit to Tonkin's restaurant was for Ben, a first in recent times, but not the others, who had visited weekdays with their mother.

'I said father would have pasty and chips,' whispered Caroline.

'There are no prizes for guessing what your father would order,' said Felicity, who agreed with Caroline earlier when she suggested that his choice could well be pasty and chips.

'How about you Erica, What would you like?' Asked Felicity.

'Those packet sandwiches, that I spotted in the cabinet, on the way in, Felicity. I'll go for cheese and onion, if you don't mind, and a tea.'

'Caroline and Justin are having pizza and chips, and this time a bottle of water to share.

'That just leaves you Felicity,' said Erica.

'I'll join you Erica, but with a prawn mayo sandwich and coffee. Have you got that dear?' This was taken as a given, since Ben was on his feet.

'Caroline, go and help your father,' said Felicity. An instruction already in progress since Caroline was stood up ready to join her father to order. A counter which sold bread and pastries, but also took orders for meals in the restaurant area. It was filling up and they were lucky to get a double table for six.

'I really don't know how you manage with work, as well,' said Erica. Out of nowhere Justin said,

'The class said you can't be my mother,' piped in Justin.

'Is that because I look so young?'

'Don't be silly,' countered Patrick.

'In my class they say that I'm a spy for the teachers.'

'Are you?' Asked Felicity.

'No of course not. They're just trying to wind me up.'

'Your mother teaches you occasionally doesn't she Justin,' said Erica.

'I expect they have difficulty understanding at that age don't they Felicity?'

'That's right. Don't make too much of it, Justin, or they'll all want their mothers to come to school.' There was a pause for consideration by Patrick.

'Why did you come to teach at our school?' He asked in in an accusatory manner.

'To annoy you dear. No, it was teaching at Brandon Fields School or travelling into Newton Abbot. And that wouldn't have worked.

'I think all three of you are lucky that your mother is at your school.' Erica didn't elaborate but probably felt the school would be wary of anything untoward happening, which would immediately get back to Felicity, their mother.

'When are you going to visit us granny?' Asked Patrick. At which point Ben returned with Caroline.

'I'm very busy with my new flat, but...' Ben who caught the question said,

'When the decks repaired, you said didn't you mother? And that could be next week.' 'Really?' Enquired Felicity.

'Yes. I see no reason why Robbie, the ship's carpenter, I told you about, won't be able to get started. He's messaged to say that he can get timber easily enough.'

'Sounds optimistic,' said Felicity, who knew her husband was capable of exaggerating claims.

'Well, if that's the case it might be soon then Patrick,' replied Erica. With a move to a new flat there was enough going on in Erica's life to occupy day- to- day considerations. A stipulation, that essential improvements were needed before she stepped aboard forestalled, inevitable demands she knew her son would make once she was in his craw, so to speak! These being, to get everything up to a standard that female passengers would find acceptable.

After their order was brought to the table, for a while, it was quiet while everyone ate. Felicity asked Erica about when she was expecting the decorator to arrive for her flat.

'He's booked for two thirty. I'll need to get on my way shortly. You'll have to excuse me,' said Erica.

'When will we see you again granny? Asked Justin.

'Quite soon, Justin, I hope. You're welcome to visit now if you'd like to.' Erica, smiled and Felicity turned to Ben, who was studying a plan of the accommodation layout of Princess Katrina.

'Perhaps me and Caroline can visit your mother's flat, while you take the boys back?'

'I can go fishing with Danny,' exclaimed Justin, who was keen on rod fishing with his friend Danny. Danny was expert at casting out from the harbour wall and Justin hoped to improve his abilities.

'And you're working on the passenger cafeteria, Ben. Patrick, you can help your father.'

Before Ben had time to suggest otherwise, he was organized into going along with Felicity's plans.

Chapter 8

A box like cafeteria cabin had been built abaft the two funnels aboard Princess Katrina. For the sake of purity of design Ben would have knocked this build down and given it back to open deck space. It would have allowed for deck golf, quoits, and other imaginative deck sporting activities, but from the commercial aspect this was not an option, as Felicity was quick to point out. It was about age demographics and passengers were likely to be young and old. The cafeteria would also bring in revenue and offer shelter on rainy days.

The boat dinghy, launched from davits, on paddle steamer Princess Katrina, to take the family ashore, was a more substantial boat than the dinghy. It was of a light fibre class construction and able to be hauled up the slipway, with small wheels beneath to assist, like the pram. Chain padlocked from its bow to a ring bolt. On departure, from the slipway, a semi-ridged protective plastic cover, over the outboard motor, needed to be unlocked and stowed in the after locker. A rising tide meant that the dinghy was nearer to the water's edge than when they left.

Patrick, assisted his father to lift the dinghy up on its inset wheels, and jointly held its bow, before a splash release, into the harbour, before it was drawn, by its painter, to the walled side of the slipway. All three, would have got trainers wet, on a clamber aboard from the slipway. Ben held the dinghy alongside while Patrick and Justin hopped aboard.

While Bed attended to starting the outboard, an oar, was released, by Patrick, to ease the dinghy clear. A push of the starter button, released a low-level whine, and after a few seconds, its motor spluttered into life. Very soon all that remained was a plume of blue smoke, over the position occupied by the dinghy, which zipped past moored yachts on its way back to Princess Katrina.

'Can you take me to the harbour steps dad?' asked Justin, who was sat on the middle thwart facing his father, while Patrick was acting a s bowman.

'I need to get my rod and bag first.' Justin shouted to be heard across the throated roar from the outboard.

'Yes, but I want you back by the slipway for five. Patrick can pick you up with the pram.'

'Do I have to?' Asked Patrick.

'No, but you'll want the generator to run, I expect when we're aboard. We could make a deal around that.'

'That's like bribery,' Patrick replied.

'Let's just call it encouragement.' Ben throttled back, as they closed in on the gangway, raised well above water level.

Patrick, thrust the boat hook toward the gangway's platform, to drag it down to boat level. Ben, hoped, no potential thief, ever watched their technique for making the gangway available. Fellow boat owners, though were watchful during the day.

Patrick, who wasn't much interested in fishing, remained with Ben, but liked to keep an eye on his young brother. Justin, grabbed the gangways roped railing, and was soon shimmying up the aluminium treaded steps to deck level.

'Don't hang about Justin,' called out Patrick. It wasn't many minutes before Justin reappeared with fishing bag strapped around his shoulders plus fibre glass rod. He called out,

'Bet Danny's already landed some bass.' Ben reassured his youngest son with,

'Danny's been fishing longer than you and has had more practice. You'll get better.'

'If you catch some whiting bring them back for tea,' said his brother. Justin scrambled back into the boat.

'More likely it'll be pollock or bass from the harbour wall.' Ben gave encouragement.

'Whichever way you look at it, Justin, it's good practice casting,' said Ben, who recognized an independent streak in his youngest son. Although, he would have enjoyed a spot of fishing, understood that Justin liked to meet up with Danny and Felicity would complain if he gave time to sea fishing rather than cracking on with the refit! The harbour steps were a hundred yards across from Princess Katrina. Danny, who was enormously impressed with his friend's living accommodation waved to Justin from a vantage point above the pier, before he returned to make a cast out to sea over the harbour wall.

Ben expertly cut the engine, to allow a slowed down approach. Patrick reached out once more, with the boat hook, from the bow, to avoid a crunch into lower steps. Pressure was exerted against the harbour wall, to stall speed before Patric took hold of a ring bolt with the boat hook.

'Careful on those steps Justin,' said Ben. The tide hadn't covered, all green slime on the wall steps.

Justin was sure footed and managed to step across a spread of green weed on to a clear step and made his way to the top. A heavy stench of drying sea weed, mixed with bright green, occupied the area beneath the steps. Small groups of mussels, lower down.

'Ten to five, Justin. Make sure you're at the slipway by ten to five,' Patrick, called out. Justin, raised an arm but did not look backwards and disappeared, from view, when he reached the top.

Patrick, twisted the boat hook from the ring bolt and pushed the dinghy's bow away, away with it. A momentary throttle on the outboard, saw them glide back alongside Princess Katrina.

Once aboard, the diesel generator was started and power made available to give light and power in the restaurant area. Ben, previously prepared and white mask-taped wall frames. These ran from deckhead to deck. Designed, to mimic a boat's ribbed frames. They were to be stained light brown, to add a wood effect, with intervening bulkheads painted, a cream emulsion to lighten the space. Patrick and Ben both put on boiler suits, over day clothes. Tables and chairs, were previously stacked, and covered with a tarpaulin on deck.

The restaurant's planked deck, was machine sanded, and varnished twice, before a final varnish cover, mixed with fine sand to give grip. Port holes, at the start were opened, to release paint fumes. Patrick was supplied with a paint brush and a paint can, in a bucket to reduce spillage, by his father.

He was to receive thirty pence for each frame painted. An old cotton sail, spread at the foot, to protect the deck area, of each frame as painted. Felicity insisted that Patrick was paid when he assisted Ben. A task negotiation payment discussed earlier in the day for thirty pence per frame. His father was called, to inspect each completed frame before Patrick moved on to the next one. There were ten on each side of the restaurant space. All three children received statutory pocket money, but rewarded for any work contribution they made toward renovation of Princess Katrina.

Power from the generator enabled Ben to drill and replace planks around the bar area, shaped like a boat's bow, with bar surface, on each side. Replacement planking, supplied via the yacht chandlers, cut to size. Old ones used as templates.

Patrick painted five frames and Ben after inspection of every completed one, decided to call a halt. The dry timber had soaked up the stain. A clear varnish coat, would give a good sheen.

'That's fine Pat, you can space it out if you want? Like continue tomorrow? I'll give you a bonus. He handed Patrick a two- pound coin.

'That's in part for fetching Justin.'

'Thanks dad. I mean I'm happy to continue.'

'No, you have some down time.' It was four fifteen.

'I'll bring the pram dinghy around to the gangway. Ready to fetch Justin later.' For Ben it was reward that his family were supportive of plans to make Princess Katrina ship-shape again. Parents can always be an embarrassment to their children in front of their friends. In general, though they recognized that school friends were quite envious about living aboard a paddle steamer, rather than in a flat or house. Although Caroline, could rail at living differently than her friends.

Ben, was able to replace, the ready-made bar structure planks, but a trained carpenter was needed to address major plank repair work. It was, a falling into place day, where well prepared paint and varnish surfaces led to good results.

Several weeks of afternoon attention, to the restaurant, had moved the area forward to this paint and varnish stage. Not so the galley. A small Calor gas cooker sufficed to cook family meals, plus a microwave, toaster and of course, an electric kettle. These ran off one of two diesel generators, housed in forward deck lockers, with cables that ran along poles, above deck space and into the accommodation.

Paddle steamer Princess Katrina, did have two generators in the engine room. When refurbishment was completed one or both would be run to provide constant power. Ben, was aware, that running costs would rise once Katrina was in commercial operation. That was apart from deck crew, engineers, and engine room staff. Necessary to reach an operational level, with Princess Katrina, ready to leave moorings, literally under her own steam.

This move from refit to fully operational Ben was aiming to achieve before next season, but this very much hinged on Jamie's boiler inspection assessment? Everything else, was achievable. Generators had been renovated, while Katrina, awaited removal from moorings, which were near to a small, marine engineers, in Portsmouth. These were mothballed, but individually would provide ample power, when Princess Katrina was back in service.

Ben, with realization of a high level of attention required to first get the paddle steamer serviceable and how future running costs would need to be met with fare revenue. The plan was to get the paddle steamer operational during March of the following year. Passenger services could be viable from the end of March, through to September, before visitor numbers at, Torbay, would fall away.

Ben was on a break in the galley, when his phone lit up, on the table nearby, followed by three buzzes, to draw attention. It was Felicity.

'We're on our way back through the fairground,' said Felicity.

'Right, I'll get to the slipway to pick you up.'

It was ten to five when he walked down the companionway to the cabin accommodation space on the main deck and knocked on Patrick's cabin door. Patrick was cutting it fine to pick up his brother from the slipway. Ben opened the door. Patrick, was lay on his bunk with his iPhone. He swung his legs from bunk to floor.

'Just about to go for Justin, dad.'

'You needn't. Mother's back with Caroline.' He placed his hand on the side of the open door.

'Kill two birds with one stone. I can pick your brother up. Could do with a bowman though,' said Ben.

'We can tow the pram behind and ship it back on the slipway.'

'Okay, be with you dad.' Ben carried keys to all padlocks and doors, but there was a glass fronted key board in the galley which Felicity insisted had duplicate keys to everything.

The ship to shore launch, was partly lifted out of the water by davits. These had been fitted to accommodate this larger dinghy, which conformed to safety regulations, but was seen as an investment should passengers need to be ferried ashore. It also provided a more suitable family dinghy for these ship to shore runs. It was convenient in that it could be rowed without the need for the outboard, which conveniently lifted and stowed under the apron of the dinghy.

This, large dinghy was lowered back into the water. Brought around to the gangway, and after the pram dinghy's painter was left attached to a stern cleat, a frothy roar from the outboard, saw the two of them in progress toward the slipway. Justin, was stood on the second deck of the car park and by the time they reached the slipway was ready to meet them and take a thrown painter from Patrick, to draw the dinghy alongside the slipway wall.

'Thanks Dad,' Justin called out as he pulled the dinghy in.'

'We came to fetch Mum and Caroline,' said Patrick, ever ready to ensure his brother did not over step his position

'And you, as well, Justin,' said Ben, in part recognition, of his taking hold of the painter

'Danny went early, he wasn't having any luck. I caught a few whiting from the inner harbour wall, though.'

'Great!'

'When are Mum and Carol due?'

'Soon, I expect,' said Ben. 'We'll get the pram stowed in its rack first.'

Chapter 9

Felicity and Caroline walked down the slipway with carrier bags. It was not intended to be a grocery forage ashore, but storage aboard was restricted, with there not being a refrigerator. One, was fitted in the galley and during summer months the plan was to run a ship's generators continuously to provide energy. Everything was to be run by electricity and the Calor gas cylinder heating and cooking system dispensed with. Felicity, refused to give in to a dependency on canned or carton milk and liked to buy fresh milk at the weekend. Vegetables and milk in a bucket of water were kept in an outside locker behind the galley and replenished from a small supermarket, recently opened above the car park. Any meat bought was cooked on the day of purchase.

It wasn't easy to carry on a conversation with the outboard motor running, but once alongside Princess Katrina, Felicity said to Ben.

'We met a guy called Robbie as we walked back. Word must get around. He asked if I knew Ben Sharpe.

'Sort of I said, I'm his wife.'

He's able to look at the planking on Monday.'

'Oh, that's good. Busy week head. There's Jamie on Tuesday to inspect the boilers. That is crucial.'

There was a pressing need to go forward with plans to develop the paddle steamer into a fully functioning vessel. It was late season and a viable future for the steamer required that the boilers were passed as safe and meeting certification standard. This process could take over three months without any delays.

The deck below the wheelhouse contained nine cabins, four of which were doubles. When Princess Katrina had been operational, cabins would have been available for Captain and crew members. Caroline had bagged a double cabin, which was more spacious, where Patrick and Justin were content with a single. They were allowed one single cabin to keep belongings in, which came aboard from the rented chalet. It was planned that Ben and Felicity would move into a spare double, but it became a storage area for their belongings. One side of the wheelhouse effectively had become a dining area and the other half curtained off for Ben and Felicity's bedroom. At breakfast next day the dining space venetian blinds were adjusted to let in light.

Felicity lay in bed and listened to the deck generator start up. The battery had discharged and Ben was having to start one of them manually. Lights, in the wheelhouse flickered on, shortly after the generator engine began its boom, boom, boom. This incentivized Felicity to get out of bed, and fling on her dressing gown. There was a toilet and shower room in the accommodation deck below, but only a wash stand and loo behind the wheelhouse. Felicity, was determined to instigate a move out of the wheelhouse, to include herself and Ben in a double cabin. With galley and restaurant area refurbished; made available for family meals. It would involve a total family move from the wheelhouse. A corner of the public restaurant space would become their dining area, with the benefit of well-appointed galley facilities. Further progress with their venture hinged on clearance for the paddle steamer's boilers. Hopefully any work able to be completed before the year end, and with Princess Katrina being registered as seaworthy before next season. Then a main generator would run constantly with no need for deck auxiliary systems. Electric power for lights and plug in equipment were dependant, on these until the paddle steamer was operational. While Felicity laid cereal bowls and spoons across a temporary wheelhouse table, Caroline arrived.

'There's a seagull that sits on the mast and poops regularly on the deck.' Caroline pointed, from the wheelhouse window to a white mark on the deck beneath the mast.

'How dare it,' said her mother. 'It's supposed to be lucky. A visit from the bird of paradise.'

'When was a seagull ever a bird of paradise?'

'You never know. It's maybe in disguise.' Your father's talking about putting some spikes around where it perches.'

'That's cruel. Couldn't he put a net over the top?' Caroline walked across and sat at the table.

'You'd better ask your father.' Felicity deflected the gull deterrent problem toward Ben just as he slid open the bridge door.

'Caroline has a question.'

'Father, you are not to put spikes on the mast. Couldn't you put a fishing net over the top?'

'What's all this about? My hands need a wash before I do much else.'

'Caroline's concerned about spikes being put on the mast to prevent the gulls from pooping,' said Felicity.

'A net's not altogether a bad idea. While we're in port.'

'In the outer harbour.' Felicity corrected Ben, who could lapse into seafaring terminology, no longer relevant to the situation.

'Yes, I'll work with that, Caroline. Leave it with me.' Ben said and exited into the chart room for the washroom at the back.

'Do you want an interpretation of that remark by your father?' asked Felicity.

'That he'll do something about it?

'No, he'll more likely not.'

'I won't let him put spikes on the mast,' said Caroline, who was likely to be the more persuasive of the two around a humane seagull deterrent plan. Felicity placed a jug of milk on the table and asked,

'Was there any sign of movement from Justin and Patrick?'

'Patrick's got a new game. They were both in his cabin before I left.'

'They'll have to see to themselves.' After pouring milk over cornflakes, Caroline asked,

'When mama, are we going to move into the restaurant for meals?' Caroline switched from "ma," to mother and then "mama," when she wanted a speedy response. Felicity, was not keen on being called mama. Mama, she considered, spoke of a class system of servants, and inequality for women. But nevertheless, "mama," could be depended on getting a response from her mother.

'Not until your father's finished the painting and anyway it's cosy enough in here, for the winter.'

'But we're like on view to everyone in the wheelhouse.'

'There are blinds and who do you mean by everyone? I suppose you mean your friends, if they happen to be down by the harbour.'

'No, I mean it's like we haven't bothered to move in properly. You and dad sleeping in here!'

'Caroline, the wheelhouse is a large enough space to live in, while work is completed in other areas. We're both working, although your father has some holiday coming up, and he plans to complete re-furbish of the restaurant and galley. Then, he'll make a start on our double cabin.' Felicity placed a tray with glasses and a carton of orange juice on the table. Ben returned to the wheelhouse when Caroline said,

'Abigail, asked if she could sleep over.'

'No reason why she can't. There are spare cabins.'

'I'll need to speak with Abigail's mother first,' said Felicity.

'Abigail said that it would be alright.'

'I expect she did. But I need to know if her mother is happy about it.'

Chapter 10

'I can be there for twelve or thereabouts.' It was Robbie, a former ships carpenter that Ben had found on a yachting website, who was looking for work, locally. Felicity's bumping into Robbie earlier brought things forward to the possibility of a deck repair going ahead.

Although Ben put up a show of resistance, in having his mother visit, Felicity was very, on board, with the prospect. Unlike some daughter-in-law relationships, where the husbands' mother can be seen to be poaching territory, regarding kitchen control and overall domestic command, Felicity was relaxed about the idea and very much in the, "bring it on," mode toward a relinquish, of some domestic responsibility to Erica, once she came aboard

Ben, had swung his bike into a lay by after he heard his phone bleep. On return from work, after an eight-hour shift at the postal depot.

'That's okay Robbie. Should make it for eleven thirty. I'm on my bike back from work.' A twenty-minute ride back to the outer harbour.

Ben, was on his approach to the road which led to the outer harbour. Fairground lorries and trailers held up traffic as they negotiated their way into the town and out on to the motorway. It did not delay him overmuch, where he could weave in and out of cars and lorries.

A meet up with carpenter Robbie, represented a new phase in that thousand-mile journey talked about. A journey needing, to start with a first step. A critical, you might say, life changing second step would be a good report from Jamie about the condition of the boilers. Progress, then could be seen possible, in preparation toward Princess Katrina's seaworthiness and issue of licence to carry passengers. All welcome progress, toward the paddle steamer's readiness for service. There were times when Ben doubted his decision to buy Princess Katrina and voiced this to Felicity, but she just said,

"You haven't heard me complaining." She did however have complaints about facilities on board and Ben's sometimes slow approach to remedy them. A major step forward was conversion of a spare cabin to a shower room. Once a month, a water barge replenished water tanks. Ben, could get behind in ordering and blue polythene drum-like containers were filled from a stand pipe, and ferried aboard.

Ben, deposited his bike, in the basement area of sail locker rooms, that belonged to the yacht club. Members had both a key to the door and were given the number 4623, which opened the padlock. Further deterrent to would be trespassers. When he walked across to the slipway, he spotted

Robbie, in conversation with an ex- sailor who had secured a task to varnish, a skiff's interior, for the owner of a motor cruiser. Ben was doubtful about this purported ex -sailors actual sea -going background, but it played well with yacht owners to act charitably, in giving work toward what was seen as a bona fide seafarer down on his luck.

'You've got accommodation then.' Ben heard Robbie ask.

'Aye, it's a cabin at the back of the hotel. I dish wash for board, in the evening, but I'd rather be out here than in that infernal kitchen.' On noticing Ben approach Robbie broke away with,

'Good luck with getting some more paint jobs then.' The ex- sailor returned to varnishing the ribs and planking, which ran along the inner frame of the racing skiff. Preparation, not high on the agenda, meant sand remained between frames and planks. Robbie greeted Ben, with,

'I cannot promise an exact match to your decking Mr Sharpe.'

'That's alright I plan to stain or paint over. Not a problem.'

'That's her over there, then.' Robbie raised his hand, in the direction of Princess Katrina, with counter stern and paddle boxes either side. A green awning covered part of the after deck.

'Yes, we've a boiler inspection tomorrow.'

'I'll wish you good luck with that, then.'

'It's a bit critical,' said Ben which was an understatement.

'Have you a crew lined up?' I mean you'll be wanting to leave the harbour; under steam I guess.' Ben warmed to Robbie's positive approach.

'That's the plan, but until the boilers are certificated, it's sort of in balance.' Ben walked across to release the padlock which held the dinghy pram in its upright cradle.

'I know an ex -Chief Engineer,' he maintains the boiler at a local store.' Robbie held the prow of the dinghy as Ben unwound the light chain around the dinghy's oars, attached to the middle thwart.

'You never know he might have itchy feet, so to speak and want to get re-acquainted with a marine boiler.'

'He just might, and that's useful to know,' Ben replied. 'Probably need at least four down the engine room.'

'Any thoughts about a ship's carpenter.'

'Are you volunteering?'

'I'll wait and see what I find on board, before I go for that decision. Lets' get out there, and view the damage.' With the tide in, no distance existed to trundle the dinghy down to the waters' edge. Oars, already in their rowlocks, it was launched.

Robbie, was wearing a pair of Nike trainers, which Ben approved of as suitable footwear to board Katrina. He would need to get accustomed to women passengers, perhaps in high heels, who would walk the decks. Ben pulled on the rope painter to retrieve the dinghy, and intuitively grabbed the bow to swing the boat around, which allowed Robbie to nip aboard and not get his feet wet. The bow dipped as he boarded. Ben, followed, and pushed the boat away with his right foot. He sat on the middle thwart and swung the bow around with a back row of the left oar, before travel across harbour, to Princess Katrina. Robbie spread his arms out and held the sides of the dinghy, as he watched Ben, lean forward, and backwards, skilfully, feathering the oars, before a return was made for the next stroke.

'You're living the dream then Mr Mate,' said Robbie, who reverted to professional seafarer terms. Aboard ship Ben would have been addressed as Mr Mate, when First Officer. It was as if lives were transferred back in time as the dinghy retreated from the shore toward Princess Katrina.

Chapter 11

Ben shipped oars, just ahead of Princess Katrina's gangway and removed a boat hook clamped to the starboard side of the dinghy. He stood up and reached upwards to catch a lower rung. This, enabled the gangway to be lowered down concertina like fashion. With dinghy painter in hand, Ben swung himself up to the gangway and drew the dinghy forward, for his passenger to disembark.

'That's neat,' said Robbie, 'without a boat hook you couldn't bring the gangway down.'

'Just have to hope the wrong sort aren't watching my technique, said Ben.' A fibrous rope threaded into stanchions on both sides of the gangway, which assisted their climb to deck level.

'Good view from here. You've a tidy bit of accommodation by the looks of things. Where's the damage then Mr Mate?'

'Follow me,' said Ben. Once clear of accommodation housing, the foredeck came into view.

'Ah, you did right to cover it with a tarp,' said Robbie. Halfway up the foredeck a tent like canvas structure covered damaged planking. Ben led the way down the companionway and untied a canvas flap to reveal three stove-in planks.

'A crane apparently dropped a loaded pallet on the decking, while laid up.'

'Nasty,' replied Robbie, as he knelt to get a better look and tapped adjoining frames, with a spike.

'No sign of rot setting in and he produced a steel measure. Ben employed to hole the tab, to measure up deck space to be replaced. The tarp was then drawn back further for photos to be taken.

'I'll need to meet and cover frames either side. You'll have new timber amongst the old, Mr Mate,' he announced.

'That'll not be a problem, once its stained or painted.'

'Wouldn't advise paint, it'll crack and discolour. You'll be okay with stain. Don't want to be holystoning too often, though'

'You've got it.'

'I can cost up the price of timber and labour, and get back to you, if that's alright?'

'Yep, that's fine.' Robbie walked forward a few paces.

'This foredeck looks in need of recaulking. I'd recommend you use a fast-drying rubber solution. Not the traditional method.'

'Thanks for the tip. Bear it in mind. Can you have a look at the restaurant. It's work in progress.' They left the foredeck and went back to the upper accommodation deck.

The restaurant butted out at the end. Ben, opened double doors, which led in, to give Robbie a view of the layout of tables, chairs and bow shaped bar, as they walked in.

'You've a fair bit of space, but I'm looking at those spaced frames, you'd benefit from some insulation between. Make for more comfort and save on heating. Yep, and an inner plywood skin would cut out noise as well.' There was a possibility that Robbie was adopting a tradesman's approach of finding work through suggestion, but these were valid observations.

'I wanted you to look at the bar,' said Ben, not to inspect his handiwork strip replacement along the front, but for Robbie to give an opinion about its laminated top which was warped by action of damp and temperature change while the vessel was laid up.

'Unless you're looking to keep some original look about it, you'd be best to replace it with stainless steel, ceramic or even quartz. You may need to get additional preference from Mrs...'

'Yes, I get where you're coming from. That's true. Could you fit these other materials?

I've someone in the kitchen trade who would assist with more domestic applications.'

'That'd be okay when we make a decision to replace the top.'

'Make it sooner than later Mr Mate, if you want to secure a price. We'll order the materials in, and store them aboard if you're happy about that?'

'That's a good idea and yes, we can store orders aboard.'

'I'll measure up the bar top area, to get an idea of quantity requirements.' After another round of tape measurement and photos, Robbie, asked,

'And can I have a look around the engine room. There aren't many old timers like this one about?'

'Certainly,' said Ben.

A walk along the accommodation to a companionway, took the two of them down a deck to a white airlocked door. Between doors there was a fitted doormat to help stop grease and oil from shoes reaching the rest of the paddle steamer. Inside, a short walkway led to a dual handled metal stairway, which led down to a gridded platform, large enough to accommodate two. A ninety-degree turn was required to descend a shiny railed stairway, to the control station. A strong memory smell, of oil and heated steam combined, swept across from three long horizontal piston arms.

'Wow,' exclaimed Robbie, 'It's a bit like a signal box. Levers, handles painted red and green faced three mighty piston arms. The middle piston poised above the others as if in anticipation of instruction to pound down and drive paddle wheels forward.

Chapter 12

Back on dry land.

'It's all on my phone,' said Robbie. 'I'll get back with a quote, for the foredeck repair, and see what you think.' They were stood on the slipway. The dinghy pulled part way up. Ben left it at that, with appreciation that work going forward awaited tomorrow's boiler inspection.

'Thanks for your time, Robbie.'

'No problem, Mr Mate or would Captain be more appropriate.'

'Not Captain until Princess Katrina is seaworthy and operational.' Robbie started calling Ben Mr Mate on his own accord. Ben, never remarked about it. After all it was a working relationship that he understood from seafarer days.

Ben, returned in the pram dinghy to the paddle steamer and heated up a steak pie in the Calor gas oven. This, teamed up with a can of carrots and peas, which soon heated up over a burner. In pursuit of a healthy eating diet a sweet was eliminated from this meal, but this could be an illusory move, since chocolate biscuits might be included with coffee, in the afternoon break.

It was refreshing, to speak with Robbie, who shared experience of deep-sea life aboard a merchant ship. It served, in a way, as displacement activity, before that crucial boiler inspection tomorrow and Ben ensured to set his phone alarm to waken him. Caroline, would then not need to call from the shore.

Across, from where Princess Katrina was moored, adjacent to the main harbour wall, a steady onshore breeze caught and lifted green tarpaulins that covered yachts on the hard, which in summer time would return to council holiday parking facility. In general, sail boat yacht cockpit areas were covered, with canvas or fitted plastic coverings. Luxurious motor cruisers similarly covered, but outnumbered by the yachts. Maintenance and repair. That of auxiliary engine overhaul, paint, and varnish work, would not see much activity until the new year. An occasional owner might be seen inspecting or at work on his or her yacht. It was like a hibernation phase in the sailing world. A stalwart group of dinghy sailors trailed their boats, to the River Teign's estuary to continue winter sail races, but in the main sailboat racing was on hold, until next year.

In the evening, after the children were settled and, Ben was drying knives, forks plates, Felicity said,

'You've not told me about the carpenter's visit?'

'I was going to, when I had a chance. Robbie's, able to repair the planks and offered some useful advice about improvements to the restaurant.'

'Well, he would, wouldn't he. He'll want to find work going forward into the winter.'

'No, he's not like that. He even mentioned crowd funding as a possible way forward.'

'I just wonder who might be up for organizing that?' Felicity, questioned Ben.

'You're a dab hand around a keyboard and it's in your line of work.'

'How do you mean? My line of work? I am not an online entrepreneur. I'm a teacher. She paused before continuing.

But it's something worth considering Ben.'

'You see where I'm coming from.' His hand reached across to hold her arm as she stacked plates on the side of the sink for him to wipe.

'I can always see where you're coming from Ben Sharpe.' His kiss on her cheek, led to a firm embrace and more determined kiss on her lips. Felicity broke away.

'This won't get the washing up done!'

'Can it help to persuade you to look at Crowd Funding?' Dried washing up, placed on the table by Ben, was stowed by Felicity in cupboards, since she preferred to take charge of final storage.

'So, there's an ulterior motive for your affection other than sex?'

'Not really, but I have the right to hope.'

'You know I admire honesty being brought to our relationship.'

'It was never not there. Was it? I mean I tell you about my hopes and dreams.'

'Yes, you do. I guess Walter Mitty didn't tell his wife about any plans or she'd have been out the door. Is there any difference?'

'We've got three children?'

'A lame excuse. You mean I stay because of the children?'

'You don't do you?'

'Got you going though. I'll have a look online later.'

'I'm not holding my breath about the boiler inspection tomorrow.'

'There's no point worrying. What will be will be. Have faith Ben Sharpe!'

Chapter 13

Ben, switched to a night shift which meant that he could meet up with Jamie first thing on Tuesday. A mist came down overnight and once they were in the dinghy and away from the slipway, harbour view and surrounds disappeared. Light bulbs strung overhead gave light to see by, while they descended ladders into the engine room. Jamie and two assistants were equipped with powerful battery torches to inspect the boilers. Ben, remained by the control platform, while work was started to remove inspection plates. He wore a white boiler suit, which gave an impression of engineering competence, whereas the other three were in jeans and tee shirts, expecting to pick up dirt from within the boilers as a matter of course. With more knowledge than Ben about boiler maintenance.

Felicity had a free lesson and called.

'You're not to let anyone into our accommodation area after they've been inspecting the boilers.'

'I wasn't planning to,' said Ben. A repeated hammering on a spanner, made conversation difficult, but Felicity was keen like Ben to know whether the boilers would need replacing.

'I'll be home early there's an end of term school rehearsal and every class will attend, which lets me off the hook. Back by three-thirty. I can't hear you that well.'

'I'll pick you up,' said Ben. Jamie called up from where they were removing a plate to enter the boiler.

'We'll be awhile, with having to look at the condition of the pipes, if you're wanting to be about something else?'

'Bye, see you soon,' Ben finished his call with Felicity.

'I've some work in progress in the restaurant. I'll be up there.'

'That's fine by us. Have a report for you once we get inside and have a close inspection.'

'Okay, I'll leave you to it then.' Ben went back up the metal rungs, through the double doors, and on to the accommodation deck where the morning mist had lifted, to be replaced by brilliant sunlight. He continued to paint the wall frames which Patrick had previously started.

An hour past by which time Ben completed, paintwork in the restaurant and was cleaning up. Jamie, with blackened clothes appeared in the frame of the restaurant's double doors.

'You're very lucky whoever shut down the boilers made a good job of protecting the pipes. There's no corrosion and with some cleaning and inspection of the operating mechanisms you should be able to steam up.'

'You mean they are going to be passed as up to safety standards?'

'With a bit of work, yes.'

'That's good news,' said Ben.

'Will you join me for a coffee?'

'That'll be me and the lads.'

'Oh, yes, but we'll have to go out on deck, to avoid paint fumes. This explanation given by Ben as reason to protect the restaurant from soot and grease on their clothing.

Jamie, said after a clean-up, that steaming up the boilers would be best completed over a week to get everything settled in. Ben, wasn't planning to take Princess Katrina out into the bay, until early Spring, but it was a weight off his shoulders to know that the paddle steamer could be operational. It gave impetus, to projects like the restaurant area and to further preparation of cabin space, with urgency, for the wheelhouse to regain its designated role. Ben, had brought table, and chairs, out of storage, and set them up on the after deck, behind the restaurant.

'You can certainly watch the world go by from here,' said one of Jamie's assistants' as they sat sipping coffee. There was a clear view of the harbour wall, with visitors to the town, strolling by. Most, stopped to look at Princess Katrina, which had a similar appeal to that of steam locomotives on a track, where now only fast diesel-electrics ran. Boats moored around the paddle steamer were of mainly fibre glass construction and although designed to convey opulence and speed, with swept back bows, large windows, and prominent cabin space, did not measure up, in appeal, to the individual, elegant lines of a twin funnelled paddle steamer. Such distinctive imagery, and historical presence, stood out in the harbour basin.

'Will you be wanting to fire up the boilers right away then?' Asked Jamie, when they were sat drinking mugs of coffee prepared by Ben.

'And, how are you managing with a shipboard generator?' As they sat on the after deck, a pulsating throb from the auxiliary generator reached their ears.

'Do you cope with having Calor for cooking?'

'We manage, but ideally I'd like the paddle steamers generator to run.'

'You're looking at an engineering crew full time to keep everything running, then?'

'Our plan is to be up and running for trips and excursions from end of March,' said Ben.

'Love your optimism,' said Jamie. His two assistants had taken their mugs of coffee and walked across to the railings to get a better view of, where visitors were walking along the harbour wall. Maybe, to get away from the boss-to-boss kind of talk between Jamie and Ben. Jamie, leant forward to speak out of the hearing of the other two.

'You're looking at a big investment just to stand still with this one.' His hand raised and with a look around where they were sat, to imply that he was talking about the paddle steamer.

'I'm happy to bill you for our two hours work today, but I'll need to give an estimate for future work to get steam up, by which time you'll need engine room staffing.'

'We're working on that. A ship's carpenter has details of a retired Chief Engineer who could be interested in offering his experience....

'And ideally, take responsibility for overall running of the engine room, I guess?' Replied Jamie.

'Well, yep. We plan to move forward, become operational with paying visitors and passengers,'

'You'll have a ship's generator running, and you'll need someone who's prepared to mind it's running on a full-time basis. Included with boiler supervision and maintenance.'

'I'm aware of that.'

'Right! Look I'm impressed with your enthusiasm and not wanting to put a damper on things. But there are several conditions going forward. Basically, I cannot fire up and get systems running, until you have experienced engine room coverage aboard, to manage safe running in the engine room.' Ben was becoming a little impatient with all the questioning.

'Yes, yes, I appreciate that. I'm looking into getting advice and assistance for engine room coverage.'

'We're aboard a piece of maritime history and guess you're exploring possibilities of fund raising, I mean, not wanting to delve into financial matters...

'No, you're right Jamie. It's something we're looking into. Not to put too fine point on it, I'd feel more at home partnering with an engineer with paddle steamer technical skills.'

'Well, that would be helpful going forward. Not to worry, though you've got a fine specimen of maritime history. No major engine room defect – that cannot be put right. How about the hull?'

'Good question. Working towards a careening, where a surveyor can go over the hull condition, at low tide in the inner harbour. That's the next major hurdle to jump.'

'Wish you every success and you know where to find me, once you've a Chief Engineer on board, to organize boiler, and engine running. Jamie produced a card and handed it to Ben.

'Here's my contact details online and by phone.'

Chapter 14

It is not, going to be easy over Christmas. I mean I won't be paid during the holiday,' said Felicity,

'I can work extra hours. It's called Christmas pressure,' said Ben.

'That could apply to wives and mothers over the Christmas holiday, I'd say,' replied Felicity.

They were sat at the table, where Ben had discussed the report about the boilers with Jamie earlier. The smell of drying paint came out on deck. A quiet time together, before Ben would need to fetch the children from the slipway as they returned from school.

Felicity, with chestnut hair, in a ponytail, was in jeans, pullover and a worn leather jacket. More comfortable attire from formal teacher clothes, of navy jacket, blouse, and skirt. Felicity made a point of dressing formally to the point of severity, when in front of a class. It helped to in still, she felt the idea that she was not going to take any playing up from those who might see her as a soft touch regarding discipline. Although occupations are not considered to define a need to act a part, there can be image expectancies that children have for adults in certain roles. Life, can imitate art, particularly where a screen portrayal is made of an occupation. Felicity, was happy to portray that image of strict disciplinarian, in the work environment, but appreciated a return to on board, partner, wife, and mother, away from school. Ben, if questioned, might be of the view that a change back to teacher mode could be an aspect of a chameleon repertoire.

'With this positive report from Jamie, about the boilers, then we could look toward life aboard a working vessel then?' Said Felicity.

'It's a relief, that's for sure! Restoring the restaurant to a good spec, and getting the deck repaired, becomes worthwhile. Katrina, was like a car without an engine before we got the go ahead with the boilers.' Ben swilled the remainder of his coffee, back. From where he was sat, he spotted Caroline, walking down the outer stairway of the car park.

'Caroline's on her way.' Ben placed his mug back on the table and got to his feet.

'You've some good news to tell her then,' said Felicity.

'Does she care about what happens to Katrina?'

'Of course she does Ben. We all do!' Ben, left the wheelhouse to row across, to fetch Caroline from the slipway. Felicity, saw this as an opportunity to phone Erica.

'Hi, Erica.' She paused.

'Felicity!' Is everything alright?'

'Yes, it's Felicity. 'No. it's good news. Two jobs are progressing. Bens, arranged for the deck to be fixed and the boilers need a service, if that's what you call it. Then, we can get ready to take passengers.'

'No. He's not here. He's just gone to fetch Caroline in the dinghy.' Erica did some explaining.

'Right, so you'll want to move out while the decorators are in.'

'Yes, the broken deck is likely to be fixed by then.' There was a pause.

'Of course, of course. I'll have a double cabin ready for you.'

'No, you won't be interfering. Justin asks when's granny coming to stay? He wants to take you fishing. He doesn't think we take enough interest. Think it could be that he's the youngest and...

'No, I make sure there's none of that. And, Caroline's protective of Justin. Patrick's been helping Ben to paint and varnish the restaurant.'

The smell of paint doesn't reach the accommodation, no.'

'In a fortnight then.'

'Yes, I'll keep in touch. The larger ship to shore ferry, with outboard, will be available to bring you aboard, yes.

Bye Erica. Speak to you, soon.'

It was a happenstance that suited Felicity well. Although she was supportive of Ben in his project to get Princess Katrina back into shape, an opportunity to have her mother -in-law on board would support a call for domestic order-liness. Erica on board would assist, where her family could be seen to not fall into line, with regard, to chores. Ben's mother, if only on board temporarily, would mean that she could call on fire power, to reel back descent into a pig heap environment!

Chapter 15

'That means granny will be here for Christmas,' said Justin, at the time. They were into November and although the decorators would be finished before then, Erica had put her belongings into storage and felt that by waiting an extra week or two it would allow the smell of paint to go away.

Erica's double cabin later became a refuge for Justin, where he liked to join his grandmother in the evenings. She listened to his chatter and they shared about the same level of game play on their iPads. The other two could exclude Justin. It was not that far off Christmas.

Ben was talking with the harbourmaster in a now restored wheelhouse.

'Yes, I'm wanting to go alongside ASAP, to complete engine room work and take on supplies.' Ben listened.

'Yes, next high tide would work well with us.' This was about taking Princess Katrina into the inner harbour. Near to an inner wall there were concrete strips embedded in the harbour bed. A large vessel, like the paddle steamer could rest on these strips while props were placed around and beneath the hull to support the vessel. This allowed for an inspection of paddle wheels, rudder, and an overall view of the otherwise under sea hull. Ben would enlist workers to scrape the bottom and others with paint rollers attached to sturdy bamboo, to red lead the lower hull. He was not expecting undue damage since Katrina had been in dry dock when he first visited her, and looked good enough then, to put his money where his mouth was and make a bank transfer purchase.

'Yes, work is complete on the boiler and engine room and, we'll have an engineer, on board when we're back on the mooring.' Ben pauses to listen to the harbourmaster's response.

'You can certainly take the wheel when we're ready to go to sea. Yes, it would be a good recommendation that you approve. See you, Jim. Bye for now.'

Ben was in jubilant mood, with progress being made to have Princess Katrina fully operational. Vicky, a teacher friend of Felicity's who was a single parent, lived with her mother. A possible sleepover was mentioned where Vicky would join her daughter and be the responsible adult on board. Vicky, earlier asked about a possible sleepover, with her daughter, aboard Princess Katrina. When Felicity told Ben about the request, nothing much was said, but Felicity was laying ground work. Ben, not overly keen on anyone joining his family on board, although Erica, after all, was his mother and family. Now that prospects for rejuvenating Princess Katrina were going forward, he sprung,

'I'd quite like a trip to the bar at the club?'

'So, would I. When?'

'This Friday.'

'That works well Vicky can stay with Abigail and baby sit.' There was a momentary quiet, before Ben replied with.

'Yes, that's sounds good. Ben, was relaxed; absorbed, on his phone screen, with photos of Mississippi paddle steamers. Felicity, in the background, made a thumbs up to register success and continued with,

'Erica asked whether we are planning a Christmas party?' Ben looked across from where he was sat and put down his phone.

'Mother does like her Christmas parties. It'll be because the restaurant is looking something like.' Felicity had plans.

'I was thinking we could run a raffle to raise funds for Katrina. I mean the trip into the inner harbour and the council fees, which go with it, are going to cost?'

'Jim,' being the harbour master, 'said he might be able to swing a deal with the council. Under the preservation of local amenities act, whatever that is?'

'There's still the gallons of paint to buy and additional labour?'

'Yes, as ever Flick you've got a better handle on finances than I have.'

'We could get a Gambling Commission Licence or you can have a raffle on the night, without registering, but we will need time to sell tickets.'

'You've already given this quite a bit of thought?'

'It's as well, Ben Sharpe, that I keep an eye on finances. Not sure your aunt Rose would wholly approve of proceeds from the house sale, going into restoration of an ancient paddle boat.'

'She would Flick, she would. Aunt Rose used to come aboard, in port to see me, None, of my immediate family showed any interest. She had to be reminded that the ship was about to sail on several occasions. Always regret that she was not able to make a trip aboard. As a passenger that is. She was planning to, until the heart attack.'

'I know the story, Ben. I sort have Aunt Rose to blame for encouraging you from the grave then, is that what you're saying?'

'Now, there's a thought.'

Chapter 16

Vicky, had a good handle on discipline. Although Ben was at first reluctant to have a baby sitter aboard, the fact that she insisted the children wore life jackets, all the time before bed, gained his approval. Really, he should have understood that minding four children aboard a paddle steamer was a doddle for a teacher, who needed to control thirty children in a class room. A competitor to Mary Poppins, in ordered discipline, that gave security of mind to children?

'We won't be that long,' Felicity said to Vicky, as they clambered aboard the dinghy. It's lights out at nine-thirty.'

'I was going to ask how long are they allowed to stay up?'

'Nine is the absolute limit with school tomorrow.'

'I'll be going for a little earlier than the absolute limit.'

'That's fine by us.' said Ben, who felt his parenting voice needed to be heard, although impact on the ongoing discussion was not that much.

'You're welcome to help yourself to a chocolate fudge cake in a cool box in the galley. I left it out.'

'I might just do that Felicity. Mother cooked us a meal, but chocolate fudge sounds tempting.' Caroline's voice could be heard laying the law down with Patrick and Justin. Her voice heard from the foredeck, where a badminton net was set up, with risk that the shuttlecock could be blown overboard on a breezy day.

'Abigail and me are in a singles game and that's, that. You two can play anytime. We've started a game now, anyhow.'

'I'd best go and referee on court, I think said Vicky. The masthead lights gave just about enough light to play by.

'Enjoy yourselves.' Vicky, waved to Ben and Felicity, with Ben back- rowing an oar to get them clear of the steamers side and on course for the slipway.

The Cliff Side Yacht Club, was not high on Felicity's list of ideal social settings. Yes, a member owned the next largest vessel in the harbour, but yacht club members would own houses and maybe even a racehorse. Trust funds enabled others, a life style, with work an optional extra. Ownership of a yacht or motor cruiser, built into their lifestyle. A sojourn to a Swiss chalet would follow the end of a summer yachting season. With daytime skiing, and ski instruction classes for beginners. Evening apres ski to follow.

None of this was on the agenda for Felicity and Ben, who lived aboard their "yacht," all year round, and life, for all the romanticism of living aboard a paddle steamer could be tough. Maintenance costs ate into their budget. Not to forget the costs associated with bringing up a family of three children.

When they settled in the snook of the Cliff Club House, Leo could be seen with Emily who seemed to be ignoring him to talk with Liz Bowers. They belonged to a world of yesteryear, in a sense, but they could be key to getting public interest, directed at achieving support for Princess Katrina. Liz, waved across to Felicity and Ben.

The bar and clubhouse was not overly busy. A bar stewardess assisted Jock, the regular club steward. It was seven-thirty when Ben and Felicity arrived. Liz, after acknowledging arrival of Ben and Felicity, with a wave, came across to talk. At the same time the club room doors opened and the bar area rapidly filled with customers.

'Why's it so busy Liz? Asked Felicity.

'It's a social committee meeting to arrange a venue for the Christmas Yacht Club Party.'

'At this time. Bit late isn't it.' Liz sat next to Felicity, She held an orange flavoured gin and tonic in her hand which she placed on the table.

'No choice in the matter. The Landsdowne, shut its doors last week and the club was booked in there.' Landsdowne Hotel, on the sea front previously hosted Christmas party venues.

'Don't suppose we could hire your paddle steamer?'

'Well...,' said Ben

'The answers no, said Felicity.

'Apart from anything else, we're not licensed and we've still massive amounts of work to turn everything around for next season.'

'Just thought I'd ask,' said Liz.

'That's okay Liz, It's just how it is.' Felicity, did not want to upset her, because there was a favour to ask. Freddie walked across from the bar after spotting Ben and Felicity with Liz.

'Good to see you two ashore and you too Liz.' It was Liz who did the talking.

'Are you available to crew on Saturday Freddie. We need one more crew member to man *Sea Dancer*,' that was Liz's cruiser.

'Around to Dartmouth for the weekend. Food and some drinks available on board, but not ashore.'

'Mention, of food and drink, clinched it for me. Yes Liz, count me in.'

'I said some drink, which will mean a can or two. In fact, we'd appreciate it Freddie, if you brought some yourself. Liz turned to Felicity, while

Freddie chatted with Ben.

'You two don't fancy a coastal pub cruise Flick?' Liz's cruiser was one of the few boats that stayed in the water until early spring. Then taken ashore on the hard for essential work before being re-floated for summer racing.

"Sounds great Liz,' but not possible this weekend, replied Felicity. Mother in law's moving in for Christmas. We're here because Vicky's stood in to baby sit.'

'Understand, but you're always welcome.'

'Thanks Liz.'

'I'll stand in as a deckhand, for you Felicity, when required, but you're not having me down the engine room.' It was Freddie.

'Anyway, I'm only offering, because I feel sorry for you Flick, and how you've been kidnapped by Captain Jack Sparrow here,' as Freddie, referred to Ben.

'And forced to forgo a normal shore-based life.'

'That's kind of you Freddie's to think of my welfare, but we're in it together.'

'You mean you're in it because you're like part of a cult movement?'

'No!' Felicity swept a hand through her hair and laughed.

'We'd love to have you help wouldn't we Ben?'

'I'll be moving along, while the press gangs ashore from Princess Katrina,' said Liz, jokingly. She got to her feet and made for a group around the bar.

'How's it going folks? Asked Freddie.

'I mean, last time I heard the boilers needed to be inspected. Pretty crucial by the sound of things?'

'We're through with that, Freddie. Could do with some help when we go into the inner harbour? Said Felicity. Freddie replied with,

'Mind if I join you?'

'Looks as if you have,' Ben remarked, as Freddie sat in the chair vacated by Liz.

'When, will you be under steam?'

'Not fully until March, but before Christmas, we'll need a stand by tug, to assist us into the inner harbour and out again once the tide is back. And, a team to clean the weed from the underside. Could probably use an extra pair of hands to do some roller painting?'

'I'm up for that,' said Freddie. 'Have you a spare boiler suit?'

'I can probably find one.' Said Felicity,

And are you still in the printing industry?' Asked Ben, knowing full well Freddie was.

'How do you mean?'

'Well, we're proposing a fund-raising raffle for Katrina.'

'Sounds good to me.'

'We don't have particular skills in like production of posters and tickets?' Continued Felicity.

'Yes. Now, that works for me! The conversationally abandoned woman who seeks assistance, where her husband doesn't give her the attention she deserves. Now, if Ben had asked,' Ben smiles and is not offended by Freddie's jokey reference, when he knew that there was no better person than Freddie to get posters and tickets printed.

'Will you be able to come up with designs for posters.'

'Yes, and I'll get an advert set up in the paper nearer to the time.'

'That's good of you Freddie,' said Ben.

'No, there's a fantastic story here. It's just the kind of wild adventure life style which will appeal to my readership who have no intention of living anywhere else, but suburbia. Headlines, perhaps? –

"Sensible teacher and mother gives up promising career to stand by her man and his dream, whose plan is to resurrect the age of the paddle steamer."

'I detect an element of jealousy creeping into your observation,' replied Felicity.

'You do, you do Flick. I really admire what you two are doing. If life isn't about building up good memories, what is it about?'

'So, we can put you on our list of inner harbour work force?

'Yes, if Liz doesn't decide to press gang me to serve aboard her vessel, yes.'

Chapter 17

There was mounting excitement, among the children, that Erica was to stay over Christmas. They liked to hear stories about their father when he was their age. With some contradiction over his strictures about what constituted good behaviour, and what was expected from them; against how granny described how he behaved as a child?

Felicity, was in tidying up mode and rather like the homeowner who tidies around before a cleaner arrives, wanted to give a good impression. That, to Erica, her housewifery skills were not wanting.

Felicity, did hang washing out on the far side of Princess Katrina away from harbour view, but mainly visited the launderette over the car park. Situated, conveniently in a new housing complex, which included a Polish grocer and a small café. A washing machine was in place, in the restaurant diner galley and Felicity or Ben would complete two washes before going ashore to the launderette. It was a family event to the extent that Ben assisted with wheeling a collapsible truck which held bags of washing to be dried, up to the Launderette. Caroline could be persuaded to accompany her mother, in that the two of them went into town to visit shops. Whereas, Justin and Patrick remained on board for the short while between Ben wheeling the trolley to the Launderette and return. No more than about twenty minutes. It was not policy to leave these two alone for long, since they could fall out over who should play a particular game. Patrick, could become exasperated with his younger brother and bully him.

The launderette was conveniently situated above the main car park in a small precinct. Five machines ran along the right side of the launderette. With five dryers at the far end. Several duvets were wrapped in polythene after their wash and dry. A pile of ten or more, in one corner waited to be washed and dried for Christmas.

When Felicity opened the door, an attendant signalled to vacant dryers in the corner of the Launderette. There were no other customers. Caroline was texting a school friend and once two dryers were filled and loaded with two-pound coins there was time for Felicity to catch up on her latest Richard and Judy recommended novel.

A few minutes passed and the door opened. It was Robbie the ship's carpenter. Caroline nudged her mother who was disturbed in her reading, but brightened up when she saw who was stood opposite the attendant.

'Can it be ready for tomorrow?' Asked Robbie.

'You can call in at five and it'll be ready for you Mr Macpherson.'

'That's good of you, but it'll be the morrow now.' He handed the attendant payment and noticed Felicity.

'Ah, he's sent the working party ashore then. I've some kitchen brochures if you'd like to have a look Mrs Sharpe.'

'Yes, I would. I'm hoping to get the restaurant galley to a better spec, but it'll be after Christmas now Robbie.'

'I completely understand, but if you place an order this side of Christmas, I can put materials ready for you. It would help keep costs down. I was explaining....'

'Oh, there's no doubt that we need the work doing. I see where you're coming from Robbie. Yes. If you've an evening next week.

'Certainly have. Tuesday be suitable? About six o'clock?'

'Yes, that'll be fine.'

'It's a date then.' He smiled at Felicity. The attendant handed over a collection chitty and change.

'I'll be in tomorrow then for the laundry.'

'It'll be ready for you, just whenever you call Mr Macpherson.' From the door he called out

'Bye now,' and gave Felicity and Caroline a discreet wave as he left.

The attendant labelled the bag, removed cigarettes and lighter from her overall pocket and walked across to go outside for a smoke.

'I'll tell daddy.'

'You'll tell him what Caroline?'

'That you met up with Robbie at the launderette.'

'Don't be silly. He just happened to arrive when we were here.'

'But that's what happens. Secret meetings.'

'You've been reading too many romantic stories, Caroline.'

'But he smiled at you?'

'People smile at each other all the time.'

'I don't think it was that sort of smile.'

'What sort of smile was it then?'

'One that said he fancied you.'

'Aren't men supposed to smile at your mother then?'

'Yes and no.'

'That's not an answer.'

'I'll not tell daddy this time.'

'So, I'm being given a first warning. Is that what you mean?'

'Mother, there's no pretending you don't find Robbie attractive.'

'Like! A woman, during her life, can find dozens of men attractive, but that's as far as it goes. Robbie's a skilled carpenter and your father's lucky to find him. Otherwise, the foredeck planking wouldn't be repaired, this side of Christmas and your granny wouldn't stay on board. I also need the galley kitchen modernized and he can find people to do that.'

'Because he likes you?'

'That doesn't come into it, Caroline! Your father met him and they get on well together, with seafaring backgrounds. Father needs someone like Robbie around to sort out practical things.'

'What does that mean mother?'

'We're hoping to employ Robbie, in the summer, as ship's carpenter and to assist with managing on deck.'

Chapter 18

On Friday Ben, assembled a trestle table, just inside double doors, which led into the restaurant. Chairs were placed around the table. It could have been laid out for a committee meeting, but he awaited the arrival of harbour master Jim Briggs.

Yesterday, while Felicity and Caroline were at the launderette, a chortling burble, came from the exhaust of the harbour masters launch as it closed in on the gangway. The harbour master's megaphone enhanced voice, called out,

"Ahoy there Katrina, anyone aboard.' Ben scrambled from where he was, in the restaurant and down the companionway, to make himself visible on the gangway deck.

'Got you a drone' eyes view of both harbours.' Jim, the harbourmaster, called out, and left the wheel to hand Ben a grey canister, which held maps.

'Is eleven, a good time to go over plans for change of mooring to the inner harbour? That'll be next Wednesday?'

'Sure, sure.' We're well forward with preparations.' Ben wanted to make a good impression.

An angle poise table lamp, threw light across two coloured photos, previously donated by harbour master Jim Briggs. Each both about three metres square. One, of the outer harbour the other, the inner. They were prevented from curling, by cut off wood chunks which held corners in place. Earlier in the week Ben visited the store where former Chief Engineer Edward Potts worked to maintain the boiler, for store heating and cooling requirements. Jamie, had told him that he was employed by the Casey store group, in town. Ben was, in any event, sent to collect a purchase of kitchen utensils, Felicity ordered. That he was a good customer may have assisted in the helpfulness of the store manager who showed him to the staff canteen, where Edward was on a morning coffee break.

'A visitor to see you, Edward. A Mr Ben Sharpe,' announced the manager as he approached the table where Edward was sat.

'Mr Potts. Chief Engineer, I believe?' Ben held out his hand.

'In a former life.' They shook hands.

Yes, Chief, I have a former life in seafaring. May I join you for a few minutes?'

'Yes, take a seat. And you are?

'Ben Sharpe. We own, that's my wife and myself own Princess Katrina. You may have seen...'

'Yes, I have.' Edward Potts reached within his boiler suit, took out a smart phone, and brought up several photos.

'I was impressed by the vessel the moment you moored up.' He smiled.

'So much so, that I've taken a few photos.'

'Really.' A recent one, he turned toward Ben, without the tarpaulin, where Robbie had repaired the deck.

'Do you know, Jamie, by any chance?'

'Yes, he completed the boiler inspection, Chief.'

'And you're nearly ready to get up steam, I guess? Look, I'm working here to fill up spare time. Not because I particularly need the money and anyhow, the store is soon to close.'

'I didn't know that.'

'Yes, they're staying open for Christmas and that's it.' It was as if Edward Potts had read Ben's mind.

'You'll, need engine room staff Mr Sharpe or should I call you. Perhaps, Captain Sharpe?'

'Ben's just fine Chief, until we get under way and it may impress the passengers, you know.'

'You've answered the question I was about to ask. That being the case, are you planning to cruise with passengers aboard?'

'That is the goal for next summer.'

'And for now. It is about getting steam up for a practice run into the inner harbour for a scrub and red lead of the bottom.

'Jamie's, willing to help I'm sure and it will need several more to assist with keeping steam up and tending the boiler. But then you've got me on board.'

Ben, could not have wanted for a better response from Chief Potts.

On the following Wednesday chairs around the trestle table in the restaurant were in position for the arrival of Harbourmaster Jim Briggs, Jamie, and Chief Engineer Edward Potts. Robbie was already at work to prepare the galley for new fitments. Another burble of exhaust noise could be heard astern of Katrina. Ben walked out on deck and saw the bow of the Harbourmasters motor cruiser closing in.

He was soon down to the gangway. It was Jamie, on the bow who threw a line across. Once secured, a throttle back by Jim, brought the motor boat closer to the gangway. Jamie as volunteer deck hand, walked to the stern, in a life jacket, while he kept hold of the guard wire, on the deck surround, and threw another line for Ben to secure. There was a drizzle, which made the deck slippery. Chief Engineer Potts head appeared from the cabin space. The Chief and Jamie had hitched a ride aboard the harbourmaster's cruiser, which was all to the good.

The children were at school, but Felicity planned a free day, to oversee work on the new galley fitments.

'You'll have to excuse any banging from the galley area, we're upgrading for when we are ready for passengers,' Ben explained to his visitors as they arrived outside the restaurant, before they entered.

'You've got some space here,' remarked Chief Potts.

'Take a seat gentlemen,' said Ben

'You've made use of my harbour plan, I see.' Harbourmaster Jim, with hands spread on the table inspected the photos spread across the table. The others sat in chairs provided. It was not crucial to the manoeuvre, but the overhead photos assisted in accessing how best to navigate through the outer harbour and into the inner one.

'I can get Jolly Jane, and Oceania on to other moorings. Two large motor cruisers that over wintered in harbour, and would have blocked a direct route into the inner harbour.

'Many, moorings are vacant, which will assist in a clearer route toward the inner harbour.'

'A good opportunity to get steam up and run the paddles,' said Jamie.

'Hold on, hold your horses, I need at least four in the engine room to run everything, Chief Potts came in with.

'You can count me in, said Jamie.' The excitement was countered by,

'That's as maybe but you'll need the services of a tug, once you're in the inner harbour,' Jim Briggs pointed out to Ben.

'Do you think so?

'Yes, I do! And your insurers will. I can find out hire costs. There may be one in the area.'

'Appreciate, that Jim. I've sourced a supply of coir fenders from the pleasure steamer company. I' m waiting on the council to get back with when they want us alongside the inner harbour wall. A repeated bang came from the galley area where Robbie was removing a unit. to make way for new ones.

'That we need to know, to get up steam, two days before and test run everything,' said Chief Potts, who had been aboard with Jamie previously, for an engine room inspection.

'We should be able to steam directly across to the inner harbour entrance?' Asked Ben. Jim the harbour master circled his hand around a cluster of small boats which blocked access for the paddle steamer.

'Not without these six boats being moved from their moorings. There's inner harbour slipway, moorings. I have an arrangement with owners to moor their vessels, as required, to these moorings temporarily. A priority will be to fix a date for the tug which matches the councils date to enter the inner harbour.

'Right,' said Ben. At least we won't need a pilot to cross the harbour.' Chief Engineer Potts and Jamie left Ben and the harbour master, to continue engine room maintenance. In preparation for Princess Katrina's move, under steam across the outer harbour, and into, the inner.

Chapter 19

Erica, wondered what her father would have made of the modern apartment she now lived in. In her handbag, she kept, a photo of their childhood home in Norway. A house well-built, to withstand cold and snow of winter months. The photo was taken in summer and in the background could be seen greenery, in front of fjords that extended northwards.

A three-story red bricked house, with an expanse of cream painted veranda, which skirted around the ground floor. A similar but smaller veranda beneath the second floor. She recalled, how she sat on the second veranda in summer and read countless books. Mainly romantic novels. She studied English and liked to read Jane Austen's Persuasion and the Bronte sisters' novels. Even Charles Dickens novels, which she found heavy going, but admired his ability to describe characters and lives of those who lived in Victorian England.

The veranda, of her modern flat caught the afternoon and evening sun. Sea, visible because her fourth floor, apartment overlooked terraced houses which led to the beach. A flying buttress effect of the veranda allowed room for a small table and chairs. Erica, could see her two small palms, which she bought to help induce calm; now on her neighbours' small veranda, immediately to the right of hers. House plants from her small lounge and kitchen were also being tended by the neighbour. Carpets, rolled up and furniture shroud covers prepared for when the decorators arrived. She was waiting, on her son Ben's call, that her cabin was ready, aboard Princess Katrina for a Christmas stay.

Forty years away from her young life the veranda evoked memories of childhood. Her eyes when tired from reading would close and it was a view from that veranda of her young life that she imagined, to be before her. Strange, now she was to leave to be with Ben and his family for a week or so, memories, far back, came to be uppermost in her mind. After marriage to husband Daniel, they lived at her Norwegian family home before they moved to live in Bristol. Her disabled sister lived with their father into old age and the house was eventually sold to cover nursing costs. A memory, like a film she re-ran through her mind, when sat in the evening sun on the mini-veranda.

Daniel, was sat in an armchair watching horse racing on a Saturday afternoon, when she discovered his slumped figure in the armchair. Erica, had finished washing up and tidying in the kitchen. It distressed her that he left suddenly, but for Daniel it was perhaps a kindly way to go.

Erica, was initially disappointed when Ben left seafaring as a profession, after so many years of training to arrive at a good salary. Daughter Anita,

68

two years younger than Ben was married to an Australian, and Erica visited them once. But did not feel that she could face another long-haul flight. Anita's husband's large family, although they welcomed Erica, she felt, lacked a certain cultural appreciation, where Felicity she felt was good for Ben. Felicity, shared similar reading tastes and Erica, was pleasantly surprised that her son had married such a well- organized, and yes, cultured young woman, after previous girlfriends. Previously to Felicity, Ben, was infatuated with a girl called Miranda. Although personable and attractive, Miranda seemed addicted to party going and led what can be euphemistically called the good life. It became a worry to Erica that Ben might ask her to marry him. Miranda, modelled for fashion magazines, in between being out of work. Erica's view was that her son was vulnerable and naïve, to the extent that he ran around after Miranda, in a dangerously obsessive manner. He was apparently heart-broken, when she left him for a manager with Coutts, the prestigious bank. Erica's, momentary, motherly sympathies, disguised inward delight that Miranda was no longer in the running to be daughter-in-law.

Happenstance was that Erica's membership of Torquay's towns woman guild meant that prominent and interesting people from the community gave talks to the group once a month. On her own after Daniel died more than ten years ago Erica joined the guild to find friends and occupation, but was not seeking another partner. She chatted with a schools' career adviser, after he previously addressed the group and mentioned how Ben was on leave from a trip to South Africa.

A week later, she received a phone call from this careers adviser to ask if Ben might be prepared to give a talk to year six, about life in the merchant service? Erica agreed on Ben's behalf.

'You're kidding me mother,' was Ben's immediate response.

'You said that you were considering a career in teaching and now you can visit a school and get a taste for it.'

'Or not.' Replied Ben.

'Yes. It could be an opportunity to make your mind up.' Erica, was keen to see her son moved on from this failed relationship, and invested in a career again.

On arrival at the school hall where he was to give the talk it was Felicity who introduced him to the assembled group of students and staff assembled in a row of chairs, near to the front. They recognized one another from membership of the yacht club and likely would have smiled politely on meeting. Following the talk, apart from Felicity making a coffee for Ben in the staff room, nothing happened until they met once more at the yacht club and, apparently, Ben bought Felicity a drink. Felicity, facilitated an opening for Ben by saying there was a performance of the Sound of Music by an operatic group, at the Princess Theatre, which was a subtle prompt to get Ben to respond with,

'Would you like to go?' The outcome was that Erica was pleasantly surprised when Ben returned home with Felicity and later married and had children. Then, Erica was living in the family home and aunt Rose still very much alive. Aunt Rose died, shortly after a visit to her nephew Ben, before he left aboard an oil tanker, bound for the Middle East on charter to Shell. News of the inheritance surprised both Ben and his mother. It was a while before his mother settled down from Ben's shock decision to buy a paddle steamer, but was compensated by the fact that he was already married to Felicity. Confident that her daughter-in-law, had ability to manage the business side of running the paddle steamer, and in particular her son! Shortly afterwards Erica down-sized to a more manageable apartment.

Chapter 20

Felicity was sat, on the starboard side of the restaurant, which caught the afternoon sun, in her favourite director style chair. It was Saturday, and Caroline was ashore with Abigail and her family. A small collapsible table, gave space for Felicity's lap top plus a coffee cup and notes that she was working from. This was down time, and she was looking through some illustrations, designed for her by a parent, who became interested in her children's book project.

Patrick, ran past and down the near companionway, followed shortly afterwards by Justin, who was breathless and stopped near to his mother, with hands on his knees. It was a competition to see who could circumnavigate the paddle steamer in the shortest time, without stopping on route. Justin had already failed on this count, but was never going to match his elder brother's, monkey like ability, to slide down companion ways and generally run faster. A classic situation, where an elder child can dominate a younger sibling, in activities, due to physical growth. Although later, the younger one may well show more prowess when he reaches the same age, later in life.

'Are you alright Justin? When you next see Patrick tell him to put his life jacket on. He'll soon need to fetch your father. Ben was ashore finalizing details for their planned move, into the inner harbour, next month.

'Are you still doing school work mum?'

'No Justin.' Justin walked across, still breathless, to where Felicity was sat. He read the heading on the screen *Adventure in Alicante.*

'It's that children's book you've been reading to me.'

'Yes, that's right.'

'I don't see the point. You might as well just talk. It's only you writing words down, and reading them out. I much prefer it when you read Roald Dahl anyway.

'I appreciate your review of my writing Justin, but it's not the same, as me just talking to you. There's a story to follow, and I need complete it soon, anyway, to enter a competition next month.' Felicity in receipt of critical comment that authors often receive from their family. Roald Dahl was a hard Childrens' author to top,

'Can I go ashore with Patrick to go fishing?

'Is Danny on the pier Justin?' Felicity removed her reading glasses. When worn in Ben's presence she received the title of marm. But it was Felicity who introduced the name of Uncle Albert, as an alternative title for their children's father.

'He will be there soon, now the tides turned. Higher tides bring in the Bass, and larger fish, Danny says.'

Patrick re-appeared after completion of another circuit.

'Have you given up Justin?'

'Your brother's never going to keep up with you Patrick and anyway you need to get ready to pick up your father in the dinghy.'

'Do I have to?'

'Yes, if you want him to buy you a new bike for your birthday. And Justin's going ashore to fish with Danny... I'll fetch you, Justin. No later than five-thirty mind, because Caroline will need a lift back.'

'Can I have a pound for some bait please mum?'

'What about me? Said Patrick.

'You and Caroline can have the same.' It was all about ensuring that all three were treated fairly. Justin had walked across to the side railing; turned and called back.

'Danny's on the pier.' Felicity noted it was twenty to four, just as her phone rang.

'Yes Ben, he's on his way.' Felicity raised her index finger toward Patrick. There was a pause as Felicity caught the message.

'You want him to assist in the sail loft with bringing the fenders down for Jim to bring aboard next week and does he want to go to the bike shop? Pause from Felicity.

'He might not want to.'

'I do mum. You know I do.' Let me talk to dad.' He reached to get the phone.

'Hi dad. Yes, I'm on my way.'

Felicity stayed near to her director's chair, while she went through a range of Yoga exercises on a mat that was kept nearby, in the restaurant. No more than ten minutes and short enough to be on her feet to see Patrick and Justin pull the dinghy up the slipway. Felicity, also spotted Ben farther up, talking to Jamie. It was always good to have time to herself on board.

Satisfied that plans for the day were working satisfactorily Felicity walked through into the restaurant. Fixed interspersed, bench seating was in place on both sides. She hoped the paint smell would vanish in time, but there would always be an individuality defined by a wooden structure with a coconut matting strip which stretched along the middle aisle. Ben was for changing the matting for a modern design. This appalled Felicity, since she considered a major part of Princess Katrina's charm was an authentic preservation of everything that was original to the paddle steamer when it was first operational. Ben was more a philistine around these matters and was not averse to incorporating modern design under the guise of improvement. There was going to be GPS and modern navigational equipment in the wheelhouse. Felicity was keen that improvements were restricted, but accepted that modern navigation equipment was required, to run the paddle steamer more safely and efficiently. Secretly she confided with Chief Potts, who was more on her wavelength with matters of authenticity and paddle steamer preservation.

Mention had already been made about taking advantage of the inner harbour visit. Princess Katrina would be opposite a busy pavement that ran along by the side of the harbour. There were shops and arcades and although out of season, still popular with visitors and locals. There was the silversmith and jewellers that for five years had displayed several "Closing Down Sale," posters, in red letters on its windows. The area remained vibrant even during winter months. Mention, of taking business advantage of the sojourn into the harbour was mentioned to Ben, when they were alone, but Felicity had not elaborated on her plans. It was, you might say, a seed sowing exercise.

It was really part of the reason that she wanted the galley operational. Not that much cooking was proposed, but the restaurant could be open to the public once the paddle steamer was secure alongside the inner harbour. Perhaps a themed French style café, rather than restaurant, with tricolour flags around the outer surround. There would need to be someone who could speak French fluently, in attendance. Felicity had already approached Alison, who was head of French, as to whether she would help out and came across as enthusiastic.

It was a courageous move on Felicity's part because she saw Alison's face light up when Ben arrived to be with her, during a parent's evening earlier. Ben seemed totally unaware, that he was, recipient, for this overt bonhomie from Alison and Felicity aimed to keep it that way. Felicity's teacher salary gave her considerable leverage over both domestic and more professional decision making around business policy to do with Princess Katrina. Ben, would be fully involved with the scrub and repaint of Princess Katrina's exposed underwater hull. Alison would be with Felicity, in the restaurant, a safe distance away.

Chapter 21

Nearly a month passed, before notification for the inner harbour move, arrived by letter. Ben's, postal address was care of the Cliff Top Club, Haldon Pier Torquay. An offshoot of the main club house, which was set back from the harbour. Ben, usually didn't call in every day, but did make a point to stop by midday or soon after, once Jim said to expect a letter from Torbay Council. The bar man, handed over a white envelope with a franked post mark with the words "Come to Sunny Devon." Ben repeated his mother's riposte, which was "rain's six days in seven." He walked out of the club house building and down to the harbour wall, before he opened the letter.

"Dear Mr Sharpe,

We are informing you that your application to proceed Vessel Princess Katrina for careening into the inner harbour has been approved, for Thursday November 14th, 2024. High tide is at 0917 and your vessel will be required to enter the inner harbour at 0900 for departure at 1930 hours, on the Thursday.

All necessary work undertaken and terminated by 1800 hours. Inability to remove, said vessel will result in additional charges of one thousand pounds daily and additional charges should the council be required to contract out the work, to remove your vessel from the docking facility provided. A deposit of five thousand pounds is required from yourselves by the 10th November, from which charges will later be deducted. A table of charges relevant to vessel length is enclosed.

Harbour master, Captain James Briggs will liaise with you, with regard, to safety and all requirements. We understand that you propose to steam across from your mooring to the inner harbour berth and maintain boiler function. One boiler may be maintained while alongside, only, where appropriate exhaust guards are in place above funnels. It is a requirement that a tug boat vessel, approved and supervised through the harbour master is in attendance, to assist in berthing, should your vessel's propulsion mode be proved ineffectual. A duplicate letter has been forwarded to Captain James Briggs Harbour Master, who will contact you shortly."

Yours sincerely,

David Markham,

Officer designate

Harbours Committee Torbay

Enclosed: (1) Charges and invoice due payment.

(2) Tidal chart for November.

'That's a bit steep.' Ben said out loud. An elderly dog walker overheard and called out,

'Electricity bill, is it? It's frightening, isn't it?' Obviously, not unduly concerned about Ben's apparent announcement to no one in particular.

'Oh yes,' sorry I was talking to myself,' he said, as if it was an everyday event for most people. Perhaps it was for the pensioner, who promptly called to his dog.

'Hold on Suzy, you can have a run on the pier.' The dog, had suddenly pulled on the harness, and wanted to go, but was at that point held back.

'I expect they'll be trying to force us to have solar panels fitted.'

'Good idea. I mean yes,' said Ben. Too preoccupied with news about the inner harbour notification to engage with a chat, aimed at passing the time of day. He folded the letter and placed it in his jacket pocket.

'Have to hope we have a mild winter.'

'It's not so bad here, but up north...' Suzy, a Rottweiler puppy, with more control of what was happening pulled forward.

'I'm looking after my son's dog for him... Bye for now,' he said, with Suzy, more than him, deciding that a walk on the pier was a better option than being stood where they were.

'Bye, then.' Ben amused by how the dog was evidently taking his dog walker for a walk, rather than the other way round. He was on his way to fetch his bike from a wire caged sail locker, large enough to hold a dinghy.

Felicity received the news in the evening.

'You could have texted me?'

'You said, that you preferred not to receive non-essential texts at work?'

'I consider that news, as in the essential category.' They were in the newly appointed galley space. Felicity paused before continuing.

'The fourteenth of November might work well though, because Erica could board from the inner harbour and that will avoid having to ferry her belongings out in the dinghy.' Ben placed his coffee mug on the table.

'You're pretty good at planning ahead.'

'Don't patronise me Ben Sharpe,' Felicity, turned with a smile to soften the implication of her remark. Bordering on thinking aloud she said

'I will have to see if Alison's free. Maybe, able to get Erica to help.'

'To do what?'

'To open up the restaurant for coffee and possibly take orders for crepes?'

'Will there be any takers?'

'It's worth a try. Sort of practice run for when we've paying passengers and guests on board. Haven't you seen how people stop and look at Princess Katrina from across the harbour. They'll be curious and want to come aboard.' Ben, did not share quite the same conviction.

'They can't be allowed free rein to wander around.'

'We can shut off access to critical parts. Although, they could walk down to the foredeck. You'll need to get accustomed, to having passengers aboard, your pride and joy. Ben Sharpe.'

'That's for when we're operational. I don't want anyone, falling overboard into the harbour mud. The restaurant deck will need to be cordoned off separately. Could put up "maintenance in progress," or something.

'So, you're okay with it?'

'Do I have the final say then?'

'No, but I would prefer that you were okay about it? It's going to be part of the what you might call, "paddle steamer experience."

'Of course, I'm okay about it, if it contributes toward funds. I'm not sure you'll get many punters.'

'Don't be such a pessimist. I'm considering placing an advert in the Herald and Express.' Ben's face registered bewilderment.

'Do people buy newspapers these days? Don't they find out about places they visit from their smart phones?

'You obviously haven't visited these websites. There can be very little information about what's actually going on, and it can be out of date. I'll be posting online, as well though. Places to eat always seem to get priority.'

'Like for one day?'

'Yes. I'm planning to include a progress report on a website. Technology, that can really help us to get noticed for the coming season. An inner harbour visit is ideal for publicising our presence and future itinerary. A photo in the Herald and Express and the Torquay Times would help get Princess Katrina in the public eye. You're not paying, are you?'

Chapter 22

Ben, was in the wheelhouse while Robbie was letting go the stern mooring. The paddle steamer was moored to buoys, at bow and stern. He was assisted by Freddie who was later going to be with the scrub and clean team, once safely secured in the inner harbour. Chief Engineer Potts had managed to contact several friends who shared his enthusiasm for paddle steamers. Jamie was his right-hand man in the engine room. It was Jamie who called Ben, via the voice pipe from the engine room.

'We're going to be turning the wheels shortly is everything clear for us to do so?' It was early in the morning and apart from Tug boat *Dancing Queen* in attendance, over by the Princess Pier, there were no other boats, moving around the outer harbour.

'I'll just check it out for you, Jamie.' Ben walked out on to the port bridge and there was clear water between the harbour wall and the paddle steamers port side. The starboard side displayed open water, save for a few moored cruisers. There was an open channel across to the mouth of the inner harbour. He returned to the wheelhouse and blew down the pipe, to get Jamie's attention.

'All clear. Will there be much forward movement?' Jamie assured Ben that a few forward turns would be countered by the same number of turns in reverse. Ben enquired about whether he would then have a Stand by capability from the engine room. Ben was told that this would be at the Chief's discretion.

A stereotypical response from a ships' engineer, who had built awareness, over time, that he was dealing with deck officers who didn't necessarily understand engineering, and required to have things spelt out! An intermittent buzz came from the radio

"Princess Katrina. How near are you to sailing? Over." Ben, warmed to the tug master's definition of this move from the mooring to the inner harbour. He picked up the ship to shore radio phone.

'No more than half an hour. Need to release our forward mooring. Over'

'We will precede you into the harbour. Once opposite your berth spot and stopped we will assist, if necessary to get you alongside. Over.'

'Hope to be able to winch rope bow and stern to get close in, but would appreciate help if fail to complete. Over,'

'Will monitor. Contact if assistance required. Over and out.' Ben was happy to leave it to be at his discretion. Not wanting the tug, to push on the hull if, at all possible. Hull plates, on the elderly paddle steamer, were unlikely to have the strength of that of an ocean-going vessel. Ben, walked out of the wheelhouse, to the bridge's afterdeck and received a cross arm wave, to signal release of after moorings. Returned to the wheelhouse to fetch the megaphone and announce,

'I'll call when ready to release the forward mooring rope.' This received a thumb's up from Robbie, and a wave from Freddie.

Felicity, and Alison were back aboard, after ferrying the children ashore for school. They would rejoin later, that afternoon, when berthed alongside. There was a slightly mutinous attitude about school attendance, from the three children, with such a momentous occasion taking place. That, of the transit for Princess Katrina from mooring to the inner harbour, under steam. But it was pointed out that they would be aboard for her return journey to the mooring. Patrick, wanted to have a go at steering the paddle steamer, back to the mooring. Albeit, supervised by his father.

Felicity, was well ahead with the restaurant presentation. Triangular red, white, and blue flags were strung around the outer walls and a menu board was placed on an easel. Intended, to display on the pavement next to the gangway. Positioning, of the paddle steamer once alongside and settled on the harbour bed, after tidal retreat would allow for a flat ridged rope nearly horizontal gangway to straddle restaurant deck to pavement.

A golden silk-like yellow fabric "restaurant," sign, on royal blue background, ran along the top on both sides. There was some debate as to whether "Restaurant," was the right word, where they were to serve crepes, teas, coffees, and knickerbocker glories. Felicity pointed out that they would be open in the afternoon, and lunch would already have been served!

A sound of paddle wheels, scooping and releasing water, could be heard from the bridge as testing was in progress. There was no noticeable forward movement, before the wheels stopped and turned three times in reverse. Intermittent bursts of steam had been blasting from the boilers, prior to this. Ben walked out to the bridge and took hold of the whistle guy rope, and purposefully pulled it downwards. A hoarse release of steam, was followed by a blast that echoed around the harbour. It caused Harbour master Jim Briggs to step out of his office, cap in hand, and wave to Ben, from the top of the car park. A signal that he was on his way to join the procession into the inner harbour.

Robbie, completed a winch of the dinghy aboard, after the return of Felicity and Alison. Freddie, meanwhile could be seen on the foredeck. Ben would need to have Robbie in charge of letting go the forward mooring rope.

Ben, allowed about fifteen minutes to pass before he re-contacted the engine room. It was eight fifteen. He was pleasantly surprised by Chief Engineer Potts reply to his question of – "How near are we to having engine power?"

'Ten Minutes at most. You can go on Stand by – with power available for eight thirty.

Once Ben could see that Robbie was on the foredeck and available to release the mooring he called the tug.

'Dancing Queen, Dancing Queen.' They were now close enough for Ben to have talked across to the tug master. However, engine and paddle noise would soon drown out opportunity for any conversation.

"Receiving you Katrina, receiving you, over." The tug master expediated by dropping Princess from his call message.

'Anticipate release of forward mooring at 0830 and departure for inner harbour berth, over.'

'Will proceed ahead of you. Please to give one blast when under way. Over.'

'Follow. Will give further blast on whistle, when under way. Over and out.' Ben previously arranged with Robbie to position himself on the foredeck, assisted by Freddie to throw a first line across to waiting harbourside council employees, who would be positioned to drag their line across to hook on a bollard. The plan was to stop Princess Katrina, directly opposite the berthing area, where steps led up to the pavement above. Ben, was concerned about the power of paddles when put astern and with an emergency, told Robbie that he would drop anchor to prevent forward motion. This he wanted to avoid, at all costs. Fenders, covered the paddle casing on the starboard paddle. The plan was to draw the vessel near enough to the harbour wall to meet with poles, either side of the central paddle. The steamer's water tanks, on the starboard side previously filled to, encourage a list to starboard. With a falling tide, the keel would settle on wooden beams spaced on the harbour sea bed, with lean toward the harbour wall supported by rows of poles lowered by chains. The poles protruded out to meet the hull. Rectangular boards attached to the poles provided a cushion effect against the ship's hull. Additional safe guard poles were to be placed upwards from the harbour sea bed. At bow, and stern, on the starboard side. Wide metal plates were cemented in place on the harbour bed to prevent poles sinking into sand. Ben, together with harbour master Jim Briggs inspected the berth position earlier.

'What if the vessel doesn't lean in toward the harbour wall, for whatever reason?' Asked Ben.

'Not a problem. Supports can be placed on the port side to prevent a topple.' Smaller vessels in the harbour were designed with flat bottoms to settle safely on the floor of the harbour when the tide retreated. Ben had dry docked aboard a cargo ship, but the dock was purpose built for the job.

'We've brought the cross-bay cruisers alongside and they settle nicely on the berth.'

'They don't have the length,' said Ben. 'I would like to measure the length available.'

'You have a tape?' Ben produced a Tefcol tape measure, and a box of chalks.

After he chalked the pavement to mark progress, it came to three hundred and fifty feet in total.

'There's plenty space and it has beams spaced along the route' Ben, wanted to visualize the site and be reassured that Princess Katrina, at 186 feet in length would easily fit into space available.

'I have organized a workforce of three, to high-speed jet wash and scrape away resistant weed. This should be completed by two o'clock.

'We then have about four hours to roller brush with red lead? That's pushing it a bit.'

'A tip I can give you Ben is to have someone available with replacement trays of paint. It can speed things up no end.'

Chapter 23

A blast, from the whistle made harbour side visitors stop their walk and to look across. Princess Katrina's paddle wheels cut the water and the swishing sound could be heard nearby ashore. Ben, held the wheel to starboard. His towed journey from dockyard to Torbay, gave experience of how to gauge amount of wheel steerage required. Tug boat Dancing Queen rapidly moved ahead of Princess Katrina to station at the inner harbour entrance.

A telegraph near to the wheel made it possible to reach out and direct the engine room to give Half Speed. Ben, was concerned about whether sufficient forward movement would be available to swing the paddle steamer's bow, clear of the outer harbour wall. Half speed gave added momentum. He was banking on assistance from an incoming tide to encourage, a swing to starboard and, get bow alignment with the inner harbour. As planned, an abrupt swing to starboard followed and Ben rang for Slow Ahead, while he gave port helm to steady the bow's swing.

Now under way, cheers came from passers-by, on the harbour wall and slipway. Ben unaware that he or rather Princess Katrina had created such interest after that first whistle blast. Excitement and a thrill for onlookers to see the paddle steamer in operation. It was like a launch event or this time a re-launch for Princess Katrina, from a period of neglect. A clatter of footsteps announced the arrival of Robbie on to the bridge. He spread his arms across the open wheelhouse door and called out,

'You're managing alright in there then?'

'So far, so far. Seem able to hold a course at slow speed. May have to let the tide take us in once at the inner harbour.' The harbour masters launch was seen to approach from out of the inner harbour mouth and in a circling swirl turned back into it, when aware that the paddle steamer was under way and on its way

'Ah, Jim's here to oversee things.'

'You mean to ensure there's someone to take our lines?'

'Yes, and clear away any boats that might impede our passage I hope.'

'Freddie's, at the stern to throw a line ashore,' said Robbie. A line, with a monkey's fist at the end to give momentum when twirled and thrown ashore. With its end attached to a larger mooring line, this gave shore recipients ability, to haul the eye of a heavy mooring rope ashore, and on to a bollard.

'If you can get a line ashore from the bow, I'll be down to give a hand,'

Ben said. In part, to reassure Robbie that more professional help would be available.

'You're reckoning to winch us in, without assistance from Dancing Queen?'

'Yes ideally.'

'I'd best get back on the fore deck. You'll be wanting the supports to keep us away from the harbour wall?'

'Yes, and providing she settles about eight to ten feet away, the props will support the hull as it leans.'

At this point Princess Katrina was closing in on the inner harbour entrance. As Robbie left down the companionway Ben rang for stop engines. He'd rather stop away from the berth than over shoot it. The clear ring, from the telegraph could be heard by those people on the inner harbour wall. A sedate twirl of the paddle wheels ended and apart from a persistent beat from the diesel generator, in the engine room, it was quiet. Ben was joined by Felicity, who left Alison in the restaurant, to be with him. She waved back to a couple, with a dog, who were stood on the quay, in front of fresh timber planks, which had been discharged from a Norwegian merchant ship.

Princess Katrina was now about one hundred and eighty metres or two hundred yards from the berth and almost stationary. There was activity on the quay, with several council employees in high vis, setting up a stand pipe from the mains water supply. Harbour master Jim Briggs's launch, was moored at a stepway past the berth position, with its pendant draped on the foredeck, in the lee of the harbour wall. He wasn't visible, but would be nearby, Ben surmised. Felicity was out on the starboard bridge and called out,

'You do know, we're stopped. Completely, as far as I can tell.'

'Right.' Before his voice was drowned by the swish of paddles, as he rang for Dead Slow Ahead.

'Wave your arm if we start to move again,' Several turns of the paddles later, and Felicity's hand was raised in a wave. Ben, angled toward the harbour wall before he rang stop engines. "Fingers crossed," that forward motion, would be sufficient to bring the bow close enough for a line to be thrown.

Robbie's first throw, fell short of the harbour wall. Freddie was detailed off to retrieve this first attempt and a second line thrown, was so successful that the monkey's fist wrapped around a railing. Ben, was relieved when one high vis employee unwound the rope and called others over to assist in the drag ashore of the mooring rope, from Princess Katrina.

'Well down Robbie,' Felicity called out. Ben not realizing that his wife had grabbed the megaphone when she heard the telegraph ring for Dead

Slow Astern. Felicity was in the wheelhouse, but walked out on the bridge to measure whether the paddle steamer was stopped. The second, her hand was raised, Ben rang Stop Engines. When the eye of their forward mooring line was on a shore bollard, Ben called out,

'I'm going down to the foredeck to help Robbie, Flick. If Chief Potts calls, can you tell him that we're not finished with engines.

'Aye, aye Captain,' said Felicity with a smile, pleased that her husband was in his element.

Chapter 24

Ben, had judged it right they were about twenty feet astern of where the paddle steamer was to be moored alongside, but only fifteen to the harbour wall. Two turns around the steam winch brought tension to the rope.

'Are you alright here Robbie?'

'You go and get a line ashore astern, Captain. I'm fine. I'll take in any slack, as it comes.'

Freddie, joined Ben and they ran to the stern to throw a line ashore. The line Ben threw, bounced on the pavement and a high vis stepped on it to stop it falling back. A stern line was coiled ready for release, with the remainder wrapped around bits. A lighter terylene line which could be controlled more effectively. Easier to pull ashore, and for its eye to be placed on a bollard. The rope ran out as Ben planned, dipped, and floated in the harbour water, ready to be pulled ashore. They returned to the foredeck.

Robbie had taken a third turn around the winch.

'Have you got the line ashore then?'

'Yep. I can hold the fort here if you and Freddie, can winch in slack, on the stern line.

'OK. Do you reckon that'll draw her alongside?'

'Here's hoping.' Ben could see that the stern needed to be winched in, for the vessel to run parallel with the harbour wall. Felicity called from the bridge by megaphone.

'I've told Chief Potts that you may still need the engines.'

Ben waved his hand in acknowledgement. It all depended on whether the stern line would take the strain or for that matter the winch?

'Hey deck hand.' It was Harbour master Jim Briggs, on the pavement.

'You're looking good.'

'Can't really tell from down here,' replied Ben.

'Another twenty minutes or so, and I'd say, and you'll be where we want you to be,'

This was like music to Ben's ears. It meant that Princess Katrina's keel was close to covering timber beams that lay out from the harbour wall to support the vessel as the tide retreated.

'Should have you settled by midday. We'll get high pressure hoses set up, to clear the hull for you.' The winch held the stern rope in tension and Robbie left Freddie to take in any slack and re-joined Ben to transfer the bow line to nearby bits. Secondary lines were run ashore from the main and after decks to give more direct purchase. There was a banging from poles being dragged forward from where the Harbour Master was stood. He called out to Ben,

'We'll have the poles lowered to meet you shortly.' These poles, wider in diameter than telegraph poles, once lowered, with wires secured to ring bolts, on the pavement, above would prevent paddle wheel casing contact, when the paddle steamer leant over. Steps, which led down to the harbour bed allowed several council employees, dressed in yellow oilskins and waders to descend with pole supports, should these be needed to provide support, where the vessel failed to lean significantly, with, out-going tide, on to the harbour wall.

Ben, relaxed, when poles were lowered from the harbour wall, to nestle against plate like boards for hull support. An afterdeck winch, manned by Robbie. warped the hull slowly toward these suspended poles. Ben, assisted by Freddie, secured wire springs, which ran fore and aft from steamer to shore. Once in place, these ensured the vessel would not move away from the harbour wall, while afloat. Ben, returned to the wheelhouse.

'Can I?' Asked Felicity when Ben announced he was finished with engines.

'If you like.' Felicity took hold of the white telegraph handle and swung it back and forth to "Finished with Engines." The ring chime, from the telegraph bell, startled two seagulls perched on the forward mast. They cawed and flew to settle, on the roof of the ice cream parlour ashore.

'Hadn't you better phone your mother to say that we're alongside? I'm surprised she hasn't phoned for an update? Felicity's phone jingled, and her pointed finger and look, gave Ben a message that said "speak of the devil."

'Where are you, Felicity. I phoned you because I won't get any sense out of Ben, while he's dancing attendance around that paddle steamer.

'I'm on the bridge now, with Ben. We're alongside. Would you like to speak to him?'

'Not particularly. I've ordered a taxi for twelve. I assume that there will be a gangway in place by then, Felicity?'

'Yes, there will be a gangway to board. It'll lead on to the restaurant deck.' She paused.

'I wondered if you might give me a hand, Erica, with running the restaurant. It's French themed. I'm calling it French Café Generalissimo. We'll Serve coffee, soft drinks, cider, gateaux de crepe, and crepe cakes.

'Of course, I will dear. How entrepreneurial of you. I'll look forward to that. See you at twelve then. Felicity, gave a thumbs up to Ben.

'Bye.'

'Bye Erica,'

85

'You're very courageous. She could frighten the customers. Don't let her gabble on about me, and how she wished I'd stayed at sea and not taken on Princess Katrina,'

'Is she likely to do that?'

'Yes, is my answer to that.'

'We get on very well.'

'Like two dragons together?'

Perhaps, it is that we can provide the fire to make it all work. Is that what you're saying Ben Sharpe?'

'Not exactly, but I'll run with that.' Ben, smiled and walked across to kiss his wife, knowing that he needed Felicity's full support to move forward with Paddle steamer Princess Katrina becoming seaworthy.

Chapter 25

'I'll be back.' Harbour master Jim Briggs called across to where Ben was stood, on the main deck, to gauge the paddle steamer's position, relative to support poles.

'Don't want to get grounded with the tide falling.' His launch needed to be moored in the outer harbour.

'I can give you a couple of hours red lead roller work. Sal, will call me if anything crops up.' Sal manned the Harbour Master's office on the top of the car park.

'That's good of you Jim. Might be a struggle to get it all covered, before the tide stops us.'

Ben, was assisted by volunteers from the engine room while he released tension on the springs, with unravelled turns on the bits fore and aft. A situation which needed constant monitoring, until the keel settled on the floor of the harbour with the paddle steamer's side leant against props. Large steel plates on the harbour wall absorbed the weight of the hull transmitted through props. Adjustments were made with lines to match the descent of the hull, as tide, took the inner harbour water, away. Fenders around the paddle wheel casing gave protection going alongside. As lines were relaxed, and distance maintained, between harbour wall and hull, to instate wall props.

It was after eleven, when the keel settled, on the harbour floor beams. A sedate lean, toward the wall, meant that even, pressure was placed on the props. Several, were positioned on the port side at bow and stern, as a safety measure, by two harbour council employees, in full length waders. These port side props fell away, once the paddle steamer leant over toward the harbour wall. Everything went to plan. A seven-degree list, gave a deck incline, which was manageable. The gangway, rolled out, roped off and a Perspex covered no entry sign affixed to shoreside.

A pair either side, set to. One jet washed and the other, eased away pockets of mussels and weeds, with a long- handled scraper. First, the rudder was cleared and then both sides working forwards. Previously, Ben had palleted twenty, five- gallon red lead and, two black paint drums, on the after deck. Ten red lead drums, for each side. Bought, on a sale or return basis. These accompanied, twenty paint trays, four hand rollers, ten long handled rollers, two four and two three-inch paint brushes and a bag of industrial waste. Plus, twelve bottles of turpentine. Robbie, questioned the amounts with,

'Are you planning to give it three coats?' knowing full well that getting one coat of red lead paint, on the hull, before the tide came in would be an achievement!

The previous day, with Princess Katrina slightly leant to starboard from full water tanks, Ben was able to mask tape the port side waterline. With a line, run alongside, he worked, with clipped-on rope attachment, to the dinghy to attach white plastic masking tape, from bow to stern. Where the red lead paint ended, before it met the black of the upper hull. The plan was to fill water tanks on the port side while alongside and use a quantity of starboard tank fresh water to create a port list for when they left the inner harbour on return to the mooring. Ben's experience, with the load and empty of oil tankers came to his assistance, in this manoeuvre, to get hull paintwork completed.

A bosun's chair, or painting stage could have been lowered over the stern, accompanied with a pot of black paint and a four-inch brush, for Ben cut in the upper hull with black paint, before Princess Katrina refloated. He felt confident that he could re-kindle experiences of painting from a Bosun's chair and was reminded of a certain First Mate's definition of a "five-minute job," which could be like – Paint the funnel! This involved swinging from a bosun chair attached to hooks around the funnel. Probably taking one or two days to complete.

An idea, which was dismissed, because (a) Felicity said it was too risky, and reminded Ben, he was married with a wife and family and (b) that time would not allow. Robbie, found the solution with the hire of a Werner 4 in 1 combination ladder. This gave sufficient reach for a stick roller to paint above the masked waterline. Ben would have preferred to use a four-inch brush, for smoother finish, but perfection toward his wanted gold standard was not an option.

Drums of red lead were lowered, from davits at bow and stern together with the combination ladder. Ben, adopted the role of Bosun and handed out rollers and trays. Felicity gave Freddie a boiler suit to wear.

The ridged sand bottom of the harbour was now scattered with runnels of water. A variety of small cabin cruisers, yachts, and row boats lay tilted, in abandoned fashion, on an empty harbour basin. A wall, by the steps which led down to the harbour, gave a zinging sound, from crustaceans, drying, deprived of water cloak. A pungent stench, from exposed seaweed, rose to where Felicity was, on the boat deck, which housed the restaurant. It was some consolation that the adjacent road reeked of seaweed smell. There was no real escape from it, until the tide returned. A more acceptable drying red lead paint smell, would filter up to maybe improve a pungent seaside aroma?

'It's the seaside, this is a smell visitors associate with being by the sea,' she said to Alison, who held her nose when she walked out on deck from the restaurant.

'I hope you're right Felicity. It's not so noticeable inside. They perhaps will prefer to escape, by coming into the restaurant. The gentle lilt of "La Mer," wafted from speakers set up, inside and outside.

A London taxi, wheeled around from the other side of the road, which caught Felicity's attention. Erica was inside, and looked across, to see if there was anyone she knew. Felicity, mindful of the need to keep in touch with Ben had smuggled the megaphone with her to the restaurant and called down.

'You're mother's arrived Ben.' He waved, came down from the ladder, and handed the paint roller to Robbie.

A stretch of the harbour road was reserved for taxis, and Erica's taxi driver drew up near, to the gangway. Erica was stood talking to the taxi driver, who then unstrapped three suitcases in descending size, from a luggage space, adjacent to his driver position.

'I can carry the small one.'

'Right you are,' said the driver who recognized his fare was best humoured rather than instructed. A relieved smile appeared when he spotted Ben, who strode from the gangway toward the cab.

The driver handed a small case to Erica.

'My son will assist you.' Erica had paid online for the taxi, but handed the driver a five -pound note.

'Thank you, mam. Hope you have a good trip.'

'Not going anywhere except across the harbour. But it does bring back memories.' Ben arrived.

'How are you managing?'

'Perfectly well, if you can carry this case as well.' The taxi driver entrepreneurially seeing further gratuity from Ben chipped in with,

'I can handle these larger ones. Where will you be wanting them to, sir?' It was a sort of done deal, since he'd unfolded a trolley. A smaller version of a sack truck and was loading the cases.

'Just the other side of the gangway on board, will do fine.' Erica's double cabin was just forward of the restaurant.

'I expect you wish you were picking up Aunt Rose and not your mother,' said Erica as she stepped on to the gangway, with buckled navy shoulder bag. Dressed in, navy jeans, white roll neck pullover, dark pink raincoat and wearing Addidas trainers.

'Don't be silly, we're all looking forward to having you aboard for Christmas mother,' said Ben, who was not going to start a family row at this point in proceedings.

'Ah Felicity, so nice to see you.' Felicity was stood, in part to welcome her mother-in-law aboard, but also to pitch a shoreside "A" board, to advertise Café Generallisimo, open. Erica, kissed Felicity on the cheek.

'Glad you could make it,' said Felicity, who was pleased to have Erica aboard.

"Mother," 'I haven't a lot of time,' said Ben, before a lengthy conversation got going, between the two of them.

'We've prepared double cabin seven for you along here.' Ben reached inside his boiler suit pocket and produced a brass fobbed key and led the way along the deck.

'I won't be long dear,' Erica smiled confidentially, back toward Felicity, who stood aside to allow the taxi driver past with his trolley.

'I expect you will need some help in the restaurant. I can unpack later.'

'We're not expecting a rush of customers, whenever you're ready, Erica.'

'That smell of paint reminds me of visiting a ship in Oslo, with your grandfather,' Erica said to Ben while he turned the key in the cabin door.

'I've got lots to do,' said Ben.

Chapter 26

Ben informed his workforce, that when the fo'c'sl'e bell sounded, a half-hour break was planned, to begin, for lunch. Felicity was instructed to ring eight bells; two at a time. In between assisting Ben with a ladder move along the port side, Robbie topped up trays with red lead paint and, offered words of advice and encouragement.

It was Chief Engineer Potts who suggested that a view of the engine room, might entice husbands or boyfriends to board, while their partners enjoyed a coffee. He offered to man the air-tight door, and escort a small number, to the upper platform, to describe, finer details of the engine room and answer questions. Leaflets, with an outer illustration of Princess Katrina, were produced with proposed sailing dates in the summer. Plus, a www. Site address, with mobile phone number for more detail and updates.

Leaflets, were placed on tables and at the serving counter. Felicity, with assistance from Freddie had a menu with price list printed out. Coffee, tea, and soft drinks listed separately.

'I do like your choice of music Felicity,' said Erica. Light jazz accordion music was playing when Erica arrived at the restaurant.

'Erica, this is Alison, who speaks French, so that I don't get caught out if we have any French customers.'

'Bonjour Alison. That's about all the French, I know. It's good that there's someone who speaks French.'

'Pleased to meet you Mrs Sharpe.'

'Oh, do call me Erica. Are you part of the crew, then Alison?'

'Not exactly.' Before a wrong impression was made, Felicity intervened.

'Alison has kindly offered to help for today. She's Head of French, where I teach.'

'Oh, I see. You may attract some French customers. What Felicity and Ben have achieved, so far, is impressive.'

Not wishing for Erica to go too far, in talking about Ben's achievements, Felicity changed the subject and turned to Alison.

'Are you okay, Alison? To hold the fort, while I show Erica the updated galley?'

'Only, so long as no customers appear. I'll call you if they do.' It had worked out well in that Erica's visit was delayed long enough to repair the foredeck and improve conditions on board. Erica, was heard to exclaim, from the galley,

'It's all very modern and up to date. I do like your primrose colour scheme, Felicity.'

Alison was not only there for her ability to speak French, but for cookery skills, with regard, to the preparation of crepe gateaux. It was partly a family affair, since Ross her brother, was assisting Chief Potts in the engine room.

Two chocolate pancake cakes were ready priced at four pound, ninety- nine a slice and a pan cake mix prepared, together with fillings. Either traditional lemon with sugar or a Nutella and fruit variation. The less elaborate crepe, on offer for three pound ninety- nine. A pre-used Bartscher Automatic coffee machine was installed behind the counter for easy access.

Chief Engineer Potts walked across to the open double doors.

'Are you open? Two young ladies would like a coffee?' The elder of the two smiled at the description, as they walked in. Mother and daughter.

'Yes, I'll just call someone.' Alison, who was booked, so to speak, in case there were French customers, but on call, if required, rather than front of house. She walked into the galley.

'Two customers have arrived and are wanting coffees, Felicity.'

'Oh good. Perhaps, you would you like to see how the coffee machine works Erica?'

'It will be a start. I hope I can be of help?'

'Of course, you can.'

'Do they only want coffees?

'As far as I know. I've chocolate crepe gateaux and some pancake mixture prepared out here, if they ask, for plain ones, that is.' Princess Katrina's newly opened Café Generalissimo's first two customers were stood at the counter when Felicity returned, with Erica. It was the daughter who said,

'Look they serve crepe gateaux.'

'What are they dear?' her mother asked.

'You'll like them. They're pan cakes, with filling and made into a cake.'

'A bit too sweet and sugary for me, but you can have one if you wish.' Felicity keen not to miss a possible sale said,

'We do a plainer French style crepe with lemon.'

'That'll do for me. You have the chocolate cake one Stephanie.' Her daughter ordered.

'Two lattes, and a chocolate and plain crepe, please.'

'Large or medium lattes? Would you like large or medium?'

'Both medium.' Felicity turned away placed a cup under the machine, and picked up their portable card machine.

'Would you like, a receipt?' She asked.

'No, that's alright.' Felicity smiled when Liz's mother made the payment.

'If you'd like to find a table. We'll, bring the lattes across. Crepes will be a few minutes.' The couple walked away toward a port side window table. Erica intervened with,

'Can I help with the coffee?'

'If you would, please, Erica. It's straightforward for lattes. Place a medium cup underneath, like so. Press the latte sign, and size required.' Felicity's deft finger touched a medium sized latte symbol, which started a gurgle and splutter from within the machine. Followed by a low intense hissing-sound, as the machine delivered a first coffee.

'Remember to put a medium cup underneath. I've to give the order to Alison, if you could...?

'Yes of course. I can manage, dear, I waitressed back in Oslo, you know, for a while.'

An order for *one chocolate Gateaux cake, and one Plain Lemon crepe* was written, in Felicity's neatest teacher writing, on to a mottled blue/black duplicate book. The top page, gently eased from its perforations, to deliver to Alison.

Mother and daughter, chose a table with a window view of pavement and road. The idea was for customers to pick up a tray and carry coffees to their table, but the system was not in place. Erica, in part, re-lived. younger waitressing days, and walked from the counter to the café area. Placed the tray with two coffees on a neighbouring table, before she picked them up to place in front of their first two customers.

'I'm not a great one for sea cruises, but it's so interesting to see these old paddle steamers,' the mother, said to Erica, who placed a blue bowl, decorated with seagulls on their table.

'Yes, it belongs to my son. He had a good career on board ships. It is like his passion, you know.'

'How exciting,' exclaimed the daughter as she ripped open a sachet of brown sugar to sprinkle on the latte.

'And you approve?' Asked the mother.

'Phew, What can I say, my daughter -in- law has the same madness!!' The daughter -in-law, in question, with this purported madness, approached.

'One chocolate cake crepe.'

'Yummy, yummy,' said the daughter, as Felicity placed a plate, together with spoons and forks, wrapped in paper napkins, on the table. Her mother decided otherwise.

'That would be a heart attack on a plate for me. Ah, that's, more my cup of tea.' Felicity, placed, icing sugar dusted, wrapped crepes, with lemon slices, down in front of her.

Meanwhile, Erica caught sight of a canary- coloured van with – **Baker – to your door** on its side, near to the paddle steamer. Parked, on double yellow lines. The driver in a white coat and straw hat got out, hurriedly.

'Felicity, there's a bakers van just arrived.'

'Oh good, that'll be the Cornish pasties I've ordered for the work force.' Just then, a man with his wife, and a child in a buggy called out from the restaurant door.

'We won't be needing life jackets with the tide out then.' His wife smiled pleasantly.

'I'll go down to see the baker,' said Erica. The van driver was by then, removing a basket wicker-sided tray, covered in cling film, from the back of his van.

'If you would ask him to bring them into the restaurant, Erica?

'How exciting,' the daughter remarked once again.

Chapter 27

Good thing, it's well out of season,' said harbour master Jim Briggs, as he walked, gingerly, across velvety green weed draped over wooden beams, that supported the paddle steamer.

'It's quiet and I've told Sal to field messages for later on or to message tomorrow.'

He wore wellington boots and khaki shorts, completed with anorak, and hood. Ben's paint roller, swept above the masking tape, and made a sound, similar, to when an adhesive strip is being removed. The red lead paint roller party were working ahead of Ben, on the starboard side.

'A start needs to be made on the port side, Jim. Robbie's rigged up some cluster lights to get light under the wall. Bit of hand brush work required around that side of the rudder.' Robbie returned from a re-fill of paint trays, carrying a half empty drum of red lead.

'Ah, we've got a professional here at last,' he said.

'That Freddie seems to paint the inner harbour, and himself, in preference to the ship's hull.'

'Don't knock it Robbie,' said Ben,

Bob Hope when asked whether he believed in God? said he needed all the help he could get.'

'Not sure young Freddie, is quite in that category.' Robbie, poured red lead paint into an empty wire handled paint can and picked up a four-inch brush.

'Just the man for the job. Can you paint, Jim around the port side of the rudder, where we can't get with rollers. I've a step ladder set up on that side. Seem to be moving ladders about and filling trays with paint, most the time.'

'Doing a grand job, Robbie. Professional, on the ground, I'd say,' said Ben.

'Flattery, for motivation is that?'

'Could be, could be.'

Good progress was made by Ben with a black paint roller brush along the port side and Harbour Master James Briggs had moved across to roller brushing the starboard side keel, when eight bells was sounded on the fo'c'sle, by Felicity.

A trestle table, several feet away from the restaurant entrance was set up to accommodate the work force. Unlike the first customers they queued at the counter with a tray.

It was Cornish pasty, chips, and peas. The Cornish pasty and chips micro-waved while the petit pois peas were poured into a bowl of boiling water.

Included were vegetarian pasties, which Felicity ordered, knowing that Alison had recently identified as vegetarian and where there might be demand among their workforce. Customers did not seem to be perturbed by the arrival of Ben's work team at the counter. It gave them a sense of participation and belonging to be on board during the refit.

'How many coffees? Felicity asked Ben who headed the queue.

'I'll see, I'll see.'

Once this was ascertained, Felicity said that they would bring them out to where they were sat outside. It was more straightforward to prepare coffees and for the group not to have to queue and wait. Felicity was hoping that café customers would not ask to buy a pasty. It was a bit tricky. A pleasant bakery smell drifted out from the galley into the café area, as two pasties were micro-waved at a time. Individually plated with added microwaved frites, plus a scoop of peas. Kept warm, in the galley's oven.

Erica surpassed herself. For the main part in management of the micro-wave process, while Alison, assisted by her brother, carried plated meals on trays, through to Ben and his work force at the counter. Chief Engineer Potts, responded to the fo'c'sl'e bell ring by posting a sign on his engine room door to notify visitors that an engine room inspection would start again at 1430 hours, before joining the work party lunch break.

'Where did you get these?' Jamie exclaimed after chewing a mouthful of pasty.

'They're brilliant.' Ben had erected a green tarpaulin outside to make a deckhead for protection, should it rain.

'A local bakery at the top of the high street. I'm glad you like them, Jamie. We could include them on the menu later.'

'If you do you can see me signing up.' Ben was ever going to agree, where possible with Jamie, who was intrinsic to the running of the engine room. It was not that Chief Potts was more figure head, but Jamie, understood steam and was able to pick up on any untoward sound, before a serious problem developed. A stickler for swabbing pistons and maintenance in general.

'Taste so much better eaten out of doors,' said Jim the harbour master.' Perhaps he'd lost his sense of smell or liked the smell of drying red lead that wafted up from below?

'*Dancing Queen's*, been called over to Brixham. Tow in a broken-down trawler,' continued Jim.

'Extravagant use of the tug's time, isn't?' replied Ben.

'Don't knock it Ben, the trawler owner can share the day's cost.' Jim Briggs finger tapped his nose, knowingly.

'You may need him back by about seven to help you off the harbour wall.'

'You're probably right, Jim.'

'You know full well I am. How are you going to short turn here, without a tug to make the bow swing in the smallest arc,'

'Can we just enjoy our lunch without too much scientific talk.' Freddie came in with. He got full backing from Felicity who'd arrived with a tray full of steaming coffee mugs.

'You tell them Freddie. Don't let them go all technical on you. And yes, Ben Sharpe, there's no tug strike for you to show off your ship handling skills.' She placed a tray filled with coffees on the trestle table. Felicity had been regaled with stories about how Ben's ship went into New Jersey without tugs, during a strike by American tug boat men.

'Thank you, Felicity,' said Jim. He was giving, a double purpose thank you for the coffees and Felicity's sensible talk.

'How's it going? How are things in Glocca Morra? Felicity asked her husband, who was painting from a ladder.

'Making a dent in it,' replied Ben.

'You can talk,' said Freddie.

'You're up a ladder, not at the coal, or mud face, like the rest of us. Are you all right in the restaurant Flick? You don't need – like a kitchen porter to help with the washing up?'

'I'll take you up on that offer Freddie, if you don't mind.'

Chapter 28

It was more than a rumour. Realisation that the tide had turned. It was still possible to keep dry by standing on the beams raised above the floor of the harbour, but only just. Ben, after completion of the cutting in of the port side with black paint, joined harbour master Jim, and volunteers, on the starboard side, to complete the red leading. The wearing of sea boots provided protection from the early incursion of tide. Last to finish, they joined the others, who were stood by a stack of pallets, which held a cradled pallet of paint drums, trays, rollers, paint brushes, turpentine, and rag waste. Robbie shouted down from above.

'Mind yourselves,' as he lowered a hook from the davit, to retrieve the wire cradled pallet.

Wooden beams which supported Princess Katrina were soon completely covered by incoming tide and those without sea boots were stood bare foot, with rolled up trousers, in the harbour, before they left to mount the harbour side steps. Towels were provided to dry their feet in the warmth of the restaurant, soon to be closed.

Felicity, was walking down the gangway to remove the café open sign when she spotted Justin on the harbour steps, with his school bag dumped, on a step above, while he twisted mussels, from the harbour wall.

'Justin, you're to get out of those school clothes, I'm not washing them before the weekend.'

'But mum, the tides coming in and you just don't get mussels like this for bait, in the outer harbour,' as he sought to justify his actions. He ripped a couple of centre pages out of an exercise book, to wrap the mussels in, picked up his school bag up and started to climb the steps.

'Where's your brother?'

'He's with father.'

'And where's that?'

'On the bridge.'

An hour later, a supporting pole fell away, then another. Robbie, was on the main deck, to clean rollers, brushes, and set aside unused paint drums, when he heard the poles crash, as they fell, and bounced against the harbour wall. He removed a marlin spike from a leather belted holster and banged an empty drum. Ben came out on to the starboard bridge.

'Captain Sharpe, we're near away.' Ben raised an arm in acknowledgement.

By six thirty, Katrina was afloat, with Dancing Queen reversed into the inner harbour. Stopped and anchored, about fifty feet from Princess Katrina's bow. This time Robbie took a line from the tug and winched a split wire rope tow line on board. Once secured around bits, the tug released the wire further to angle the tow rope back from the paddle steamer and weighed anchor.

Fore and aft springs were back on board, and a forward line released from its bollard. Left to trail in the water, while Robbie went to assist Freddie, and two volunteers, accompanied by Patrick. Robbie transferred the after line, from its wrap around bits, to the winch. Ben was informed by shouts of,

'We're ready, we're ready,' from Robbie at the stern. Acknowledged by Ben on the bridge. The tug was ready to take in slack from the forward tow rope, and swing the bow to port; while the paddle steamer was held at the stern. Once, a swing to port was achieved, the tug reversed to create slack, for the wire spring to be released and winched back aboard. Ben rang for Dead Slow Ahead, which made little impression, against the tide, Then Slow Ahead, followed by Stop. Lines were in the water and Ben wanted these aboard before he left the inner harbour.

Caroline, earlier, phoned her mother and it was agreed she could stay with Abigail and return when they were back on the mooring. Felicity insisted on speaking with Abigail's mother to confirm that she was happy about this.

When, the tug was let go, and lines aboard, Ben rang for Slow Ahead and, once in the outer harbour, gave port wheel to complete an arc swing, to line up with the mooring. Patrick was given the task of holding the wheel midships once lined up with the mooring buoy.

With the paddle steamer stopped yards from the mooring, Harbour master Jim, aboard his launch, took a line from the paddle steamer's bow to thread through the mooring hook for return to Robbie. This procedure was repeated at the stern, where Freddie and Patrick stood, to let out a stern line for the other buoy. Winches on board, took in slack line from buoys to paddle steamer.

Justin, meanwhile was with Granny. Pleased, that he had her all to himself. Especially, when Erica unpacked a Game Boy Advance Nintendo and set it up, in her cabin.

'Half an hour and then it's bath time.' His mother stuck her head into the cabin. While, previously alongside water tanks were re-filled to enable supply of hot water, courtesy of the engine room.

Ben, was relieved, that they were successfully back on the moorings, and rang Finished with Engines, on return to the bridge. The plan was to keep the ship's generator running until the weekend. Chief Potts volunteered to stay aboard with two volunteers plus Alison's brother to assist. Felicity told Alison that there were no spare berths when she asked if she might sleep the night, but offered to run her ashore, when Caroline needed picking up. It was not exactly true, but sensed that she might be angling for opportunity to meet with Ben, beyond an introduction level.

'You can have a bath Ben Sharpe, after Justin. I'm not going to bed with that smell of paint, turpentine, and mooring ropes.' After a gracious period of politeness and decorum toward customers in the restaurant, Felicity, switched into teacher mode when she entered the wheelhouse. Ben, in boiler suit was, knelt, on the wheelhouse floor to read a GPS instruction manual.

'It'll be difficult getting used to the ship generator and boilers being shut down, once more.'

'But we're nearer to being fully operational.' Ben said, as he got to his feet. A move made to kiss Felicity thwarted. She held out an arm, hand held to nose and offered a cheek to peck.

'I feel more confident in my role as wife and mother now that Erica is aboard.'

'You mean that you'll have womanly back up?'

'Caroline has become more understanding than she used to be.'

'But she's a young girl.'

'Girls are innately able to empathise at an earlier age. Look at you Ben, you're, still like a small boy with his first train set. No Erica is a sympathetic ear. No woman knows as much about a man as his mother.'

It is that some proverb? I'm not reckoning on that as a plus. Mother didn't frighten the customers away then?'

'Of course not! I'm not sure we could have managed very well, without her.'

Chapter 29

It was an interlude, but also a preview of how it would be during the summer, when Princess Katrina was not in semi-mothballed state. All systems would be functioning. Deck area and restaurant would be open to the public.

Lifeboats, either side of the bridge needed inspection and a run down into harbour water, to test davit gear. On the foredeck and after decks there were rafts, disguised, in the form of seats. Also, cylinder rafts were to be installed on either side of the mid- deck. Ejected overboard, they inflated, when the line attached was yanked from on board. Work, and maintenance that needed completion, to obtain a certificate of sea-worthiness and an operator's licence.

It was agreed that Robbie would be paid for two days work a week. Mainly to oversee a team of volunteers that came from a variety of occupational background.

It was Erica, who suggested that they should have a Christmas party. Princess Katrina was moored about sixty feet from the outer harbour wall. It was possible to run lines across and winch the vessel alongside. When Erica heard that Ben planned to go alongside, to refill water and fuel tanks, she voiced the idea to Felicity, when they were sat outside the restaurant.

'It would be an opportunity to sell raffle tickets and advertise the summer cruise schedules, wouldn't it?

'I don't want a boozy yacht club event,' said Felicity.

'You'll have to be selective who you invite dear. Perhaps colleagues from school?

'They might be more, risky than yacht club members! Just because teachers are the only adult in a class room of students, it doesn't follow, that they behave like responsible adults outside the class room.'

'Alison, is a very pleasant young woman?'

'High risk around Ben, though.'

'I see where you're coming from there. Men can be like clay in the hands of a woman, determined enough in her pursuit. My son is an innocent ashore, in more ways than one.'

'Are you saying that I captured him?'

'You had my backing, you know that, Felicity. It was a pursuit that I wanted you to win. A pursuit, that led to an adventure in madness, maybe?' They were stood outside the restaurant and Erica spread her hand across a view of the after deck, to encompass what she saw as a madness, in taking on the restoration of Princess Katrina. Justin could be seen to cast, from his fishing rod in to the harbour.

'What would my life be without you Felicity, Ben and the children near to me?' Felicity smiled and said,

'Then Cinderella shall go to the ball. Erica, we'll have a Christmas party. One for the children and one for adults. My husband will have to put on his social face.'

'It'll do good to make Ben socialize. I've thought about his decision to leave a career at sea and have decided that it was a right move for a long-term future. A family should take priority over all else, for future happiness.'

A clatter of footsteps on the companionway led to the arrival of Ben.

'That's another box to tick.' He said, while he held a letter in his hand.

'The life-saving has passed inspection. Do I qualify for a coffee?'

'What you are saying is will I make you a coffee?'

'Not in so many words, I can...'

'It's alright, I could do with a coffee myself,' said Erica.

'To avoid marital disagreement, I'll make it.' Erica, got to her feet and walked into the restaurant and across to the bar, to fill two Lattes from the machine. Ben, sat opposite Felicity. Without delay she decided to broach the subject about a Christmas party.

'You know, I wasn't keen on a Christmas party, Ben. Part of the reason was that everyone would need ferrying out to the mooring, but now we're going alongside the harbour, it would work.'

'Is that your view?'

'It is now. I mean, have to admit that Erica suggested the idea first. But it makes sense. We can invite anyone who might be influential towards our hiring out next Spring.'

'You have a way of turning every activity into a commercial venture.'

'Someone, has to promote our future aboard this boat.'

'How plebian, calling Katrina a boat.'

'Don't get all clever with me Ben Sharpe. A passenger liner can be called a boat. A paddle steamer is down below a liner in status.'

'I beg to differ.'

'I beg to differ, in that married couples should squabble privately.' Erica caught up on their chat on her return with the coffees.

'Granny, you said you'd set up the Nintendo Game Boy again,' Justin, had given up on enticing harbour fish on to a baited hook and appeared in the restaurant, rod packed back in its carrying bag.

'What it is to be in demand?' said Ben

'No complaints from me,' said Felicity. It was half-term and both Patrick and Caroline were ashore with friends. Justin's friend Danny was on holiday in Majorca and Justin, had resorted to fishing off the paddle steamer, instead of the outer harbour wall.

'Granny's having a coffee,' Felicity, called to Justin.

'Alright, sweetheart I can bring my coffee with me.'

'You're the tops gran. I'll let you win a game.'

'Cheeky rascal! I won the last two.'

'I know granny's very competitive,' said Ben. 'She gave up playing table tennis when I started beating her.'

'I should think so. You were four years older than Justin I seem to remember.'

'Lunch is at one sharp, you two, so don't get too engrossed.'

'That's right teacher,' said Ben. Keep the youngsters in order.'

Ben, did not see the finger point from his mother.

Chapter 30

It was mild weather into November, which gave good conditions for Ben to manoeuvre Princess Katrina from her moorings to the harbour wall. A Norwegian timber cargo vessel was moored further forward, but there was ample harbour stretch for the paddle steamer to winch into. Chief Potts, came aboard to give the boilers a test run and once alongside the main diesel generator was started up. It was Friday and the plan was to remain alongside for the weekend.

The Christmas party was by ticket invitation. Felicity had applied for and received a Temporary Event Notice (TEN) to enable alcohol to be served for the late evening party.

A previous family reunion at a village hall had fallen flat because the hall was not licensed to sell alcohol and spirits. Ben was sent to the yacht club to scout out a price list. Felicity, decided on a ten per cent increase on prices and a twenty on soft drinks.

'That's over the top, isn't it?' questioned Ben.

'We're not running a charity. It's like a charge for the ambience. How often do people have opportunity to Christmas party, aboard a paddle steamer? I think we'll need more open space in the restaurant area. Tables can be removed and taken to the after deck. Provided it's dry, it'll allow extra space. Freddie's volunteered to be Father Christmas.'

'That let's me off that hook then. That'll be for the Children's party in the afternoon?'

'No, he'll compere proceedings in the evening.'

'You mean like a disc jockey?'

'Sort of, but also to call out raffle winners and game results.'

'He'll organize raffles?'

'Not exactly. Everyone will have a numbered entrance ticket and a man or woman, who wins, certain games for example will be allowed to kiss the woman or man of choice.'

'Dangerous stuff?'

'Only where a married woman doesn't kiss her husband.'

'That's, exactly what I mean.'

'You're not allowed to kiss the bulkhead of Princess Katrina, if you win.'

'It all sounds a bit risqué.'

'No Ben, men will be monitored as to suitability to be a winner of this prize.'

'Very sexist.'

'No, just sensible. I' don't want our Christmas party to be cause of marital disharmony.' There was a pause, before Ben asked.

'Is the restaurant to be open for food?'

'Possibly a buffet style. Do you think we should include it in the ticket price?'

'Why are you asking me?'

'Because, you're some random person I met last night who ended up living aboard! No, I'm having you fully invested in this Christmas party. I think you should welcome everyone aboard in Captain's uniform.'

'Do I have to?'

'The answer to that is yes. It's all part of the experience. It will go down well with the children.'

'You've got Freddie as Father Christmas. I wouldn't want to steal his thunder.'

'It's either that or you double up as Father Christmas yourself.'

'I'll maybe run with the first option.'

'I thought you might.'

'I've talked with the Torquay Librarian. She wasn't interested in my children's book, Adventure in Alicante, but I can have a table inside to promote trips around the bay and sell raffle tickets for the restoration fund. Provided we feature books about paddle steamers. That's the library element.

'I can sort of tell what's coming next.'

'Yes, it would be helpful if you could be there in uniform. Robbie's built a model of Princess Katrina, which will be display on the table and you can answer questions. There will be an hour, just after school when you can attend and, I'll man the table prior to that.'

'You're taking me way out of my comfort zone.'

'That's what wives are for.'

'You've just made that up. I've never heard that said before?'

'Are you going to sell Christmas Party tickets at the Library?'

I was politely told, that the library was not a commercial venture, but an educational one.'

No, yacht club members, husbands, wives, and friends are our likely best customers for the Christmas party. I may have to allow Liz to have a yacht club social meeting aboard, after all. In fact, she's probably the best one to contact,' said Felicity, thinking aloud.

'The children's party will be restricted to twenty.'

'Right. Are, you going to charge for that, as well?'

'No of course not, but the parents may be persuaded to buy raffle tickets and bring some prizes. I've managed to persuade Esplanade Travel, in Fleet Street to offer a week's family holiday in Biarritz, as a prize. Provided that we display for them aboard, and online.'

'That's a bit counter-productive. I mean we're offering a holiday experience.'

'Not really the same is it, Ben? I mean it's a good first prize. Bit worried that punters may feel cheated if they only win a cruise to Elberry Cove as a runner up prize.'

'I know which prize I'd rather win?'

'The meal for two at the Cottage Inn? Be careful how you answer that.'

'I'll run with that. Mother can baby sit.'

'I'll need then to tell the world, that I've squeezed a bit of romanticism out of my husband.'

Chapter 31

Rise and fall of the tide, in the outer harbour, did not leave boats stranded, like in the inner harbour and Ben arranged with Torbay Council to go alongside for Thursday, Friday, and Saturday, in the first week of December. Felicity having planned for the children's party on the Thursday and the adults for Friday. A conclusion reached that both on the same day would be too demanding.

A Christmas makeover of the restaurant with regard, to decorations, was in progress. The after deck, home to Santa's tent grotto, was covered with greenery. Ben and Felicity with assistance from Patrick and Caroline were putting up decorations, in the restaurant. Erica, was taken ashore by Ben earlier for an apartment visit to update on progress and as she said,

"To resample a world of normality."

'It's good, don't you think that we have a mix of Christmas party goers? I mean the yacht club members won't sort of hold the floor.' Felicity cheerfully announced.

'Don't count on it.' An original figure of fifty invites was reduced to thirty

'Local people are unlikely to want to take a cruise around the bay or visit somewhere like Dartmouth, anyhow.'

'Don't be such a party pooper father.'

'Caroline, I couldn't have expressed that opinion better myself,' said Felicity.

'Dad's right though,' said Patrick, in support of freedom expression for male members of a family, who could have less speech input than females, over domestic matters or anything for that matter.

'It'll be Grockles who will want to come aboard for a cruise.'

'I do wish you wouldn't use that name for tourists, Patrick. Especially now they'll be essential for us to have good passenger lists in the summer. Anyway, it'll get the message out that we'll be up and running for cruises and visits next summer.'

'How are we expected to run our lives when Princess Katrina, is going out of the harbour, when we still live aboard?' Asked Caroline. This was a realistic question, from Caroline about the future and one that Felicity had not fully given attention to. It was Ben who answered.

'We'll be back in harbour for when you finish school.'

'I'll go and live with granny I think said Patrick. It'll be like living in a fair ground when there are passengers aboard. Justin will most likely stay to go fishing,' he said, in a matter-of-fact way. Patrick, joined in with the complaint, but of the three was the most enthusiastic, about living aboard. However, children can collaborate collectively to wind parents up

'Come on,' said Felicity. 'It's not a big problem. Your school friends' parents have hotels and it's part of their lives, when guests are staying.'

'Yes, but if they go anywhere, during the day the hotel doesn't leave the street.'

'I'll speak with granny. She has spare bedrooms in her flat,' said Ben.

'That's if you don't want to be on board any longer.'

'Look. Now you've upset your father,' said Felicity.' She smiled and protectively placed an arm around Ben.

'We do father.' Caroline ran across and joined in a mother daughter embrace of Ben. Patrick, staunchly remained where he was, not willing to indulge it what he saw as girlish behaviour, with no real purpose other than to attention seek.

'I was just talking out loud,' said Caroline.

'It was Abigail who said that she wouldn't want to live in a home that could float away.'

'I expect she's really jealous of the life you lead aboard a paddle steamer. Don't you think?' Felicity looked at her husband for agreement, and to give reassurance.

'She doesn't get to see seagulls pooping on the deck, does she?' A moment of child, adult sabre rattling came to an end, with laughter.

Chapter 32

'Get those fenders over.' Freddie, acknowledged Ben in his role as Captain, when on the bridge, but was less reverential in everyday life, He flipped attached fenders over, to cover the port paddle wheel casing. Ben assessed progress from Princess Katrina's port bridge, where Jamie operated a forward winch and Robbie an after one. Ben, blasted out, by megaphone,

'Stop the winch, and release all tension.' To first Robbie and then Jamie at the bow.

An extended paddle box was at risk of being crushed by too rapid an approach. With this consideration Ben had lined-up to a wooden beam, which offered softer impact, than harbour wall concrete pillars.

'Within moments of fenders being lifted over the side to offer protection, they started to absorb pressure. Several squelched against the wood beam, which emitted a creak on impact. It was close run manoeuvre, but the paddle box was undamaged.

'Take up slack and secure.' Ben gave megaphone instructions to bow and stern. Only for Robbie to shout back.

We'll need more hands.' Freddie was detailed off to assist Robbie. Ben made for the bow to help Jamie.

Earlier, that morning, orange polypropylene bow, and stern ropes were run across, attached to the motor- powered shore dinghy. Floating lines, which gave visibility, when the mooring ropes were winched in, to bring the vessel alongside. A line attached to each polypropylene rope was thrown ashore, from the dinghy, and enabled both mooring ropes to be pulled in from the water, and looped around bollards.

Two more lines were run ashore, later before the gangway was lowered. Visitors by then walking were from the car park to get a better view of the paddle steamer.

Felicity, was without supply work and could give to attention to party preparation, after they were safely alongside. Erica's boarding earlier that week, pleased Justin since he could play Nintendo on his granny's consul. Felicity, was relieved, because Erica said she could help or be in attendance, at the children's party and was curious to know, who would attend the adult Christmas party. It was high tide, They were sat outside making the most of the sun and its reflection on to the after deck, when Erica asked,

'Who's on the adult party list Felicity?

'We weren't going to have a house warming party, but it seems there are yacht club members that we both know. They make up about twelve with partners.' Felicity read out other names from a list that she'd prepared.

'Commander Blenkinsop and partner. Geoffery Moore; Alison Stroud and friend. That's the Alison who helped at the restaurant when we were alongside.'

'There's one person that I know, at least.'

'The friend is her brother. I don't know why she didn't just write that it was her brother!'

'Might frighten away suitors. Friend could be girl- friend, maybe?'

'I hope she finds someone. As long as it's not my husband.'

'I don't think you have anything to fear my dear. Ben's too much in love.'

'What with a paddle steamer?'

'No, don't be silly my dear. I didn't mean that. You know that.'

'Shall I continue?'

'Oh, yes, there maybe someone I know. If they've nothing to do with the yacht club.'

'Here's one. Edward Potts.'

'Do I know him?'

'Yes, he's our Chief Engineer.'

'I only know him as Teddie.'

'Already on first name terms. That sounds promising.'

'And what do you mean by that Felicity?'

'Well, nothing really. Just that you'll both have someone to talk with.'

'More that we have a common interest, than anything else.' Felicity continued,

'Geoff Winterton and partner.'

'I do know those two. They run an electrical store in town. They might be interesting to get to know.'

'Good. James Briggs plus two. That's interesting the Harbour Master has two guests.

I'm getting vibes that there may be an emphasis on male guests over females.'

'I don't' have a problem with that. Do you? Said Erica.

'Only, that could cause an imbalance. Oh wait a minute. Olivia, Charlotte, and Sophia Vanter. They own a racing dinghy. I hope they won't be disappointed by a lack of young stud talent.'

'How old are they Felicity?'

'In early to mid- twenties.'

'From the yacht club?'

'No not this one. They race at Dartmouth. They could be useful contacts. Ben plans to run trips to the River Dart.

'That's ambitious, isn't it?'

'Not really. We'll need to sell more than trips in Torbay and around warships at anchor.' Erica was enthusiastic about Dartmouth.

'I'll be able to have a look around the shops in Dartmouth then.' Felicity scanned the list.

'Oh, they might be in luck. Tom Banbury plus two. That's Torquay Rugby Club. That'll be Ben, he follows the rugby.'

'You could be in need of some bouncers Felicity.'

'I've thought that one through. Robbie and Jamie are on board Friday evening to complete some maintenance work. I wouldn't fancy anyone's chances. Robbie's arm muscles are the size of other people's thighs. I saw him lift Freddie up with one arm.'

Chapter 33

A sprinkling of snow fell, the night, before the children's party. Tarpaulin yacht cabin covers on the hard, transformed a uniform white.

Decks aboard Princess Katrina were brushed clear of snow. Snow, that remained gave a feel of Christmas in harbour surround. In a change of plan, Felicity decided to bring in outside caterers to provide party food. A round robin to parents, for a contribution did not meet with resistance. It was Erica who suggested that it would relieve pressure, and give more time to arranging the party side of things. A parent committee meeting was held on board a week before. That brought a level of commitment from participating parents and families. It was to seek volunteers who would help to organize games and assist Felicity with the running of the party.

It was decided that the children could invite one friend each and that there was to be no sneaking away from the party. Patrick, with supervision from Freddie was allowed to gas fill, ticketed balloons. These to be released from the foredeck. Provided there was an onshore westerly wind. It would be pointless if the balloons landed in the sea. Each balloon with a pre- paid stamped card with the Paddle steamers address on. A first, second and third prize for each ticket returned farthest away from the harbour.

Unsurprisingly Caroline invited Abigail and Justin his friend Danny. Instructions given that there was no opting out to go fishing over the stern for grey mullet. Fish that like to congregate around the side of a harbour wall or in this case a paddle steamer's hull. They could be caught, when they swallowed bread attached to a hook. Patrick, said that his friends were too adult to attend children's parties, but consensus, of opinion was that he did not want competition over his role aboard. Now that he had assisted his father with the steering of the paddle steamer back from the inner harbour to the mooring, he felt that he was more integral to the manning of the paddle steamer than his brother and sister.

Felicity and Erica ended the children's party with musical chairs, before they all walked down to the after deck, for the younger children to see Father Christmas, with parents in attendance. Every child that went out during the playing of musical chairs received a goody bag. The winner received a family ticket to McDonalds. One of the parents contributed this, as a prize for the party. Caroline, said that she would have tried harder if she'd known that was the prize.

'I wish you had Caroline,' said Felicity, 'but then it might have been inappropriate, for one of the family to walk away with a top prize.'

'Yes, we used to be told it was family step back,' said Erica.

'We've already done that by letting all these kids on board.'

'It's a way of making guests welcome, not grabbing all the goodies first.'

'So, if I had won you would have made me hand the prize back. How unfair.'

'You, haven't won Caroline. Anyway, we'd best get down to the after deck to assist. Chief Potts will need support.' Chief Potts, assisted by Patrick was filling coloured balloons with gas, ready to attach a participant's ticket before balloon release. With the strong westerly wind, it might allow a balloon to reach Dartmoor or fly even further afield. Each child was given a two- pound coin from a parent whip around, at an earlier committee meeting. Patrick and Justin decided that the coin offered more attraction, than punting it on a balloon. Felicity was pleased that Caroline did buy a balloon ticket, possibly to join Abigail. Both girls were that bit older.

Felicity was rewarded when Ben arrived at the party, halfway through, in Captain's uniform and was able to take the boys and one or two of the older girls on an escorted tour of the wheelhouse. Chief Potts supervised a visit to the engine room. This dove- tailed in with a catering prepared buffet choice, of fruit juices, triangle sandwiches, sausages on sticks, cup- cakes and ice cream. After a final game of musical chairs, the children were given crackers to pull open. Felicity, selected motto jokes and was joined by parents who had arrived to fetch their children and immediately recruited to read out jokes from the crackers.

The first one brought groans – "What did Adam say on the day before Christmas?"- "It's Christmas, Eve." The second was better received by the children. "How do snowmen get around?"- "They ride an icicle." After the third reading – "What do reindeer say before they tell a joke?"- "This one's gonna sleigh you," a megaphone call from Freddie, ended the read of further howlers.

"Balloons are ready to be released. All competitors to assemble on the after deck."

Each competitor held a stringed balloon, ready for release. Grouped, on the after deck. An additional fifty were sponsored from raffle ticket sales and released by Felicity and Erica.

Freddie, in Father Christmas dress acted as starter.

'Ready balloonists; steady! Release your balloons.'

Spotlights on the after deck caught the batch of coloured balloons as they flew up into the night sky.

The girls Christmas gift from Santa was sorted by a donation of rattan shoulder bags, from a parent who owned a gift shop. The boys were given a solar toy to assemble. Patrick later said the boys were short changed, because you needed to be scientifically minded. However, Justin and Danny were quite happy with the gift. Each gift -wrapped present depicted a paddle steamer on the stamped card with the child's name. Addressed for return to Princess Katrina with a free cruise available to the child, accompanied by parents.

Freddie, rolled a barrel out of the grotto on to deck. Caroline assisted by taking out any Christmas gift to hand to Freddie who called out the child's name. A selection of Christmas music, played in the background, which included songs by Beyonce and Taylor Swift, requested by Caroline. The process speeded up when a light drizzle could be felt. Seen to sweep through the spotlight glow. Parents had their child thank Felicity and Erica as they departed. By the gangway, a board, with sailing times was prepared, with a start date on 25th March. Trips around the Bay and a once weekly cruise to the River Dart.

Felicity persuaded Ben And Chief Potts to stand by the gangway and wish both adults and children a Happy Christmas, and to say

'Look forward to seeing you in the New Year for a cruise.'

Chapter 34

'Ed.' Ben called across from his position overseeing proceedings on the after deck, to catch Chief Potts, after they'd seen all guest visitors ashore. He was about to open the engine room and turned to face Ben, who was in Captain's uniform.'

'Yes, Captain Sharpe.' A formality which seemed out of synch with Ben's first name address, but a Captain's uniform realized shipboard roles, and Chief Potts responded accordingly.

'Fancy a swift half ashore?'

'Now that is an offer hard to refuse. Jamie and Ross,' Alison's brother, 'are working on number two generator, until nine. Should be able to take an hour or so shore leave.

'Where you planning to go?' Ben pointed across to the Cliff club bar.

'No distance. Just over there.'

'I'm not a member.'

'That's not a problem. I'll sign you in as my guest. Got to get out of these togs. Not my idea but the better half...

'Felicity has a business head and you're lucky to have a wife who understands the power of advertising.'

'You two, Ed, do seem to be on a similar wavelength.'

'More into authentic restoration than the paddle steamer's Captain, I suspect?'

'Should I grow a beard and smoke a pipe to be more authentic?'

'Well, there you are.' Ben nodded his head.

'No that's unlikely.'

'Give me twenty-minutes and I'll be with you, Ben.'

'Got to square it with Felicity. That our Chief Engineer's gasping for a beer.'

'Now, don't go upsetting Felicity on my account.'

'No, she wants me to sort out some work for Katrina next year. Not sure I'd be let of the hook so easily otherwise.

Ben, ten minutes later made a re-appearance in jeans and jumper at the paddle steamers restaurant.

'Does this mean you're off duty?' Felicity called across to where she was assisting the caterers to pack away.

'The Chief Engineers in need of refreshment and well, we need to keep the crew happy.'

'That's the lamest excuse for a drink ashore, as ever, I've heard. You are

going to follow up on work for Princess Katrina during the summer months?'
Freddie, suggested to Felicity that Katrina could have a role in laying buoys for
yacht racing and maybe, if anchored out in the bay, as a starting platform for
race supervision. Felicity, was au fait with the buoy laying, because this would
be pre- summer, but later-on cruises for holidaymakers would, hopefully, be
in full swing.

'I will if there's anyone in official capacity there.'

'If Liz is there, tell her, she can have a committee meeting on board... I'll
rephrase that. Felicity says that should alternative premises be required for
committee and social club meetings our restaurant is available for hire.'

'That's a change of tune.'

'Look Ben, if we're to run a successful steam boat business we'll need to be
open for hire business in and out of season.'

Felicity didn't mention it to Ben but Erica had said she would be willing
to help after Christmas. They were in tune, in understanding of the challenges
that Ben could present, in a woman's life, be it as wife or mother.

'Okay, okay, I'll put out feelers.'

'We could run a yacht club special and take members to Paignton, Brixham,
and Dartmouth during the regatta season.' Felicity picked up a box.

'Here, ask Jock at the bar if he would hand these out.' Felicity handed the
small red box to Ben, which he opened.

'They're business cards.'

I've already shown you the proofs.'

'My clever wife.'

'Freddie gave them to me as a Christmas present from the printing works.
He was happy to do them if we mentioned the print works email at the end.'

'How many are there in here?'

'One hundred. I've five more boxes. Business cards are a bit old- fashioned.'

'But we live in an old-fashioned part of the world?'

'Yes, I kinda thought that. Tell Jock, I'll get in some haggis for him.'

'That should do the trick.' A silhouette of Chief Potts, now dressed in a
navy coat, grey flannels and matching flat cap, appeared in the door entrance
to the restaurant. Felicity greeted him.

'Thanks so much for all, your help today, Edward. The balloon Race event
went down a treat.'

'That's what matters, Felicity. The children all seemed to be enjoying
themselves. Christmas is for them mainly I always think.'

'It's wonderful to have Katrina's generator going again.' A persistent pulse of the generator could be heard in the restaurant. When at sea, the whirr of paddle wheels would become dominant. Then, near to the engine room would be heard the scythe back and forth of pistons punctuated with steam pressure gasps, to inform passers-by, of the working engines beneath. It was reassuring for Chief Potts, that Felicity appreciated all the work.

'Your husband invited me ashore for a drink. You're still busy. Do you need some help?' Felicity smiled in appreciation of the Chief's concern for her well- being. Ben, could take her for granted, and there was hope that the concern shown for general well- being by other men might permeate into a greater appreciation from Ben – more than "You know I love you."

'No Edward, you've more than earned a break. We wouldn't have been able to manage these parties without the engine room contribution. It's given a taste of how it will be when we're ready to take passengers with a fully functioning engine room.'

'Could do with a proper run in the bay, before that happens,' replied Chief Potts. More directed at Ben than Felicity.

'Can't see that happening this side of New Year. But you never know.'

'Are you having other parties?'

Ben and Felicity looked at one another. It was Felicity who answered.

'No plans, at the, moment. We've tomorrow night to contend with.'

Chapter 35

The tide was in and the gangway was near flat with the deck, when Chief Pots followed Ben across to go ashore. A Norwegian timber ship, one berth, up from Princess Katrina was working into the evening, to discharge slings of timber on to a flat-bed lorry. Powerful spotlights were trained on to deck and lorry. A torch was trained at a sling, as it swung across, by a deck officer who wore a white roll neck jumper, under a uniform jacket. He was able to direct his winch men aboard by a wave of the torch, to lower or stop a sling, which held a bundle of planks. In a large dock, overhead cranes would have handled larger amounts. Movement of the wood planks released a pungent wood pine scent on to the pier. The driver on the flat bed lorry, was assisted by a crew member, who in turn talked in English to the driver and replied to the officer in Norwegian.

'Brings back memories,' said Chief Potts.

'Only on a larger scale' said Ben, as they walked along Haldon pier, toward steps which led up to the Cliff Club yacht club bar. A club house, that projected outwards into the bay; mimicking, in a way the overhang of a ship's bridge to afford a better view. An outer part extended to provide a start platform for race meetings. A halyard which held the club flag, twanged, as strong breeze, repeatedly caught a blue flag with the words "Cliff Club Bar." in yellow, above a silhouetted sail boat. Taken down when the bar was closed. A club house door, that faced possible sea onslaught, could be blanked with a waterproof cover to exclude waves breaking in.

A rectangular club bar room was furnished with arm chairs around tables, which were positioned, next to floor to ceiling windows, which gave a panoramic view of the bay, in the day. A winding stairway near to the bar, gave access, in season, to a race start platform. Four young members, were playing pool, while a couple of regulars, were sat at the bar, sipping drinks while scrolling a phone.

'Good evening, Captain Sharpe.' Jock turned to greet Ben as he walked across with Chief Potts.

'And how have I become Captain, Jock?'

'Well, there you are. My youngest daughter, Gisela was at a Christmas party and she told me about a dashing Captain who came to visit them. She was very impressed and asked her teacher, who was running the party what the Captain's name was and, what's more, was he married? I think Gisela has her priorities right, you see, in lining up Captains as possible husband material.'

'And how old is Gisela?'

'She's just turned ten.'

'Right. And what did the teacher say?'

'That she was married to the paddle steamer captain and her teacher I know is a Mrs Sharpe.

'Very impressed Gisela is, that her teacher is married to a paddle steamer's captain.'

'Your fame goes before you Ben.' Chief Potts joined the conversation.

Ah, you haven't met Chief Engineer Edward Potts.'

'We've the top brass in tonight then. You'll just need to sign the guest book.' Jock turned to a shelf behind the bar and produced a leather edged hard cover book, which to judge, by the crumpled corners had been in use for some years. He flicked through gold edged pages and faced it in front of Ben.

'I have a pen.'

'If The Chief Engineer would fill in the guest column. Name and address etc...

'We just need your signature at the end. Your guest will be allowed in on future occasions, without requiring to sign the book, provided you accompany him.

'That's a change in rules.'

'Ah, the social committee rear commodore sees it as an opportunity to find new members.'

'You mean the guest, may like the club so much that he will pay a full membership fee?'

'There's country membership at half-price, Captain Sharpe.' Ben hadn't become accustomed to the elevation from Mr to Captain and realized it might become permanent.

'I'm not a yachtie, but you never know, I might have need of membership,' said Chief Potts as he filled in the details required.

'You've a beautiful position here for your club house bar.'

Aye, sometimes when it's still in the morning I can imagine that I'm a lookin' over Loch Lomond.' That wasn't what Chief Potts had in mind.

'You donna have to be that active on the sailing front There's lots going on that's not sailing.'

'What like Bingo?'

'Now, Captain Sharpe, you know that's not a Cliff Yacht Club activity. No, the social committee chairman is to organize a coach run to a west end show.

'Now that might interest me.' Chief Potts replied.

'Good.'

'Your guest has good taste.'

'What'll you be having Eddie?'

'A pint of beer shandy would help re-lubricate me, Ben.

'A pint of beer shandy and a pint of Guinness Jock, and will you be having one?'

'I'll join the Chief with a half of shandy, if that's alright?'

'Sure. It's a tad quiet in here isn't it for a Thursday?' Questioned Ben.

'There's a social committee meeting, in the top room at the Royal Club apartment. They'll be down here like flies once the meeting's over. Not wanting to pay Royal Club bar prices. Ben paid for the drinks.

I'll bring them over, if you're wanting to have a view of the bay.' Berry Head's light, made visible at window table windows, with its two-flash sequence, every fifteen seconds.

'Thanks for that Jock,' said Ben. A tanker's shadowy form, anchored in the bay, with deck lights ablaze, appeared surrounded by black ink, when viewed from their window. Near to the harbour entrance a green navigation light of a returning fishing vessel could be seen, as they sat down.

'Very comfy these,' said Chief Potts after he sank into a textured cushion, of a leather upholstered armchair.

'By the by, we've tanker lorries due tomorrow morning at eight-thirty. There'll be a bit of an oil stench.'

'No problem for me Eddie. Felicity, Erica, and children are going into town. It'll be completed by the time they return in the afternoon?

'I definitely, hope so. Like to get a run out into the bay sometime to see how everything holds together.'

'Now that doesn't sound like engineering terminology.'

'It'll do. There will be adjustments to be made and I'd like to check out the paddle wheel synchronicity and pitch at varied speeds.'

'That sounds more like engineer speak. I'm with you, though. Next year we'll be operating out of Princess Pier. Like, to work through manoeuvring in and out. Provided, we can get clear from the pier, we should be able to exit under our own steam. Need to catch up with harbour master, Jim Briggs. We'll likely need a lookout at the end of the pier to warn of approaching vessels, with minimal manoeuvrability.' Jock, arrived with a tray of drinks. He looked at his watch while he placed the drinks down in front of them.

'I should make the most of the quiet before the committee arrive.'

'Thanks Jock. I'm on a sort of mission to speak with them.'

'Anyone in particular?'

'The Rear Commodore for starters.'

'I'll mention that you'd like to speak with her.'

'Thanks for that Jock.' Ben, noted that he was getting more attention than expected, maybe through, recommendation from Gisele to her father?

'Not expecting any problems, but a run into the bay would help to get familiar with any quirks that might present themselves.'

'I was kind of hoping you would be keen to get operational,' replied Ben.

The club door burst open and a stream of committee members made for the bar. Some had pre-ordered on their phones, and Jock was in the midst, of preparing orders. Liz Bowers was one of these and evidently Jock mentioned that Ben would like to speak with her. Liz, collected her drink and walked across to their window table.

'Introduce me then Ben.'

'Edward Potts, Chief Engineer aboard Princess Katrina. May I introduce you to Rear Commodore Liz Bowers Chair of the Cliff and Royal Yacht Club, social committee.

'Very pleased to meet you, Edward. No don't bother to stand up.' Chief Potts had made to lift himself up from his armchair and continued to do so. He reached across to shake Liz's hand, before she sat in a third seat, which looked toward the window and out on to the bay.

'How's the Sharpe sea-going family then?' She asked

'We're all fine Liz. Felicity has asked me to put out feelers for next year.'

'Right,' said Liz.

'Mention has been made that a suitable vessel is required to lay race buoys?'

'Right yes Ben. After, Colonel Spalding sold his open motor yacht Matilda, and left to live permanently in the Bahamas we don't have a replacement.'

'I guess the Colonel volunteered the use of his motor yacht?'

'Oh, no. We had to pay the wages of a helmsman, bowman, and engineer plus an hourly higher charge. It was tricky, since the Colonel leases the Royal Yacht Club premises to us at a below market price. Its always been a case of keeping him sweet. He argued that he could lease the premises to a hotel chain at a higher rate.'

'We have a restaurant and overall, more amenities, and could most likely offer a competitive daily hire.'

'That would help the club out Ben.'

'Good operational test for the engines,' Chief Potts came in with.'

'Are you attending the Christmas party Liz?' Asked Ben.

'You bet. Tom Banbury and two of the rugby club are going. I'm looking for some sturdy crew members. They would fit the bill.' Emily, also had already decided that she wanted to accompany Liz, but for the male rugby talent. Not for any shared interest in sailing.

'Felicity handles new contracts for Princess Katrina, Liz.'

'I'll mention the availability for buoy laying in March to Vice Commodore Dan Richards. I'm sure he'll grab at a chance to have Princess Katrina. It would be ideal for a floating regatta starting platform, you know Ben.

'Certainly, give it consideration Liz.' Ben knew that Felicity had already vetoed this role, but wanted to keep everything on a positive note.

Chapter 36

On Friday, although bunkering from two BP tankers, parked on the pier was completed before Felicity returned, there was spillage, on the port deck, near the manifolds. This was evident, from the sand and saw dust thrown down to help soak it up.

'That's got to go before this evening.' Felicity pointed to the sand, where oil could be seen to have seeped through.

'Right, we can sweep it up.' Ben included Patrick and Justin, in his decision.

'It'll need more than that.' Felicity replied in best First Mate speak.

'Like?'

'Like. A scrub down with hot soapy water and pine disinfectant.'

'I've got a drum of Atlas.'

'That won't take the smell away.'

'It needs pine disinfectant mixed into the soap.'

'Are you sure you weren't a First Mate or Bosun in a previous life?'

'Mother, might have been a pirate king,' said Justin.' Justin, was very into pirate ships and imagined a possibility that the paddle steamer could be converted into one.

'I might just have been that, Justin. Someone, needs to shake things up. The yacht chandlers were open when we walked past.'

'I'll go get a bottle of pine disinfectant, then.'

'Two.'

'Right.'

'Before you go, can we have Chief Potts get some hot water on deck?'

'Good thinking.' Ben quite liked the distraction away from focus on the Christmas party. After a visit to Chief Potts and Jamie in the engine room, accompanied by Patrick. Ben walked back on deck, and saw Abigail and her mother walking toward the gangway. It was decided that Caroline, Patrick, and Justin would be better berthed ashore, rather than on board, with an adult party in full swing. Patrick and Justin were not that keen, but there was a scheduled visit to the multiplex cinema next week, which Felicity suggested could be in jeopardy if they did not comply.

Erica, was explaining the coffee machine to the caterers, when Felicity returned. Tables and chairs had been carried into the afterdeck awning space, to make room, in front of the bar for lightweight trestle tables. These were to be removed after a buffet planned for eight o'clock ended. Felicity, had changed into denim jeans and jacket. More appropriate for working in galley and restaurant to prepare for the upcoming party.

Freddie, was to return as father Christmas but also disc jockey. As a semi-professional, it was agreed that he should be paid the rate that he charged at other venues. On payment of five pounds, individual tickets collected on boarding Princess Katrina, would be entered into a raffle, to be held that evening. Payment, either with cash or by phone transfer. Ben was a bit flabbergasted that guests could effectively be arm-twisted to fork out a further five pounds. Felicity, said it would delay them from leaving early, and help with bar sales. Ben could not fault the logic, or an appreciation that his wife was similar, to a canny ship's steward, who could always engineer a best deal, and run into a cash surplus.

'Isn't eight o'clock a bit early for the buffet?' Erica questioned Felicity, while they took a break from assisting Freddie, with assembly of speakers, at the far end of the restaurant. They were sat on the port side of the after deck and Justin decided to run up to see Felicity and Erica. The other two, made do with a wave, as they prepared to leave with Abigail and her mother.

'Save some balloons for me Mum,' said Justin. 'And cracker jokes. I've started writing a joke book collection.'

'Taking after your mother then, writing a book?'

'Mine's going to be a proper book not a children's one, granny.'

'Quite right. Do I get a kiss?' Justin had just kissed his mother on the cheek. 'If you like.'

'I do.' He walked around the table to kiss his granny.'

"Come on Justin." It was Patrick, who was stood on the pier with the group.

'I'll do my best Justin,' said Felicity. Justin, gave a wave before he disappeared down the companionway.

'Make the most of it. It's not long before he'll be criticizing his mother for short comings.'

'I know. Caroline is already finding fault.'

'It's a case of making the most of it before they get taken in by school and teachers who are seen as far more capable than their mother.'

'Very much aware of the situation Erica.' An oil -stained, boiler suited figure, walked across from the engine room door. It was Jamie.

'Where's Ben?'

'He's next deck down, as far as I know, scrubbing away oil spillage, Jamie.'

'We're changing over generators and need an extra pair of hands.'

'He'll be up for that. It'll be a get-out from party preparation.'

'Right. I mean is that alright?'

'Jamie, we need light and if you need help then of course it is. You have permission to press gang my husband. Doubt whether he'll put up resistance.'

'It might go dark for ten minutes or so.'

'Better now than later Jamie.'

He smiled, and went down the companionway to find Ben.

The catering manager and owner, walked into the restaurant wearing a full-length apron with a large stencilled knife and fork on the top with the words,

Mary and Peter Johnson.

Catering, for that Special Event

below and asked,

'Would you like to view the buffet Mrs Sharpe?'

Felicity smiled, and got to her feet.

'Yes,' I certainly would. She joined the catering manager and followed her through the open restaurant floor space to a display on trestle tables. Assistant Anita, carefully removed a light table covering. Trays, were positioned at the end of the tables. Plates and bowls were stacked on the left side, together with trays of light wooden knives, forks, and spoons. Several plates with cold meat and pastry were interspersed covered with Pyrex bowls.

'Perhaps the knives, forks and spoons would be better at the other end,' suggested Felicity.

'Yes, you're right,' said Mary Johnson, catering manager.

'Can you alter the layout to put them at the other end please Anita.'

'Of course, Mrs Johnson.'

'Otherwise, it's looking good,' said Felicity. Not wishing to interfere.

'I wanted you to see the layout before we cover everything, to protect it. Cold meats; Vol au vents; sausage rolls; veggie rolls; scotch eggs; rice dishes with sweetcorn, and peas are stored in the fridge. We've prepared a selection of dips and salads and will add them to the table near to the start of the buffet.' An additional trestle table had been allocated to the galley where her team were at work, when Felicity walked in.

'We have four ice cream tubs of each flavour- vanilla, strawberry, chocolate, and toffee in the freezer. We'll take two tubs of each flavour out an hour before the buffet. They'll be scoopable then, when needed. You wanted an uncomplicated sweet choice and we've gone for banana split. Fresh cream on the split banana topped with chocolate sauce and a scoop of ice cream. Alternatively, a plain fruit cocktail or a knickerbocker glory.

'That seems quite a selection.'

'We have a display board, which can go in front of the bar, as required.' The catering manager smiled and walked across to a long rectangular board leant against the bulkhead. When turned around it displayed the three sweets described.

'Sometimes there's a run on one sweet. She lifted a white card tab which covered the knickerbocker glory. We find it best to be able to restrict the choice if there's an over demand for a particular sweet.'

'That seems sensible, said Felicity.

'It's all very much in hand then.'

'We're hoping so, Mrs Sharpe.' The lights went out and overhead emergency lights came on.

'It's alright they're just switching generators. The lights will be back on in ten minutes.'

Chapter 37

It was not beyond the realms of possibility that Alison texted Felicity to be part of the hospitality group, when she learnt that Tom Banbury and team members from the rugby were on the Christmas party guest list. It sort of cleared the decks being with her brother and from Felicity's perspective it meant that Alison was under supervision rather than free roaming. Ben and Felicity were happily married but she was under no illusions about how men can be distracted and stupefied, by a woman, intent on getting attention and even devotion. Wiles of listening to a man's chatter and to give voluminous praise for skills and abilities!

'You'll need to be here by seven.' Felicity replied, to the text by phone.

'What about Ross?'

'He's ducked out and is helping Jamie in the engine room.'

'He can't do that.'

'Apparently, after the buffet.'

'Oh, I see. No, you're welcome to help-out Alison. Desperately need someone on the coffee machine.

'Will I be taking payments?'

'No. Coffees are included in the buffet. First one, anyway. A second coffee, and they'll need a receipt from the bar.' That satisfied Alison.

Freddie, completed the set-up of speakers and decks. The Blue Danube was playing in the restaurant.

'You're not playing Strauss all evening, are you Jamie? Asked Felicity.

'No, but I find the music calming before a session. Do you want disco dance music throughout?'

'Glad you asked Freddie. No. At nine, we want to wrap up the buffet. We would like you to announce that there will be party games.'

'Like what?'

'Charades.' Felicity picked up an egg timer, notepad, and biro from the bar, and handed these to Freddie.

'They can have three minutes. You set the egg timer. The player needs to enact a film, book, or TV programme. Explain how they wind their hand forward to indicate a film; open their hands to show, a book title and make a TV screen with forefingers and thumbs.'

'Like this.' Freddie held up his hands and formed a small rectangle, which he held before his eyes.

'Don't forget that they hold up their fingers to indicate how many words in the title,' said Erica.

'That's right. You've played charades before.'

'Will everyone get to play?'

'No only ten. Six men and four women guests.'

'Their names are in folded slips of paper in the cap.' Felicity picked up Ben's cap from the bar and placed it on her head.'

'it suits you dear,' said Erica.

'Not random then?' Said Freddie.

'The four winning men will take part in a game of "Are you there Moriarty?"

'And will they play that stood up.'

'No.' Felicity pointed to a roll of carpet against the starboard bulkhead.

'We'll lay the rug down and they can grip wrists on the floor.'

'Don't each have a rolled newspaper,' said Freddie, 'and call out – "Are you there Moriarty." Whoever, achieves the best number of hits out of –

'Five.' Said Felicity. 'A semi -final will follow, and then a final between the two winners.'

'And a winner's prize.'

'Oh yes, he gets to kiss the woman of his choice.'

'Tricky if he's married dear,' said Erica.

'Don't worry, they'll nearly all be single. The dice you might say is loaded.'

Chapter 38

Chief Potts had filled three clusters of twenty large stringed-balloons with helium. One cluster was tied to a flag pole on the fo'c'sl'e; another at the top of the first funnel, and a third cluster tugged from the stern flag pole. It gave an illusion, when viewed from the approach, to Haldon pier, that the paddle steamer could float away into the sky.

Earlier, in the week, Freddie with his connections inveigled the Herald Express to send a camera person to take a photo of Princess Katrina, preparatory to the Friday Christmas party.

'They like to upset the apple cart.'

'How do you mean?' Asked Felicity.

'Show photos of how the other half live.'

'They want to take a photo of the gin palace motor cruisers in the marina if that's the case. This is a working vessel!'

'Knew that would get you going.'

'It's publicity, whichever way Freddie. Thanks for getting them down to take a photo.'

'That's alright I managed to get a contract for two pallets of paper out of it.'

'Father Christmas, with a business nose.'

'Like to think so.'

Felicity, asked Freddie to turn down the non-stop medley of Christmas songs, which followed on from Blue Danube. Speakers, were placed on the fore and after deck, which invited walks on deck. It was dark and the coloured lights which ran from bow to stern gave a good Christmas vibe. A relatively small tree was lit, and attached to the top of the foremast. Steam exited from the foremost funnel, ahead of a whistle blast, that broke the still night air.

'Bloody hell, what does that mean?' Asked Freddie.

'Ben said he would sound the whistle for seven, to alert yacht club members, that the party's scheduled for a seven thirty start, and if they're not aboard before eight they'll miss the buffet.'

'That sounds very organized. More like your idea than Bens.'

'No. It was Ben's suggestion, that a whistle signal make a statement, and they would have no excuses for not being aboard on time for the buffet

A card table and chair was positioned to face the gangway and Freddie together with back up from Robbie was seated in Father Christmas garb to welcome guests aboard. He'd prepared a stamp which stated – "Santa Claus says Yes!"

Liz Bowers and Emily were first to arrive.

'Do we get to tell Father Christmas what we want for Christmas?' asked Emily.

'No, my work permit only allows wish present requests to be made by children.' Replied Freddie as he stamped diagonally across Emily's ticket.

'We have a raffle included for five pounds.'

'You can pay on the app.'

'It's extra then?' Asked Emily.

'Not exactly.' Freddie pointed to the ticket now crossed over with "Santa Claus says yes."

'It's for a good cause. And you might win a turkey.'

I'm getting to feel like the turkey who votes for Christmas,' said Emily.

Liz Bowers intervened.

'It's alright Freddie I'll have two raffle tickets. That'll cover Emily.'

'Thanks Liz. That's the spirit of Christmas.' Robbie directed Liz and Emily to the companionway, which led to the restaurant deck.

Chief Potts, arrived to replace Freddie, who was wanted in his role of both Father Christmas and disc jockey at the restaurant. He was not disappointed, after his encounter with Emily. Chief Potts would be less likely to get back chat from yacht club members.

Guests, Liz, and Emily were offered a Prosecco or a glass of chilled orange or lemon juice, on arrival. They both choose a Prosecco.

'Glad you could make it Liz, Emily.' Felicity came out from behind the bar to greet the two of them.

'Hi Liz, Emily.' Ben appeared in the door way behind dressed in a boiler suit, after assisting Jamie in the engine room.

'Excuse my husband he's been helping down the engine room and he's on his way to getting suitably attired to receive guests.'

Liz smiled and said,

'I understand. Essential work has, to be completed.'

'That's supportive of you Liz. I was on my way to get changed, but was diverted to help in the engine room.'

Freddie walked out from the galley, carrying a tray of food, for the trestle table, followed by Erica,

'You've found your real role in life then,' said Liz to Freddie.

'I'm more a trainee in the galley,'

'You do very well Freddie. We have not met I'm Ben's mother,' said Erica.

'My son had a good position aboard a ship, and now he is like a jack of all trades.'

'Mother, Liz and Emily don't want to hear about my past life.'

'Very pleased to meet you Mrs Sharpe,' said Liz.

'Erica, please call me Erica. Then there isn't any mix up with Felicity, the new Mrs Sharpe.'

'Hi, you two.' Alison, walked out with paper coffee cups stacked on a tray for the machine.

Other guests started arriving, and Ben returned to the restaurant, after he swapped boiler suit and working clothes, for blazer, polo shirt and jeans. His instructions from Felicity were, to work the room. Fortunately, one or two pairs decided to dance to Freddie's medley of Christmas songs. A small selection of chairs and tables, were positioned around the outer rim of the restaurant, which left dance floor space. Freddie, encouraged guests to dance from his pedestal disc jockey podium, near the far-right corner, by the bar. Guests, quite happy to chat and watch the few couples who braved the floor. Ben, decided to join Robbie and Chief Potts at the bar.

Chapter 39

'Ladies and gentlemen,' Freddie stopped the music to make an announcement.

'Our hosts, Captain and Mrs Ben Sharpe have asked me to request assistance from male guests with the transfer of tables and chairs, now on the after deck, onto the dance floor area. Captain Sharpe and Chief Engineer Potts, will supervise.' Freddie, unexpectedly spotlighted the two of them , when he turned the high intensity light over the turntable in their direction.

'The buffet bar will then be open.' Freddie turned up, dimmed overhead lights. Ben and Chief Potts walked across the floor, with James Briggs, to be joined by Tom Banbury and rugby club members, plus Ross, Geoff Winterton and all the men.

Ben, removed a stitched canvas cover from a stack of wooden-folded chairs, on the after deck and handed chairs out, while Chief Potts corralled two volunteers, to carry a folded table into the restaurant.

'How many Captain?' Called across Chief Potts.

'Six should be plenty, with four chairs per table.'

Before the tables and chairs were set up in the dance floor space, a queue formed by the uncovered trestle buffet bar. Two tables were set up on the after deck for those who smoked. Fortunately, it was dry although breezy.

Once the queue started to move Alison pored coffees for those who wanted one. Bar sales, found support from rugby club members and other guests later as the evening progressed. Felicity, benefitted through Jock, being present, who added familiarity to yacht club members. It was card payment only, at the bar. This was noted on entry tickets.

Felicity, from behind the bar called across to Freddie, just before he was about to announce a new medley of songs.

'Freddie, you can stop the music and have a buffet break. You'll need to join the queue like everyone else. Freddie nodded, smiled, and switched off the music, keen to get a break. Two tables, were set up each side of the bar, with a "reserved" notice. It was fair to say that the one to the left of the bar was like the captain's table. Buffet plates were prepared earlier for those involved with the running of Princess Katrina and the party itself. Freddie, joined the queue and was asked by Tom Banbury whether he would be having traditional Father Christmas fayre of mince pies and a sherry? To which he replied that he was at a dress rehearsal, with Christmas a few days away and was allowed to go off piste, on this occasion. Light hearted banter, replaced the music as tables filled with guests.

It was near to half past eight when Freddie was instructed by Felicity to announce, that a game of charades was to follow. With the Captain's cap, which belonged to Ben, in hand, Freddie announced.

'From within this Captain's cap, ten names are to be chosen for charades. I do not wish to be seen to influence the decision in any way. I will ask our hostess to randomly choose who shall play.' Names were restricted to eleven chosen guests. These were – Chief Potts, Tom Banbury, Dave Smith (rugby player), Ross, Robbie, James Briggs, and Ben, Felicity's husband. Women – Olivia Vanter, Alison, Erica, and Liz Bowers.

'Shake that cap Father Christmas,' said Felicity. 'We want a good mix of competitors.' Freddie, shook the cap, and grabbed a few screwed-up name slips, in his free hand and replaced these, before he gave the cap a swirl and shake.

'Okay, okay that should do, Father Christmas,' she said, and Freddie walked down from his disc jockey position, with cap held high, mainly to disguise, how few slip entrants were really inside the cap. Felicity reached up and withdrew one. Opened, the screwed-up paper and read out,

'Ben Sharpe.'

'It's a fix,' called out Ben, in protest. Felicity nodded her head in disagreement and said,

'Not at all.' It was an overall fix, but a chance event, for Ben's name to be selected first. Felicity's inclusion of Ben sort of anchored others named afterwards that Ben was included.

When the pre-planned ten contestants were announced Felicity explained that four men from charades would be chosen for the next game.

'The prize for the winner of the next game, is a kiss with a woman of his choice. Provided, that the chosen woman is agreeable.' She looked across at Ben.

'It goes without saying, that should the winner be a married man, he can only choose his wife to kiss.'

'But of course,' replied Ben.

'Alison would you be so good as to start.' Felicity had spoken to Alison earlier as to whether she was okay to be chosen for charades. Pleased to learn that it was a game of choice, in Alison's family.

'I'll have a go.' Alison walked out from the coffee making area, by the bar. Freddie, started to clap which encouraged guests to follow his lead. Alison stood in front of the buffet table.

A twirl of the hand, released a chorus of "Film." Alison hid her thumb behind her right hand and held it up.

'Four words,' was the reply. Alison nodded. It was all very short-lived after Alison placed her hands together, as if to read from a book and mimed with her mouth, the words. There were one or two calls of 'reading a book,' but a single call from the far side of the restaurant, from Sophia Vanter won the day with 'singing.' Alison immediately pointed across to acknowledge the call.

A practised hands over the head followed by the action of opening an umbrella, to wave about in a dance routine, and mimed singing led to several calling out "Singin' in the Rain.'

Alison duly pointed, to those who called out the film title, and pretended to clap.

'Thank you, Alison for such an excellent demonstration,' said Felicity.

The film "Top Gun," from Ben was picked up quite quickly after Ben mimicked to fly a plane with arms outstretched. He unholstered a gun and made to fire it. The Film was being shown in local cinemas.

'Too easy,' called out Robbie.

'Another.'

'We haven't time,' said Felicity.

'Can we have something other than a film?' Called out Erica. This led to a very well- acted version of Treasure Island from Liz Bowers. Liz, knelt to unlock a treasure chest and gave a wide- eyed gloat, while she pretended to stack gold coins and mimicked the use of a crutch, with one leg held up, before she hopped about to mimic Long John Silver.

'Is it Treasure Island?' Called out Emily. There was no apparent collusion, but Emily may have seen Liz perform – a Treasure Island charade, before?

The men did not fare as well as the women. Several attempts were made by Dave Smith, the rugby player and Ross, but they were unable to convince anyone of their film or book. It worked well though, so far as Felicity was concerned. Ross wanted to go to the engine room to assist Jamie, and four men were left for the next competition.

Chapter 40

'Ladies and gentleman. We are appreciative of the fine acting skills displayed to us in this game of charades. Casting agents for next seasons Princess Theatre show production, unfortunately are not in attendance, otherwise a new career would have surely beckoned for all contestants.' Sporadic clapping followed.

'Now, lets' have a more enthusiastic round of applause,' said Freddie. This followed through with a better response.

'It is my pleasure to welcome your hostess for the evening to address you – Felicity Sharpe.' There was increased clapping, which seemed to surprise Felicity, who did not expect to receive applause, but the guests were obviously enjoying the entertainment.

'Good evening to everyone and welcome aboard Princess Katrina for the Christmas party. We will need to clear tables from the centre of the floor for our next game activity – "Are you there Moriarty?"'

'I will read out the names of the four contestants. Edward Potts, James Briggs, Tom Banbury, and Ben Sharpe. Will all contestants report to Father Christmas for instructions. Let's have a fair competition and may the best man win. The winners prize, will be an opportunity to kiss the princess of his choice. Provided, of course she is willing to be a princess, for that moment, in recognition of champion status. Should Ben Sharpe be the winner then he will be required to kiss the promoter of the competition, and the runner up will be declared winner.' Ben, held his hands up, gave a thumbs up, to stay on the right side of Felicity, in this public arena.

Tables were folded and taken outside, while chairs, were spread out to the sides of the restaurant, with supervision from Felicity.

The rolled wall rug was unravelled and revealed a golden dragon on red back ground. A rug bought by Ben, in Singapore, when he served aboard a tanker. It was for Erica, but returned because she said it did not match the décor in her flat and suggested it be donated to a worthwhile charity. Felicity, saved the rug and said,

"It could be Princess Katrina's magic carpet." Justin's secretly imagined plan was to stand on it, fishing rod in hand and make a wish to hover over the outer edge of the pier, to catch bass on an incoming tide. He would have been disappointed to miss this spread of the "magic carpet," on the restaurant floor.

This, golden dragon design not apparent to the contestants. Felicity, and Erica having wrapped bandana blindfolds around their eyes and double knotted, at the back. Triangular cuts, from faded blue curtains, in Erica's apartment served as blindfolds. It was decided that all four should be blind-folded, to avoid technique study by the two who waiting to compete.

First two contestants Tom Bradbury and Chief Potts were handed a truncheon of rolled newspapers, wrapped with Christmas tape. Rolled newspapers are usually not solid enough to bruise or injure combatants, but a thwack on the front or side of the face could sting.

'It was worse at the Coliseum for gladiators,' called out one of Tom's rugby playing friends.

'How do you know,' replied Tom. Were you there?'

'He probably was. He would have been Nero,' called out Liz Bowers, to mix things. Freddie, assisted by Robbie, guided the first pair to the "magic" carpet. Blindfolds adjusted to ensure they could not see anything, once on the floor. Each combatant held the others left hand while they lay to face each other across the carpet.

It became clear that Chief Potts was skilled at the game. After the call of "Are you there Moriarty," by Tom, he twisted his hand in the opposite direction to which he turned, as he answered.

"Yes," It worked in that Tom Bradbury struck an empty floor space, after Chief Potts rolled in the opposite direction to that expected. When Tom called and rolled to the right, Chief Potts's paper smacked his shoulder. The Chief managed to win a third call and won the contest.

Ben was knocked out by James Briggs and again Chief Potts deceived the Harbour Master with his clever twisted hand deception. Felicity stood within the group after masks were removed and raised Chief Potts right arm, like a referee after a boxing tournament.

'I declare Edward the winner.' There was a round of applause from the guests, gathered around the outer edge of the restaurant. Chief Potts could be seen questioning Felicity, who smiled and nodded her head, before she announced that he would pick the princess of his choice to kiss. He walked across to the coffee bar area where Alison was with Erica who was making a coffee for a guest. There was a wide- eyed moment when Erica realized that she was the one chosen. She left Alison, to continue handing the coffee to a guest and walked out from behind the counter. Several quests with phone cameras came forward to capture the kiss. There was a kind of "wow," like sound from those watching. Eric and Edward Potts were both in their late fifties. Both single. Felicity smiled at Ben. It seemed that there was possibility of a first romance in progress, aboard Princess Katrina.

'Thank you to all the gallant contestants in the contest. Now I'll return you to Father Christmas and some more dance music.

'They'd better dance! Freddie cost a bit to hire,' said Ben.

'Don't get at Freddie, he's doing a great job,' replied Felicity. Perhaps it was that the guests were more relaxed after the buffet, followed by charades and the contest. The floor filled, after the mat was rolled up and returned to the bulkhead. (wall)

'Look, Chief Potts is s on the floor with your mother.'

'Do you think we're about to acquire a father- in- law?'

'And another grand-parent for the children, maybe?'

'We'll have to wait and see.' Emily walked across to chat with Freddie. Shortly afterwards they left together to go out on deck. Freddie no longer needed to call out encouragement for dancers to leave their tables and "Get those sea legs dancing," as he put it.

'Another romantic assignation,' perhaps remarked Felicity.

'Good job that Leo's not here tonight.'

'Is that going anywhere?'

'Emily needs to get her skates on otherwise Leo will be all that's left.'

'Was I all that was left? I mean were there no alternatives lined up?'

'Perhaps, but you appeared a more demanding project Ben Sharpe, than a teacher, with fixed career prospects? Even Erica was stunned that I wanted to marry you, I remember.'

'Mother tried to put you off?'

'No. She wanted to test whether I was "really," serious about wanting to marry her son.'

Emily rushed in. When she caught sight of Felicity and Ben she shouted, 'Freddie's fallen in the drink!'

Chapter 41

'Where? Which side? Ben demanded to know.

'The harbour side.'

'Quick show me.' They both ran from the restaurant. Out on deck, Emily pointed out and down from the deck railings.

'There. He's there.' Freddie's red Father Christmas gown was ballooned across the water and he was struggling to remove it. The red hat floated some distance away from where he was, together with fake white beard. Ben directed a deck light on to the water.

'It's freezing.' Freddie's shrill voice came back.

'Freddie. Tread water. I'm going to launch an inflatable. It'll open near you.

'Hold on boy, you're doing great.' White plastic, cylinder inflatables, fortuitously, had been fitted on both sides of the restaurant deck, to beef up safety provision. Ben, decided to have them mounted on a turntable, to facilitate directional launch. Although Freddie was almost directly below the inflatable raft with deck rails removed, the cylinder was directed to fall astern of where he was.

Previously, to its launch, Ben extricated a coil of nylon line from the cylinder and wrapped its end three times around a top rail, before he pushed it free of its chocks, to splashed down a few feet away from Freddie. It was like a capsule return to earth from space, save that Freddie wasn't in it!

'Stay where you are Freddie. Stay where you are! It'll burst open.' Ben tugged and pulled the cord as quickly as he could to trigger the gas cylinder switch.

'Freddie. Is he going to be alright?' Asked Emily,

'He will be, once he gets into the raft.' Just as Ben spoke, the white cylinder burst apart and an orange blur viewed from the paddle steamer grew as it filled with gas. The line lay across the water.

'Grab the line if you can and flap your legs. Draw yourself to the raft.'

Emily shouted,

'You can do it Freddie.'

'It's freezing and the waters oily.' Freddie called back. Although, he'd rid himself of the Father Christmas gown, he made slow progress toward the raft, in sodden jeans and tee shirt.

Music and a gentle lilt of Moon River drifted out from the restaurant. It seemed like no one else knew of Freddie's fall, from funnel to harbour. Afterwards, it was revealed that Emily wanted a green, red, and white balloon to match her hockey team colours. It was this choice that made Freddie's situation near the top of the ladder precarious. He did not follow the seafarer's motto – one hand for the ship and one for yourself, as he attempted to disentangle appropriate balloons from a large group near the funnel top. A sudden breeze, blew Freddie and ladder away from the funnel, and down into the cold, oily water below.

Ben, during an update of safety requirements decided on these additional safety life rafts, for both sides of the restaurant. He had not envisaged launching one so soon!

'When you reach the raft-work your way around to the boarding area.' Ben, called down to Freddie who was now feet away from the raft.

A high, volume ambulance wail broke into the night air. Felicity dialled nine, nine, nine, after Ben left with Emily. A siren wail near to Princess Katrina did see guests walk out on to, the deck, harbourside. An ambulance, with blue lights flashing had a clear run along the harbourside. Ben had reversed a spotlight on to the water, where Freddie could be seen to pulled himself out, and into the life raft

'It's Freddie,' called out Emily, to Liz who joined her by the railing.

'Bet it's freezing in there.' Robbie was at Ben's side. Followed by James Briggs, Harbour Master.

'Can you come with me, Robbie, we'll need to get Freddie out of the life raft?' The ambulance crew had opened the doors and were removing a stretcher. They had seen the orange life raft, and Felicity messaged, that there was someone in the water.

'What next Ben?' Asked Jim.

'I'm going to lower the outboard motor dinghy, with Robbie and get Freddie out of the life raft.

'I'll go down and put the ambulance crew in the picture.'

'Good man,' said Robbie, as they made for the companionway, to get to the dinghy. Felicity, had Jock, call out last orders, from the restaurant doorway, although there was half an hour to go. This helped to encourage some of the gawping guests back inside.

Within minutes Ben and Robbie had Princess Katrina's ship to shore dinghy lowered, and next to the gangway. A whirr of starter motor followed, before it burst into life and eclipsed a chatter of voices, on the deck above.

Ben and Robbie once alongside the life raft, helped a shivering Freddie aboard. A falling tide exposed a lower concrete platform of steps, where Harbour master James Briggs and ambulance, crew were stood, as the dinghy appeared, from the other side of the paddle steamer, with a shivering Freddie aboard, flinging his arms back and forth to get warm.

The harbour master caught Robbie's thrown painter, and drew the dinghy alongside. Ambulance crew held out a blanket to wrap around Freddie, as he was helped shakingly from dinghy to steps. Made to lie on a prepared blanketed stretcher, although he first protested that he was alright, but realized he wasn't when he tried to walk, possibly in a semi-delirious state.

Emily, concerned for Freddie, appeared at the top of the steps, maybe in part, because she was the one, who encouraged him to climb the ladder, in the first place, to fetch balloons?

'Is Freddie going to be alright.'

The Harbour Master, reassured her.

'It's cold-water shock. Don't worry he's in safe hands now, my dear.'

Attention from the paddle steamer viewers platform had moved from the starboard side to the after, port side. Darkness hid a view of the early step descent to the platform below.

First, a torch's wavering light, shone up from the depths and then an ambulance person with fluorescent jacket could be seen as she negotiated her way to the top, one step at a time, with firm grip on stretcher handles.

'He's not drowned then,' said one of the rugby players. It was meant to be light-hearted banter, but came across as inappropriate.

'Danny boy, Danny boy the pipes are calling,' drifted through the open restaurant doors. A plaintiff song. A lament that seemed to chime with Freddie's friends and their concern for his safety.

Freddie, was immediately unstrapped from the stretcher, when they reached the ambulance and helped to his feet. He started coughing and it was evident that the paramedic in attendance wanted to take Freddie to the Torbay Hospital.

Felicity, saw Ben take hold of Freddie's arm from where she was stood on the after deck. He raised a hand and directed it toward the ambulance. Ben wanted Freddie to get into the ambulance. Hesitation ended when Emily ran across from the gangway. Unzipped puffer jacket with handbag flying, from hurried departure.

'I'll go with you Freddie,' Emily called out. I'll text Liz later, she'll drive over to fetch us.'

'Will you Emily?' Freddie coughed, and shook his head to try and stop a coughing fit. Evidence, that he might have swallowed harbour water. Swimming was banned, due to the risk of typhoid.

'That's good of you, young lady,' said the older of the two ambulance persons.'

'You're happy with that sir? Your girlfriend accompanying you?'

'She's,' but a coughing spasm stopped Freddie from denying the relationship. Emily, grabbed his hand and led Freddie to the ambulance's stairway. A young ambulance crew member, a woman of about Emily's age accompanied the two of them into the back compartment. The siren sounded immediately; the ambulance wheeled around to exit the harbour pier.

Activity, around Freddie's recovery from the harbours water, hid the arrival of a nearby duty police car, called to investigate the reason for an ambulance at Haldon Pier?

Previously, Felicity, persuaded Ben to put on his uniform jacket. The plan was for the two of them to thank guests for attending the party. Ben suitably attired as Princess Katrina's Captain.

A slam of the police car door alerted Ben to its arrival. Ben was under the spotlight intended, to throw light on ambulance crew and para-medics. Four gold braid arm bands sparkled under the light.

'Good evening,' the police constable hesitated.

'Captain. Will you be the Captain of this vessel, sir?'

'That's correct officer.'

'Can you explain the recent call out of an ambulance. Are there serious injuries that may have resulted from foul play may I ask? We will require a statement, you understand?'

'No foul play officer. A man overboard situation, but he was successfully rescued.'

Chapter 42

A band of rain swept across from the south west. Other, than Ben, who gave details to the police about Freddie's fall and rescue, there was little for party guests to gawp at. They returned to the paddle steamer's restaurant.

Felicity, interrupted chatter, when she sounded eight bells on a miniature ship's bell. Bar steward Jock called out,

"Last orders, ladies and gentlemen, if you please," and lowered the bar shutter, to halfway.

'Everyone, have your raffle-tickets, ready, for our main Christmas Party raffle.' Felicity, announced as she stood behind Freddie's disc jockey desk.

Several feet in front of the bar, a red cotton mainsail covered a trestle table. Sail, streaked white, from wind, rain, and sun.

It lay forgotten, in Ben's sail locker by a previous occupant. Destined, to be a deck cover paint protection sheet. Now used to hide prizes from view. Raffle entries were posted in the children's Santa letter box. Felicity continued,

'Unfortunately, not everyone can win our First Prize of a weeks' family holiday in Biarritz, but we have a selection of fantastic prizes, kindly donated by club members and followers of Princess Katrina.' She turned to look at the silver- rimmed ship's clock, above the bar and followed with,

'We will draw raffle tickets for winners, in approximately twenty minutes, after the bar is closed. I know everyone will want to wish Freddie well, and a speedy recovery. He is in the best of hands.' A spontaneous clap followed, and stopped as abruptly as it started.

A queue formed at the bar. Evidently, recent excitement had developed a thirst among guests. Felicity, assisted by Erica, called out ten guest names and requested they join her, in the selection of raffle winners.

On Haldon Pier, Ben was explaining to police, the man overboard situation, when Harbour Master James Briggs arrived and said that he was satisfied with safety procedures being followed and should they require further information about the health of Freddie they needed to contact Torbay Hospital. His jurisdiction over harbour matters gave reassurance, and said they would make further enquiries. Ben, was able to return and assist in the restaurant. Felicity, pleased that he took charge of the running of the raffle.

"We're looking for volunteers to empty our post box." Ben, looked across at where guests were seated, and saw Commander and Mrs Blenkinsop, sat a little way from the others.

'Commander and Mrs Blenkinsop would you be so kind – to assist?'

Surprised, but pleased they got up and walked across the floor.

'Applause for Commander and Mrs Blenkinsop.' Ben called out.

Mrs Blenkinsop not wishing to be over formal said to Ben, amidst the clapping.

'It's Bill and Jean.' Ben handed a key to Jean, and a small replica postal bag, to the commander. A bag, which more resembled a ventilator cover, with a base, had been worked from duck canvas by Robbie. He said it was a better shape to select tickets from, than a postal bag. Ben went along with his suggestion. Robbie's carpentry skills were irreplaceable.

'Jean if you could open the post box, please? And Bill, fill the bags with raffle tickets, that would be great.' Ben spoke loudly to include the guest audience, in proceedings.

'Thanks, so much to Bill and Jean for their help.' Ben's hand was raised to initiate more applause. Felicity, delighted with her husband's skill in the role, meant that Ben would likely be called upon to be Master of Ceremonies again. At a signal from Felicity, Robbie, Jamie, and Chief Potts took hold of the sail corners and lifted it clear, to reveal raffle prizes.

Displayed on the table, was a red envelope with "Biarritz," in gold letters. Details about a week's family holiday prize. Secondary prizes, were a meal for two at the Cottage Restaurant; cinema tickets for a family. Individual bottles of champagne, gin, rum, vodka, whisky. Also, a Dundee cake, giant Toblerone, fruit hamper and boxes of Black Magic chocolates. A few booby prizes, included a baler for a dinghy; set of clothes pegs; plastic bath duck; car wash sponge, and three kitchen towels with a photo of Princess Katrina emblazoned on the front.

This main raffle advertised online, with a proviso that winners needed to collect prizes, within a week from the Cliff Yacht Club Office. Entrants, were likely to be confined to the area, with a list of winning numbers posted online.

A separate raffle was set up at the bar, because Ben was concerned that there might be no winners that evening, in the restaurant! Steward Jock, and Robbie, were to draw winners, from an empty ice bucket filled with raffle tickets, which had been sold from the bar. A carry over from a raffle started at the yacht club.

An ongoing dispute with certain members, was that this raffle conflicted with a yacht club Christmas raffle. Liz Bowers, social club chairman said that their club raffle could be extended through to the New Year. Not quite what members wanted, but the yacht clubs social committee decided, and that was that!

The bar raffle gave opportunity to win Christmas fayre. W. H. Hallam a local butcher, supplied a turkey, ham, and fillet of beef. Additionally, a shopping basket, contained apples, tangerines; a red netted bag of mixed nuts; boxes of dates and figs; Fox's classic biscuit selection; after eight dark-mints; tinned fruit cake and a boxed selection of Walkers luxury shortbread. Assorted, Green and Black, miniature chocolates, displayed under protective, blue tinged cellophane, made for a colourful appearance. The curved basket handle, covered with inter twinned, red, white, and blue ribbon. Presentation, completed with a red crinkly, cellophane bow.

Felicity's master plan, to delay their main raffle draw until the end was paying off. No one would have wished for Freddie to fall from funnel to harbour, but launch of the raft and ambulance arrival, added unexpected excitement, which revived a Christmas party atmosphere.

Apart from Emily, who went with Freddie, to the Torbay Hospital, party guests remained to find out who the winners would be.

Chapter 43

'Will you please read out our first winner.' Sophie, one of the guests chosen to pick a ticket read the name,

"John Delaney." There was a hush for a moment. Robbie, who held the raffle bag came to the rescue.

'I know who that is. John runs the Launderette. Sold him the ticket I did. He can buy me a drink for that!' It was a relief, in a sense, that the first prize winner was known. Someone called out.

'Has the ticket been through the wash? This remark led to some merriment. It was a good start to the raffle. The Bank of England are known to give reasonable, consideration to notes damaged in a wash. A raffle ticket perhaps another matter!

A bottle of gin and champagne were also won by party guests. Harbour Master James Briggs won the large Toblerone. Tom Banbury, the set of towels with Princess Katrina on, and Robbie a set of clothes pegs, which he appeared pleased to win. It was not the wipe-out for party guests, from online entries that Ben had feared.

The bar raffle which started a fortnight earlier, at the Cliff Yacht club, bar saw the turkey and ham go to club member Steve Cookson. Steve, was known to regularly buy tickets when he visited the club house. His odds of winning prizes perhaps heightened by the number of tickets he had bought. Liz Bowers, who bought tickets for the bar raffle just before the bar closed won the hamper. Ben, won the plastic duck, from the main raffle and decided to auction it.

'How much can I ask for an irreplaceable bath companion?' Harry Sturgis called out,

'Fifty.'

'That's very generous. Fifty pounds from Harry,'

'No, Ben. Fifty pence!'

'Doesn't reach the reserve price, Harry. I'm afraid we will have to withdraw
—

Thank you, Ollie.' A raised finger was taken to be a pound and the sale price went forward a pound at a time. One of Tom Banbury's rugby mates, was hung out to dry, when the price reached ten pounds with no more bidders. Liz Bowers received a call from Emily to say that Freddie was alright and was to stay in hospital overnight, with a message to Ben and Felicity to leave the DJ equipment for him to dismantle, when he was let out.

It was eleven fifteen by the time the bar raffle was completed and Ben had auctioned his plastic duck win. Both restaurant doors were open. Taylor Swifts "It's a love story babe, just say yes," was ending, when Felicity sounded the miniature ship's bell once more.

'Ladies and gentlemen, friends, and guests of *Princess Katrina*: Liz Bowers has received a call from Emily. Freddie I'm pleased to say is fine, but is to stay in hospital overnight, with instructions for me to leave his DJ equipment for him to dismantle. That suggests that he is in good form!'

It just remains for me to say thank you to everyone for attending our first Christmas party aboard and to wish you all a very Happy Christmas. And.... please be careful, out on deck, after the rain. The gangway will be manned, to assist anyone who needs extra help to negotiate it.'

Ben was with a group, which included, harbour master James Briggs, and stood near to the bar when Chief Engineer Potts, on direction from Felicity, dimmed the lights in the restaurant. The music continued playing but it marked a point where the party was ending. Guests walked out on to the deck, and were making their way to the gangway.

'It went well. That's apart from Freddie falling in,' Felicity remarked to Ben as together with Erica and Alison they cleared tables of empty glasses. The caterers left before the raffle got going. Remains from the buffet were placed on a table in the galley, covered in cling film, with salads returned to the fridge.

'That's probably what everyone will remember about the party. Don't really want it to become a news item in the Herald and Express. Do we.' Replied Ben.

'Nor will Freddie.'

'Don't you think you two should be at the gangway to say goodbye to your guests?'

'You could be right mother,' said Ben.

'If we go down the other side, we'll catch them before they get to the gangway,' said Felicity.

When they arrived, they met up with Chief Engineer Potts and Robbie. There, to help guests down the gangway, now more angled with the tide going out.

Robbie walked, half way down, to assist those disembarking, while Felicity and Ben together with Chief Engineer Potts wished them goodbye.

'Hope to see you in the summer for a cruise,' Felicity said to departing guests. Although visitors were likely to be the main passengers, there were guests with holiday apartments and houses to let, who might pass on the message.

Geoff Winterton and partner, from the electrical store, were effusive about how much they'd enjoyed the evening.

'If you're needing replacement bulbs or lighting for Princess Katrina, be sure to contact us. I'm sure we'll be able to offer competitive rates,' said Geoff.

'Thank you, Geoff. So pleased you enjoyed the evening,' replied Felicity.

Harbour master James Briggs stopped to chat with Ben by the gangway.

'Still keen to have a trial tomorrow, Ben?'

'You make it sound like preparation for some record breaking.'

'It kind of will be, to have those paddles turning at full-speed, after years of lay -up,' said Chief Engineer Potts.

'High tides at about eleven-twenty.'

'If we leave at eleven-thirty we'll be in slack water then?'

'Yes. I can be there to escort you out. Although there won't be much harbour traffic to contend with.'

Chapter 44

'That's alright by me, Vicky. Only if it's not too much trouble for you?' Felicity was in the wheelhouse with Ben, who was checking out the radar. The scanner picked out a tanker anchored, in the bay and fishing boats, out of Brixham. Apparently, Caroline had arranged to stay with Abigail.

'We are- leaving the harbour for,' Felicity resisted saying "a spin," knowing that Ben would see that as inappropriate and said, 'an engine trial at eleven-twenty. If you could get Justin and Patrick down here for ten thirty Vicky, that would be great.' There was a pause.

'You must come aboard for a meal with Matt and Abigail. It seems a bit uneven you having our three. Hold a sec Vick.' She turned to Ben.

'What time are you planning to return. Caroline's staying with Abigail?'

'Plan to return to Princess Pier by,' – Ben examined his wrist watch – 'four at the latest.' Ben, silently disappointed that Caroline preferred to be with her friend.

'We should be back by four this afternoon Vicky. That's moored at the Princess Pier. But if I message you when we're alongside?' Another pause.

'That's so good of you Vicky, bye.' Felicity, reached out to return the mobile back to her handbag, slung across the telegraph handle.

The electric kettle clicked off, and she walked to a foldable table that Robbie had built in the wheelhouse. This accommodated, kettle, toaster, mugs, secured in holders, and plates in a magazine- like rack. With a separate compartment for knives and spoons. Instant coffee, tea bags, seeded multi-grain sandwich bread, Perspex- covered butter dish and a selection of miniature jams on a tray were protected by a tea towel.

'It's toast and coffee for breakfast. We can lunch on the remains of the buffet.'

'Fine by me'

'It's quite like old times, before we re-furbished the cabins, being in the wheelhouse.'

'That was too work-related for me,' said Ben. His mind was focused on the day ahead.

'The others are having a cooked breakfast in the restaurant curtesy of your mother.'

'Hope they're on their best behaviour.'

'Perhaps Erica's getting in some training, cooking breakfast for Chief Potts?'

'There's a surprise for you. That kiss.'

'Probably doesn't mean anything. Erica and Edward are about the same age. He was being diplomatic.'

'Oh yes.' Felicity's womanly intuition told her otherwise.

'I said to Edward that you would like to go on Standby at 1045.'

'And?'

'He's perfectly happy with that.'

Several volunteers were aboard, to assist in the engine room, but there was more of a skeleton deck crew. Freddie had been told to rest, in case symptoms appeared from his dip in the harbour water. Robbie had already extended his role of ship's carpenter to include that of Bosun. Liz Bowers and Emily were keen to be aboard, on this first bay excursion. Harry and Ollie, volunteered to assist a fortnight earlier and would be available muscle power. Ben, needed a wheelman and it was agreed that Robbie would take that role once they'd let go moorings and were heading out into the bay. Liz Bowers had said she would like to then step into the role. The most experienced yachtsman aboard.

Felicity, said she was happy to be a passenger. There was consideration given to a husband and wife, relationship where orders were needed to be one way, in the wheelhouse, with no discussion or input by recipient. Passenger was never an appropriate title, with Felicity's role as wife and mother. There was always maintenance work required. Additional passenger seats needed varnishing before the season started and railings required painting. Felicity, found ship maintenance, a therapeutic escape, from multi-faceted role, of mother, wife, and school teacher.

Chapter 45

Ben and Felicity's morning quiet time was interrupted by Justin, who opened the port bridge door and called out,

'Mum, can Danny come with us?'

'Only if his parents know where he is and Danny wears a lifejacket.'

'He's with his dad by the gangway.'

'Perhaps, you'd better ask your father?' Felicity spoke as if Ben was somehow absent. He might have been. His eyes were buried in the cowl of the radar, positioned to shut out daylight. Ben heard what was said.

'Justin, I'll come down and see Danny's dad. He might like to join us?' Ben was latching on to the possibility of another deck hand.

'Where's your brother?'

'In the restaurant.' Judy Garland's voice sang – "Somewhere over the Rainbow," out of Felicity's handbag. She answered the phone.

Hi Vicky... yes, I've got one of them with me. I'll be right down.' When Felicity left the wheel house she waved in reply to Vicky, who was stood a little way back from the gangway, accompanied by Abigail and Caroline. Ben was first to get to the gangway, followed by Felicity. Danny, took the opportunity to grab a chair from the chart room to stand on, and get a view of the radar screen

'You're welcome to join us sir,' Ben, smiled as he addressed Danny's dad, after he'd stepped from gangway to pier. Danny, not wishing to miss a possibility of casting a line overside held his fibre-glass fishing rod, topped with red and white float. A rod, significantly taller than him. Khaki strap of fishing bag, crossed over red anorak.

'Really?' Danny's dad exclaimed.

'I'll need to phone the boss.'

'I understand. We plan to be back by four and would welcome some deck assistance, if you feel up to it?'

'I'm a tiler by trade. Used to hanging on ladders, scaffolding and such like. Guess I can make myself useful.'

'That's great. Mr –

'Pete Tompkins.' Most people call me Pete. Do I need to speak with the Captain or anything?'

'It's alright Pete, we've jumped that hoop.' Pete, returned to his mobile.

Hello Shirl,' and smiled to himself, when he realized that he was speaking with Princess Katrina's Captain.

'Yes, Danny's with me. Justin has asked if Danny wants to go for a trip on the paddle steamer.

Apparently, there's room for me.' There was a pause.

'Well, yes if you are happy to go to mothers on your own?'

'Of course not. I was looking forward to catching up on things. Give my apologies to Fran.'

'Yes, will catch up when we return. Bye.' Pete replied,

'All clear on the home front Captain.'

'Great. Not sure we'll be able manage rod fishing Danny, but we could throw a couple of mackerel spinners overboard.'

'That would be fun. Never done any mackerel fishing.'

'Danny!' Justin scrambled down the gangway.

'Danny, and his father are joining us. Perhaps you would like to show them to the restaurant area Justin.'

'Sure. Grannies got a game consul Danny.'

'Not sure they'll be much time for that,' said Ben.

'I'll catch up with you, in the restaurant, Pete, if that's alright?'

'That's fine by me, captain.' Ben walked across to see Caroline, who was staying ashore.

Hoses, to fill water tanks were being uncoupled on board. Steam was raised in boilers, to power twin engines.

'We'll be on the Princess Pier Caroline. Not at the mooring when we return,' said Ben.

'Yes dad, I know. It'll be better, for getting aboard.'

'It's not permanent, but good practise for the summer.'

'You don't need me on board, do you?'

'I'll miss you.'

'We both will,' said Felicity,

'But have a good time. It's good of you, Vicky, to have Caroline for the day?'

'Felicity it's fine. It'll be easier for me with the two, instead of just Abigail.' said Vicky.

'I'll call message, as soon as we're back at the Princess Pier.'

Chapter 46

'We're ready to leave.' Ben called Harbour master James Briggs by mobile, at eleven ten.

Forward lines had been let go, aboard the paddle steamer. A rising tide, assisted bow movement away from the harbour wall.

'You're clear to leave. Harbour mouths clear of traffic. Let me know when you return and we'll have someone to take lines, on Princess Pier. As explained earlier, we've a Dutch mine sweeper due and space will be tight on Haldon. Looking forward, Ben, to seeing you under steam in the bay.' From the upper car park, the Harbour Masters glass -fronted office overlooked the harbour.

'Same for me. Thanks for support, Jim. Getting everything organized harbour-wise.'

'No problem. All part of the service. Bon Voyage Ben.'

Patrick was on the wheel temporarily, while Robbie organized, winching stern lines aboard. No risk of ropes getting caught in a propellor, but he wanted to make sure that ropes were correctly coiled and helpers, kept clear of both winch and return shore ropes. Felicity, mentioned that Patrick was keen to practice his wheelman skills.

'Ten degrees starboard helm, wheelman,' Ben called across to Patrick.

'Ten degrees starboard helm, it is,' replied Patrick. Ben walked from wheel-house to bridge. Robbie waved to signal that all stern lines were clear. On return to the wheelhouse Ben rang "Dead Slow Ahead." Felicity from the starboard side of the wheelhouse, called out,

'I can do that.'

'You said you wanted a passenger role?'

'I was joking. That's never an option, is it?'

Once the paddles started turning, the bow moved further away from the harbour wall. Ben, satisfied that passage could be made toward the mouth, gave one short-blast on the whistle, which startled harbour visitors. A dog barked.

'Midships,' he called to Patrick from his position in front of the wheel and "Slow Ahead," to Felicity. It was only at slow ahead that steerage could be maintained. A run of two hundred metres toward the mouth, allowed speed to be gathered. It was a fine judgement, that at about sixty metres Ben called for five degrees port helm and half speed. A sweep was needed to turn the bow into the middle of the harbour mouth. Two short blasts were given to indicate the paddle steamers swing alteration to port. Whistle signals that appertained more to warn ships, to be aware of dramatic course alteration, at sea, than in a harbour environment. But if any vessel was close to the harbour mouth it would be made aware of Princess Katrina's approach. A return to slow speed once the course was secured and the paddle steamer settled, into the middle of the harbour mouth. Once clear of the harbour, Ben instructed Felicity to ring half ahead, and took over the wheel from Patrick. With five degrees port helm, Ben altered course toward Berry Head. and countered with a momentary starboard five- degree helm, to halt bow swing. Ten minutes later and Robbie arrived on the bridge, followed by Liz Bowers, who was to receive instructions on steering.

'Are we going around Berry Head?' Asked Robbie.

'Not that far. A four-mile run to Elberry Cove. Chief Potts said he would like a full ahead speed trial,' replied Ben.

'Real Formula one stuff then,' said Robbie.

Felicity, stayed to chat with Liz for a while but left the wheelhouse with Patrick, who was under direction from his mother to tidy his cabin.

'Course is175 degrees Robbie. Need to alter to 220.' Ben handed the wheel over to Robbie with Liz stood next to him. They were well out into the bay and clear of other vessels, which allowed Robbie to get a feel of the wheel. Considerably more starboard wheel was needed than expected to get the bow to starboard. Once settled on the new course, Ben rang for – full ahead. From a quiet water feathering of the wheels moved to a seething crescendo, that drowned out conversation when near to either wheel.

Robbie, was stood by Liz who was quick to get accustomed to the amount of adjustment to keep the course close to 220 degrees.

'We're well clear of that tanker, at anchor.' Ben scanned across the bay to spot any vessels that might be coming into the bay. Several vessels, could be at anchor, to shelter in stormy conditions. Tankers, at anchor, effectively acted as storage tanks, while the price of oil crept up on the markets.

'We'll head for Elberry Cove and drop anchor. Have a bite to eat and head back.'

'Sounds good to me,' said Robbie.

'You'll be okay on the wheel?'

'Reckon so.'

'Twenty- six minutes to Elberry at nine knots,' said Ben

'Do you reckon we're doing nine knots?'

'Don't see why not. It's four miles to Brixham. We're be not far away. Can check time on arrival, which will give us speed.' Ben blew through the voice pipe to gain the attention of Chief Engineer Potts.

'How's it with you Chief?'

'Another five minutes and we'll need to go on Stand By. Plan to drop anchor off Elberry for lunch.' Ben listened to the Chief.

'Yes, we'll likely need astern movement to anchor.'

Out of the engine room Ben could hear a pumping motion of the steam engines' pistons. A rhythmic clank of steam power in action. Like giant sewing machines pulsing in the bowels of the vessel.

'Ben had contacted Chief Potts with some trepidation. Not wanting to hear that there were any mechanical or steam related problems below decks.

'Will that be alright? – slow astern at the anchorage?' He received affirmation. Chief Engineer Potts was getting both a trial at full speed, and astern movement of the paddle wheels when anchoring.

Felicity returned to the bridge, with Patrick

'Justin and Danny have asked about putting mackerel lines over the stern?'

'Perhaps on the way back.' Ben rang the telegraph to Stand By. The engine room reply caught up with his instruction almost immediately.

'They'll be able to fish with their rods. We're about to anchor.'

'Ben. Ollie and Harry have brought their wet suits and would like to cold water swim from the gangway?'

'This isn't Pontins, Felicity. But I'll lower the shore launch, when we're at anchor. They can swim, but only with lines attached, tell them. There's a strong tidal current from around Berry Head.' Ben was scanning the approach to Elberry and rang half speed.

'Five degrees starboard, Robbie.'

'Five degrees, it is Skip.' Only Robbie got away with "Skip." Anyone else was told in no uncertain terms. " We're not aboard a fishing trawler out of Brixham. It's either Captain or sir."

'Can I have a go on the wheel dad?' asked Patrick.

'Come over here laddie.' Robbie called out. Patrick walked across to the wheelman position.

'Take a hold of the top of the wheel.' Your father's got five degrees starboard helm – see.' Robbie pointed to the indicator. Patrick did as he was told. Liz left her position by the wheel, to talk with Felicity.

'Midships,' Ben called out and rang slow ahead. They were running parallel on an approach to Elberry beach.

'Midships, it is, said Robbie taking off the starboard helm. Ben looked at the compass which read 280 degrees.

'That'll do us.'

'Two-eighty degrees it is then Skip. I'd best be getting up to the fo'c'sl'e' once we're settled. Do you think you can hold this course? Robbie called across to Liz Bowers, who returned to the wheel, while Patrick on a signal from his father stepped away.

'I reckon I can Robbie,' said Liz.

'That's what a bit of expert training does.' Ben said and rang for "Stop Engines." A sand and pebble sea bed might not allow grip for the anchor in a tidal surge. On occasion "Dead Slow Ahead," engine instructions were implemented to keep an anchored vessel in position, against high winds and tidal surge, and remove strain exerted on cable and anchor.

Chapter 47

An easterly swell was reduced under the lee of the coast. Ben suspected there could be a powerful tidal swirl. When anchored Princess Katrina's bow would be turned seawards.

Patrick, was sent to the port bridge to note when forward movement was slowed.

'We're nearly stopped.' he called out. Ben walked over to the bridge, to see for himself and returned to ring slow astern. After another look over the port bridge, with megaphone in hand, called out,

"Let go the port anchor," and received a wave from Robbie.

Sound of a slow clatter, reached the bridge. This quickened into a staccato rattle as the anchor plummeted to the sea bed. Princess Katrina drew astern and Ben stopped engines. An out flowing tide meant that the paddle steamer, in this light breeze, lay back on the cable. Once satisfied that they were anchored, and unlikely to move out of position, Robbie let go the starboard anchor, which ran dropped to the sea bed.

A binnacle compass housed on the top of the wheelhouse enabled Ben to take three bearings. Elberry Cove, The Princess Theatre and Haldon pier. Back in the chart room these gave a near perfect intersection on the Torbay chart. Ben noted bearings on his phone for future reference. Patrick, caught sight of Justin and Danny, who were preparing to cast lines over the stern and decided to join them.

'Is that the time?' Said Felicity. The wheelhouse clock was at quarter past one.

'I can't leave Erica on her own in the restaurant.'

'And I can't really leave the wheelhouse,' said Ben.

'Unless you'd be happy to take bearings Liz?'

'That's something I'm capable of Ben.'

'There's a strong tidal flow,' and we need regular bearings. He pointed toward Paignton and Haldon pier and gave the bearings to Liz.

'If you take in the beach this gives a good intersection. Every ten minutes. Ben left the engines on Stand By, after he informed Chief Potts that they were secure at anchor. Engines remained on Stand By.

'You two get a bite to eat,' said Liz. Liz Bowers was familiar with three-point bearings and was happy to stay in the wheelhouse and make a check every ten minutes to see that the anchor position was being held. Ben sounded the whistle. Startled gulls flew from the foredeck.

'One blast on the whistle, if you detect any movement or you, need me back on the bridge.'

'We won't be long. No more than half an hour,' said Felicity.

'I can have a read on my phone. It's nice and peaceful up here. I've got seagulls for company,' said Liz. Two had landed to strut about the foredeck and others circled above in anticipation that, food might be available from this new arrival.

'Thanks Liz.'

'Save me some of those veggie rolls and ice cream.'

'Will do.'

An overhead screen in the restaurant was showing "Ground Hog Day." A situation that Ben hoped not to be caught in, while getting Princess Katrina up and running for the summer.

The screen was effectively a panel fitted in the starboard bulkhead. A blind, with a red ensign design could be lowered to hide its presence. On board entertainment for when it was raining, windy and cold. An alternative to phone scanning, which was every day. Weather conditions, met the "windy and cold," category, but hadn't stopped Justin and Danny from casting lines over the stern.

Sound, was turned back on the film while the paddle steamer was settled at the anchorage. On the way across a rolling corkscrew motion induced sea -sickness in some. Food held no attraction then, but at anchor the motion almost disappeared. Felicity arrived with Ben and said,

'Do help yourself to the pies and crab sandwiches, won't you?' Harry, Ollie, and several paddle steamer volunteers got up and walked across to the trestle table, set up in front of the bar. Felicity joined them to secure two veggie rolls for Liz, while Erica complained to Ben that she'd run out of fresh milk and had to add diluted instant to the coffee machine. A complaint that could be levelled effectively, at a captain of a paddle steamer by his mother.

'I quite like instant,' said Ben.

'It's not really what you like. I'm sure passengers would prefer fresh.'

'I'll make a note for future reference.'

Robbie, walked in and asked husband and wife team Ben and Felicity,

'Will it be alright to take a snack to the foredeck I've a bit of re-caulking I'd like to complete before we up anchor?

'Of course it will, Robbie,' said Felicity, who was on the way to the galley to fetch ice cream to go with Liz's veggie rolls. Ben was with Harry and Ollie giving explanation about a launch of the outboard motor dinghy to monitor their swim. Felicity departed with a tray of food and coffees to chat with Liz about the world outside Princess Katrina.

Chief Engineer Potts, in white boiler suit and cap, looked for Ben inside the restaurant and when he spotted him walked over, and caught Ben's eye.

'Need to have a chat.'

'Sure Chief. Be with you guys in a bit,' he said to Harry and Ollie.

'Can we go outside. It's not dire, but need to talk more privately.' Ben was hoping for an event free trial, but this he was about to discover was not to be.

'Right, let's go outside, on the afterdeck,' said Ben.

'Don't look so worried, it's not that serious,' said Chief Potts when they were outside.

'Jamie put dye on the port and starboard connecting rods.'

'And?'

A port rod has shown numerous cracks. They showed up after we anchored. Probably there, before we went on full speed.'

'We're not stranded here?' Chief Engineer Potts smiled and reached out to reassure Ben with a gentle arm touch.

'No, but we'll need to keep at half speed on our return.' Ben gave some thought to this.

'The tide turns in an hour and will be behind us.'

'There's some luck.'

'We've still got astern capability in the paddles,' said the Chief.

'I can probably give you up to half speed. Jamie's been online and there's a firm in Leicester that has supplied Waverley with connecting rods. We can most likely get one ordered.'

'I'll need to alert the Harbour master that we won't be back for four.'

Chapter 48

The sea temperature measured seven degrees.

'Positively toastie for time of year said Ollie.' They were on the gangway just above the waters' edge. Danny's dad had volunteered to be in the dinghy tied alongside. Ben previously launched the dinghy, and threw the painter to Robbie who brought the dinghy alongside the gangway.

Before Ben returned aboard, he made a rolling hitch with the two, orange, one-inch lines. Loops made to circle under the shoulders of Ollie and Harry.

'We're like dogs on a leash,' said Harry,'

'Do you want to go in or not? One tidal surge and you'll be gone. Pete! Can you give them about thirty feet of line and wrap each coil around a thwart. This enabled a release of extra line as required, but also limited total line flow.

'Don't expect you two will want to be in for long.' The news about the engine had unsettled Ben and he was more abrupt with Ollie and Harry than he would normally have been. Out of hearing of the two swimmers he said,

'They can pull themselves back Pete, if they start to drift. We're not having a Commander Crabb incident here.' Lionel Crabb was a naval frogman who went missing while diving near a soviet vessel in 1956.

'No more than half an hour, we're going back at half speed to see how the engines manage.' Ben made the engine emergency into part of the sea trial.

Ben, went to see how Justin and Danny were getting on fishing from the after deck.

'Danny's caught a sea bass and I've caught two pollock. Can we come back here dad the fishing's really, good? Said Justin. The fish were in a bucket.

'Well done, you two. I'd like to join in, but I've got to get back to the bridge. We'll probably return in the summer, when there'll be passengers aboard. Perhaps you and Danny could give some fishing lessons.

'Don't fancy that,' said Justin.

'Danny, Your father's helping the swimmers at the gangway.'

'Yes, I know Captain Sharpe. I'm going to join him.' They were both winding in their fishing reels.'

'Have you two eaten anything?'

'No Dad,' said Justin.

'You'd both better get up to the restaurant, before you do anything else.'

'Okay dad. But the fishing is good.' Ben smiled to himself thinking he would likely have done the same and forgotten about lunch at Danny's age.

Ben, left the two of them, on the after deck and made his way up over the accommodation and down to the foredeck to see Robbie.

A smell of melting pitch wafted up from the foredeck. An acrid, but not wholly unpleasant stench, like that of hot tar grit laid on a road surface. Crevices, in three outer lines of planks, on the starboard side glowed with its black trail. Robbie was running the squeezed spout of a metal kettle deftly toward the end of a fourth plank.

'That's a great job you're doing there Robbie, said Ben.

'They'll look way tidier when the surplus is scraped away.'

'Can't think of a job that needed doing more.'

'I wanted to use a rubber solution,' but that'll have to wait.'

'It's authentic. If there's a paddle steamer preservation society they'd approve.'

'By the by, we'll be going back at half speed.'

'And why is that?'

'Cracks, have appeared, in a connecting rod. It's not desperate, but the Chief doesn't want to place strain on the faulty rod.' Robbie was quick to pick up on what this might mean.

'And will this affect docking time skipper?'

'Yes, we'll need to anchor some distance from the pier and ferry anyone ashore who needs to go.' Not ideal, but with an engine trial these things can happen.'

'I've a cupboard to fit in Higher Warberry Road for a customers' house tomorrow. So long as I can get back for that I'm alright.'

'Should be no problem.' It was two-fifteen. Ben sensed a need to get moving.

'Can you give us a hand Robbie with getting the shore launch back aboard? We'll weigh anchor straight afterwards.' Robbie placed the pouring kettle back on its stand and asked?

'Have they finished their swim?'

'They'll have to.'

'Be with you in five Skip. Just need to tidy up.' Ben walked aft. Two black wet suited-figures, could be seen making their way across from gangway to deck. Fifteen minutes in the cold water evidently, was sufficient. A warm shower would now be welcome. Ben walked across to the gangway and called out,

'Alright are they Pete.' Danny was sat in a life jacket on the stern transom of the boat.

'Bit colder than they expected Captain Sharpe.'

'Thanks very much for helping-out. Are you up for bringing in the gangway?'

'Does it require muscle power?'

'No, you just need to keep your hand on a lever to keep the electric motor running. The ship's carpenter will assist in getting our go- ashore dinghy back aboard.'

Chapter 49

A dominant cloud formation was building over Berry Head when Ben arrived in the wheelhouse.

'Shouldn't we be getting back?' Asked Felicity.

'It's in hand. Robbie's stowing the shore dinghy before we weigh anchor, but we'll be going back at half ahead.'

'And why is that?'

'Cracks have shown up in a connecting rod and the Chief doesn't want to risk full ahead.'

'Is that serious? I mean we will get back?'

'It's alright. Just a precaution. Probably put thirty to forty minutes on the trip. We'll anchor off Princess Pier, I'm not going alongside in the dark. We'll anchor and ferry people ashore.' Liz returned from the small monkey island space after taking bearings.

'What time do you reckon we'll be able to pick Caroline up then?'

'Aim to be at anchor by five. Looking at five -thirty.' Felicity walked out on to the port bridge to get a good signal to talk with Vicky about change of plans.

A slow clunk from the fo'c'sle windlass signalled that the starboard anchor was being lifted from the sea bed.

'How's the lay?' Ben called on the megaphone to Robbie who left Pete on the windlass while he inspected the lay of the cable. He flung his arm out to indicate it was well forward. Once the starboard cable, which lay directly on the sea bed was clear, of the water-signalled by Robbie with a rapid criss-cross of his arms, Ben rang for Dead Slow Ahead, to take pressure from the Windlass as it took in the port anchor. The paddles made a gentle swish sound, as they turned, at the pace of a slow turning mill, water wheel. Ben messaged Harbour Master James Briggs to say that he was anchoring and not going alongside.

Brooding clouds from the west brought a sweep of rain mixed with hail, and drove those on deck into the restaurant space. Robbie, sent Pete down the fo'c'sle ladder and into the housing. He returned with yellow smocks and trousers for him and Robbie, who walked to the bow, leant over and returned to give a rapid bell to signal to Ben that the port anchor had broken from the sea bed. Ben waited for twenty minutes before he ordered,

'Ten degrees starboard helm,' Ben called back to Liz from where his binoculars were trained on the fo'c'sle.

'Ten degrees starboard helm it is "Captain." Liz received a look of approval from Felicity.

A rapid clatter slowed as it indicated that the windlass was taking the anchor cable back to its housing.

Ben, stopped engines and rang for slow astern. This slowed stalled forward movement, and affected a more abrupt swing to starboard. He needed the bow to turn away from the shore and find deep water. This was an aspect of the trial that gave Ben better appreciation, of the paddle steamer's manoeuvrability.

After going for a course of 030 degrees Ben found cross bearings on the chart which would give an appropriate anchorage west of Princess Pier, to minimize ferry run distance to the pier. At half ahead there was more of a rolling motion, but the course could be maintained. Ben had switched the mast head and port and starboard navigation lights on. The rain stopped and within fifteen minutes white bulbed lights were visible from the paddle steamer along Princess Pier. Coloured fairy lights along the sea front were switched off for the winter months.

Berry Head Lighthouse, with its two white flashes gave a reliable bearing. A lit cross, on St John's Church and a flood lit Princess Theatre made three good bearings for a position. This determined Ben to make a course alteration to 035 degrees. Motor cruiser owners would doubtless not even bother with compass headings, and position bearings, and just head for landmarks, but Ben took this as an opportunity to practice his professional experience once more. A coastal cruise would require a high degree of professionalism.

It was five-ten when Ben rang slow astern and had Robbie "Let go," the starboard anchor, off Princess Pier.

163

Chapter 50

Masthead, and funnel lights were switched on to highlight Princess Katrina at anchor. Fortunately, there was no mist to obscure the steamer's presence. The ship to shore motorised dinghy was equipped to run from ship to shore with port and starboard navigation lights midships and a spotlight on the bow canopy.

It was proposed that two runs would be made to the pier's inner steps. Felicity, called Vicky to update her on the situation and spoke with Caroline.

'We're anchored off Princess Pier.'

'Why's that?'

'Your father doesn't want to berth in the dark.'

'Can Abigail stay over?' Felicity expected an objection to being ferried aboard and the fact of being at anchor.

'What does Abigail's mother think about her being afloat for the night.'

'Abigail sails a cadet like me. Her mother doesn't mind.' It sounded like Abigail had enthusiasm for Princess Katrina, which made it okay.

'Let me speak with Caroline's mother.'.... There was a pause, before Vicky answered.

'Vicky are you alright with Abigail staying over? Vicky was, apparently, okay about it.

'Ben need to run me ashore for school and there's a bus right by the theatre. ... Yes, it's fine by me. We've a spare double cabin.' Vicky asked what Abigail should bring.

'Some night clothes. We've got towels, soap. A floating hotel. We're landing on Princess Pier. First steps on the left, in front of the theatre. Hold on Vick, I'll get a time from Ben.'

'Floating hotel!' Exaggeration for effect? Tell Vicky.' Ben glanced at the wheelhouse clock.

'Seven. We should have managed two runs by then. Robbie will be ashore. Could do with a bow man.'

'Girl?' Replied Felicity and Felicity returned to Vicky.

'Seven, if that's alright? Ben's making two runs to the pier...

'No, it's fine. I'll see them on to the bus tomorrow. Ben will be at Princess Pier for seven.'

'Tell Vicky, probably earlier,' said Ben.

'He'll likely be there before seven.

Bye, bye Vicky.'

The temperature had plummeted since they left Elberry Cove and apart from Ben and Felicity everyone else was in the restaurant. Hot air was pumped from the engine room, through a duct system that circled the restaurant. Several portholes were open to reduce a situation of suffocating heat.

Emily and Liz Bowers had Patrick, Justin and Danny join them in a game of charades. A list of well-known films and books were listed on Liz's iPad and they choose one to perform. Five volunteers from the engine room were sat drinking coffee at a table, by the door, when Ben walked in. He went straight over to thank them, for their contribution.

'Couldn't manage without you guys.'

'Ah we're disappointed that we had to reduce to slow coming across,' one replied.

'Nothing that serious according to the Chief,' another said.

'It would have been good if we'd been able to keep at full speed, though.' Ben enthusiastically replied,

'Yep, but you got us back. You're welcome to be aboard for our first passenger cruise.'

'Where will you be going?' another asked.

'Possibly Dartmouth.'

'Up for that Captain Sharpe. Arran's been asking about boiler suits. Sort of look the part more?

'Sure, we can manage that. My wife has your email addresses. We'll be in contact. Look forward to you aboard again, when we're sea -going in March. Expect the Chief would welcome assistance before then.

'Weekends, it'll have to be for me,' said one from the group.'

'We'll make a call for help mid-week then if that's okay with all of you.'

'Saturday, but not Sunday,' said one.

'That's fine. I'll get the Chief to get in touch, going forward. We've a boat going ashore, in about twenty minutes. Thanks very much guys. Really appreciate your enthusiasm and commitment.'

Ben walked across to the far corner where Patrick was acting out a charade. He appeared to be mimicking climbing with his hands.

Ben called out – "Spider Man – Across the Spider Verse."

'Dad, you're not in the game,' said Patrick.

'Is that it?' Asked Justin?'

"Spider Man -Across the Spider Verse," Danny, called out.

'Danny you "are in the game," and get a point.' Said Emily.

'That's not fair.'

'Probably not,' said Ben. Perhaps they should all get a point.' Ben said diplomatically.

'Captain Sharpe has spoken,' said Liz. Ben spoke to Liz and Emily to sound them out about shore -going.

'Are you two okay to take the second boat. I've said that I'll take the engine room work force on the first one.'

'That's fine Ben,' said Liz. Emily came in with,

'Up the Workers.'

'Can I come dad?' Asked Patrick. This, games boring.'

'Yes, Patrick I could do with a bow man to go ashore at the steps.

With Robbie, that'll be a boat load.

'Who have you got on board overnight?' Asked Liz?

There's the Chief, Jamie; my mother, Felicity, and the children. I've to pick up Caroline at seven.

'I can stay over to help. You're going to need an anchor watch, aren't you? Working from home tomorrow. Slight variation, I can work from a paddle steamer.'

'That would be great Liz. We could stagger the anchor watch around the three of us.'

Chapter 51

A cowl came forward from the small cabin at the bow. It was a necessary addition, and gave spray protection, when the dinghy pitched through open sea, for passengers sat in the fore-part. Ben, throttled back, as the boat swung into the shelter of the outer harbour. It was transformational, a move from the exposed sea, in the bay, to an inside calm by the pier. It gave Ben an opportunity to get sight of his mooring space, behind a River Dart ferry, named River Princess. Laid-up for the winter months. Unlike, the Western Lady ferries, painted in a cream yellow, its white hull, gave an appearance more of a luxury yacht, with varnished upper cabin space, which led to a bridge and wheelhouse. Like a miniature liner in profile. Ben reckoned that he could run a faster service, with more entertainment and better stability for passengers, than those who sailed aboard River Princess.

A trial run across to Berry Head and back, had not exposed any major problems other than that a tarpaulin canopy built out on the after deck, would be a useful addition, to give passenger protection in squally conditions, for those who liked to be outside rather than shut in the restaurant. A worn connecting rod was a service problem, which needed addressing. Nothing, of a serious mechanical nature.

Ben, gave instructions, before he left for shore, to sound the whistle, should there be any drift at anchorage, but he also remained in mobile phone contact. The paddle steamer's bow faced out to sea. Any drift would be westwards away from the pier. A light easterly wind, and slack water between tides, meant risk of anchor slippage was minimal.

Ben, cut the motor, when they closed in on the steps, while Robbie, reached the boat hook out and caught a ring bolt, to draw the bow inwards. Patrick, took hold of the painter, stepped ashore, and drew the boat alongside. Ben's plan was to take Princess Katrina alongside in daylight. With leave ending on Thursday, he wanted to be alongside Princess Pier, for Tuesday

'You'll be wanting me aboard then?' Robbie was first to step on to the steps, after Patrick.

'It'll be Tuesday midday most likely. Need to finalize with the Harbour Master, Robbie.'

'That's a sensible time of day.'

'I'll let you know for sure tomorrow morning.

On return to Princess Katrina, he was met with news that Emily had contacted Freddie and could he bunk aboard overnight, to get his disco equipment packed away? Emily had cleared it with Felicity that she could share a double berth with Liz. When Emily messaged back to Freddie Ben spoke to him. He said that he was pleased that he'd made a good recovery from his dunking, in the harbour and that would he like to stay two nights aboard and assist with the docking on Tuesday? Freddie asked,

'Will Emily be aboard Ben?'

'Do you want me to see?' There was a pause, and Ben turned to Emily.

'Emily, will you be able to manage Monday night? More hands the merrier for going in.'

'I can. I'm working from home like Liz quite like this life afloat. Envious of you all.' Ben returned to Freddie.

'Yes, Emily's staying for a couple more days. Value, having both of you aboard.

Ben looked at his watch.

'You'll need to be by the inner steps of the Princess Pier by seven. I'm running Harry and Ollie ashore. Six- thirty. Can you manage that?'

'Good. See you at seven then Freddie. Hand you over to Emily.' Ben smiled to himself.

'That's if you want to speak to her? He received a sickly type smile from Emily. A visit was made to the bridge to check anchor bearings, before another run back to the pier to pick up Caroline and now, Freddie.

There was quite a gathering, when Ben walked through the bridge door, Felicity, his mother, Liz Bowers, and Chief Engineer Potts.

'Interrupted, a special meeting or something have I?'

'No, said Erica. But I'm shutting the restaurant in a few minutes and there won't be any food unless it's ordered now!' Chief Potts came in with,

'Just here to find out what your plans are Captain. Myself, Jamie, and Ross can run a night watch in the engine room, but we'll need more help to dock.'

'That's fine. I've arranged for a few volunteers to come aboard to dock on Tuesday. Everything's in hand Chief. Where are Justin and Patrick?'

'In my cabin on the game consul. They're quite happy.' said Erica.

'I don't have a bow man then?'

'You'll manage with Harry and Ollie. You've a daughter waiting to be fetched from the pier,' said Felicity.

'There'll be me some crab sandwiches and salad covered in cling in the fridge,' said Erica.

'What about Caroline?'

They'll be some for her as well and ice cream.

As they approached the pier, Caroline, with Abigail and her mother could be seen near to the pier. Ben, throttled back on the outboard. When they arrived at the top of the steps, Harry and Ollie went ashore and held the boat alongside, while water slurped noisily against its sides.

'Hi dad,' called out Caroline. He waved and smiled, as he scrambled forward to take hold of Abigail's overnight bag to place in the boat and then Caroline's. Abigail, like Caroline, was dressed in jeans, jumper, and anorak. She smiled and said,

'Thanks for having me aboard Captain Sharpe.' Her mother, stood a few feet back, on the barnacle and limpet clustered landing strip. Raised, her free arm, and waved to acknowledge Ben, while on her phone to finalize plans with Felicity. Light from the phone lit a smiling face. Ben, superfluous to the ongoing discussion.

Harry and Ollie meanwhile, removed their lifejackets, and gave them to Caroline, and Abigail. Waved goodbye to Ben as they walked up the steps. For Ben, it was good to see Caroline happy and keen to return aboard with Abigail.

Chapter 52

Jamie, with assistance from Ross, was in charge, of the engine room. Abigail and Caroline joined Justin and Patrick on the games' consul, in Erica's double cabin, with a proviso that bed time was to be eight-thirty for all four. Liz Bowers volunteered to take an early bridge anchor watch, while Emily assisted Freddie with his removal and pack away of disc jockey equipment from the Christmas party.

Chief Engineer Potts joined Ben and Felicity in the restaurant, no longer in a white boiler suit with "Chief Eng," embroidered in red silk across a top pocket, but dressed in navy chinos, paisley shirt, and blazer. Ben greeted the Chief with,

'You've got us back Chief. Are you happy with how it went? Had to anchor off shore, with night closing in.'

'In general, a success, apart from the faulty connecting rod. Speed reduction was Just a precaution,' said the Chief.

'That worn connecting rod may have thousands of miles of more life in it, but best to not take the risk of a breakage.' Ben keen for assurance about the state of the engines asked,

'Can we go alongside at Slow, provided there's Slow Astern available, then Chief?' Ben knew the answer was yes, but wanted opportunity for the Chief to voice his opinion.

'Once in the harbour you can have half astern, if needs be.'

'Good to hear that. You're happy with overall running then?'

'Good as we'll get. I mean there'll be a learning curve. Every triple expansion engine, an individual with regard, to its quirks." Erica entered the restaurant after she'd closed- down the game consul, a bit earlier than recommended. Felicity picked up on her arrival.

'Erica's prepared a crab salad, with buttered whole grain bread slices as requested,' said Felicity.

'That sounds sensational.'

'You might prefer to eat in the galley, with all the clearing up going.' Felicity waved a hand toward where Freddie and Emily had lights and cable strewn over tables.

'Felicity, the galley will be fine.'

'Edward, would you like coffee?' Erica called out from by the coffee machine. He responded with,

'Just the medicine, Erica,' and walked across to join her.

'Are you having a coffee?'

'A hot chocolate, Teddie. Coffee keeps me awake.'

'Can I change to chocolate?

'By all means.' The Chief advanced with,

'And will you be having a meal? I mean would you like to join me?'

'I'll just be having a sandwich but yes, of course.' After the chocolate drinks were made, they left, for the galley.

'That's given me an idea,' said Felicity, out of hearing of Freddie and Emily.

'What's that?' Asked Ben.

'We could set up a casual dating site, once we're operational. Far more romantic than a first meeting, at a Costa Coffee or local pub.'

'Are you serious?'

'It would need to be advertised as available only when alongside. Wouldn't want to trap couples aboard, on a trip to Dartmouth if they decide they aren't compatible.' Ben interjected with,

'Have you paid Jamie and Robbie for the weekend?' Chief Engineer Potts was paid an honorarium, when the Paddle steamer was fully operational, like now. Unlike Jamie and Robbie, he was allowed a double cabin, with a brass plaque overhead, which announced in red letters "Chief Engineer." A cabin, feet away from the engine room door.

Felicity allowed a twenty per cent discount on food and drink for paid-crew members. It was card or cash payment up front. Ben, was for handing out free food to volunteers, but Felicity said the budget could not afford and she said that they might just come aboard for the freebies, anyhow! It was a hard-headed appreciation of overheads and cost that Felicity gleaned from her online spread sheet, printed out every week to keep everything financial, on an even keel. An hourly rate of pay, with agreement that pay off was registered the moment a crew member went ashore and departed for home.

Felicity's laptop was open on the bar.

'Are you a mind reader Captain Sharpe? I am, you'll be pleased to know, in the process of doing just that. Any profit from the Christmas party and raffle monies will be eaten up by this jaunt. You do know that?

'Register that as a win.' Ben was pleased overall with their trip to Elberry Cove and back.

'Do you think so. Neither of us can give up our day job. I'll need to take any supply work that comes along. Once alongside it'll be back then to rations, portable generators and Calor gas.

'Yes, but it's a positive step toward being ready to take passengers. Aunt

Rose would be pleased.'

'What about your wife?' Ben held Felicity by the waist and looked into her eyes.

'And what about my wife?'

'Well, she's not petitioning for divorce.'

'That's good to hear.'

'We should be grateful, for all the support we've received over the weekend,' Felicity reminded Ben.

'How should we show our gratitude?'

'We could fit in a ship's crew and supporters dinner party before Christmas?'

'That means a dip into Aunt Rose's house legacy. It's not a magic money pot. We could t have been better off financially if we'd let that house out as a buy to let.

'Is that what you would have liked?' Ben ducked a straight answer.

'As long as I have you, that's all that matters.'

'You do think soft soaping will get you anywhere, Ben Sharpe. But it's what I like to hear,' she said, and leant forward to be kissed by Ben.

Chapter 53

The short four-mile trip to Elberry Cove was deemed a success. Triple expansion engines, which turned the paddle wheels, were capable, of maintaining, an average cruising speed of above fourteen knots. Oil consumption higher than propellor driven-motor engines, like the Western Lady Ferries and River Princes, but historic charm and passenger experience of sailing aboard a paddle steamer, Ben, and Felicity, felt would likely have more appeal.

Innovative cruises, to the River Dart and possible beach barbeques at Elberry Cove could offer variety, and entice a younger passenger profile. There were nine passenger cabins, but apart from family and restricted crew members. There were no plans to have passengers sleep aboard overnight. Ben remarked to Felicity that large liners did on occasion have long-standing passengers. Wealthy widows, who preferred to enjoy amenities offered by a cruise liner to that of a shore-based hotel. Even known to stay aboard when the liner went into dry dock. Erica, his mother was a possible candidate, but she had already said that as soon as her apartment which overlooked Torbay was decorated, she would be ashore!

A night anchor watch was shared. Liz Bowers said she was happy to keep watch on the bridge, until four. Felicity joined her. Ben, after a few hours' sleep returned to the bridge, to later witness sunrise. Shore light references, like lights on Princess and Haldon Pier, plus the flash of light from Berry Head, reassured Ben that Princess Katrina was securely at anchor. An outgoing tide and easterly breeze meant that any drift, Ben anticipated would be westwards and away from the harbour area.

It was eight o'clock, on Monday 9th December, after Ben made an entry in Princess Katrina's log book –

"at anchor, in calm seas," that his mobile buzzed.

'Hi Ben, it's your Harbour Master speaking.' James Briggs, after arrival at his office, scanned the bay to see what traffic was about and picked up Princess Katrina at anchor, not far off shore.

'Hi Jim,' replied Ben.

'Yes, change of plan. We'd like you back on your former mooring. The Vlissingen has been directed up channel to join a NATO force, apparently. The crew won't be able to enjoy the delights of Torquay. There's space to skirt around and come up on your mooring. If you're alright with that Ben?

'Yes sure.'

'How did it go then?'

'Very well, apart from discovery of wear on a connecting rod. Had to steam back at half-ahead. A service problem. Nothing serious, Jim.' Ben didn't want to suggest there might be any significant engineering problems.

'Decided not to risk berthing during the dark. Looks like it's worked out for the best.'

'Yep. You'll get more privacy back on that mooring. We've no further planned warship visits to Haldon, until May, by which time you'll be berthed on Princess Pier and running cruises, Ben.'

'Fingers crossed, Jim. Midday? Is midday, Tuesday still on the cards for us to pick up on our mooring then?' The Harbour Master was happy about this.

'That'll suit me fine. I'll Make a circuit, in the launch, ensure you've got a clear run to pick up. Message about eleven, to give all clear to enter

'Good on you Jim. Over and out.' Although on his mobile Ben responded as if on a ship to shore radio, with his signing off. A conversation, with no social chit chat and specific to the situation in hand. An hour earlier Ben launched the dinghy with the outboard and brought it to the port gangway.

After running Felicity, children, and Abigail ashore, Liz, Emily and Freddie were left on the bridge as anchor watchkeepers. Liz, would take charge as the most responsible of the three. A yacht owner herself.

Ben, wanted to inspect the forward deck area and lie of the anchor cable. He was armed with Vim, a can of Brasso and cloths to clean and polish the ship's bell, which was bolted to a fo'c'sle stanchion. Encrusted with salt and green verdigris, after exposure to salt and spray.

He was reminded of a saying, attributed to Pliny the Elder. (AD 29) That copper becomes covered with verdigris when cleaned. This bell would have been cleaned numerous times, but maybe it was an excuse on Pliny's part to avoid the task of cleaning? It was the job of ships' apprentices to clean bells, binnacles. Anything brass- like in a ship's wheelhouse and generally aboard ship. It was years since Ben cleaned a ship's bell, but it was affirmation that Princess Katrina was like awakening from slumber and near ready for active service. After half an hours' application of elbow grease, the fo'c'sle' bell gleamed in the afternoon sun.

On his return to the wheelhouse, he was greeted by

'Can't get the staff these days then Ben,' from Liz.

'Depends Liz, When you want a job completed to a high specification you sometimes have to do it yourself. You could also call it multi-tasking. Are you guys okay to keep this anchor watch, for half an hour while I fetch the family back aboard?'

'Not a problem Ben. I like this working from home venue. I'll toot, the whistle like you said if anything happens which needs you back aboard straight away,' replied Liz.

Ben, appreciated assistance from Liz, Emily, and Freddie, but also was aware that going forward, Princess Katrina would be dependent on a regular crew. He did not want to put pressure on volunteers that would make them feel that they were in any way exploited. This situation was getting near the mark.

Chapter 54

A return to the mooring, next to Haldon Pier did mean main boilers and the engine room diesel generators were mothballed. Every occupied cabin was supplied with a fan heater which ran off one of two silenced-generators. These were positioned on the foredeck in protective well -ventilated boxed housings. Muffle proof adhesive tiles were fitted by Robbie. These tiles, a more recent addition, reduced noise further. Felicity remarked that the protective boxing around the generators gave an, aesthetically more pleasing look. When fully operational the clatter from a shipboard generator's was, however, a constant, but reassuring presence.

Normality, or the routine experienced, before the sea trial came back, with Ben's return to work on Thursday. Felicity, had picked up supply work at Abbey School for the following week. That Saturday, became a family trip ashore, to stock up on grocery supplies and for Erica, an opportunity to visit her flat to see how work was progressing. Whether smell of fresh paint was too pungent for an early return!

Erica, loaned Felicity a shopping trolley, which was deemed unfashionable and old people, by her children, but allowed heavier items to be stored and wheeled back to Princess Katrina.

Ben, ferried everyone ashore, in the large outboard dinghy and then returned for the pram dinghy, which, when on the slipway, was upended, stowed and pad locked in the slipway rack. A walk along past the inner harbour took them to the Strand, where they parted company with Erica, before they caught a bus to the upper end of town. It was decided to eat at Tonkins before shopping in the market area.

'Why do we have to always have to eat here?' Asked Caroline. It was busy, but they'd found a table at the back, which could seat five.

'It is dependable and the café has happy memories for your father.' Patrick and Justin were with Ben at the counter placing the orders.

'What memories?'

'Granny used to bring your father here when he was about your age, as a treat during the holidays.'

'But that was years and years ago.'

'Perhaps it will be the same for you when you're older?'

'I don't think so. But I don't mind, really.' Caroline was at an age where she cared about her father's welfare and was more aware of his crucial role in the family.

'Good. I work on the basis that it saves risking going somewhere else and being disappointed. That's something you can do on holiday when there's time to be adventurous and anyway Caroline, it puts your father in a good mood for the rest of the day.'

'Father is in a good mood.'

'Well, it's working then.' That it was working was probably as much due to being together as a family, but Felicity felt the need to consider family finance management. They were, later ashore than planned but it did mean there wasn't a stop at Macaris, Ice Cream Parlour, for morning coffee and drinks for the children.

'I'm going to help father,' said Caroline. Immediately after Felicity's phone started. Felicity had contacted Devon Radio for a possible interview to talk about her children's book. They said that they might get back for an afternoon interview. It was when she gave her address as Princess Katrina, c/o The Cliff Yacht Club that there was what seemed like genuine interest.

'Are you connected with paddle steamer Princess Katrina?'

'I'm married to the Captain, as it happens,' she replied.

'Really. Do you actually live aboard?'

'Yes,' Felicity was unsure where this was going.

'How exciting. Just the two of you?'

'No, no, we have three children. We're due to run cruises in the holiday months.' Felicity considered it worth giving the cruise element a plug.

'Will you be getting back to me about a possible book interview?'

'Adrian, he's our programme editor. He'll decide, if there's a two-minute space, in the 1400, hour afternoon show. It sounds really, good, and we have interviewed local authors. Can't promise anything, Felicity, but thanks so much for contacting us.' Felicity didn't feel overly confident from the reply about getting an interview.

When Felicity heard that it was Devon Radio this time, she immediately expected any news to be about a possible interview to talk about her book.

'Adrian Fargo here. Is that Felicity Sharpe?

'Yes, speaking.

'Hi there. I've just seen a photo, in the Herald and Express of Princess Katrina, with water flowing from her paddle wheels. It's great, like a look back in history. Bethany, explained that you're married to the paddle steamers captain. We'd love to have you and your husband in a slot on the show. If you would like to incorporate it with a chat about your book, is it – Alicante Holiday?' This was not what Felicity planned, particularly as she felt the conversation would be more about Princess Katrina and life on board, than her book!

'That would be fine Adrian. Thanks for getting back. When might a slot be available?'

'It would be next year, Felicity. January. Most likely Friday 24th. If you can be available for the 1400 afternoon show?

'I'm sure we can.'

'That's just great Felicity, May I call you Felicity?'

'By all means Adrian.' Felicity didn't mind first names, but felt that there was a faux familiarity attached to the show business side of things.

'I'll have Bethany message you with confirmation and more details.'

'Look forward to being on the show in January,' Felicity, replied.

'Bye for now Felicity.'

'Bye.'

Felicity had looked, into radio advertising and knew it could be expensive. This would be like a freebie. Radio Devon was possibly not a top advertising medium, but maybe it attracted listeners from further afield who were considering an English Rivera holiday experience or even a children's book?

Chapter 55

'Hi Erica.' A visit to the metro supermarket had covered a number, of items, which were in short supply. Online grocery orders were ended prior to the trial run to Elberry Cove, but Felicity planned to re-instate them now that they were back on the mooring and not at Princess Pier. Felicity decided to phone Erica to update her on where they were, with the shore shopping expedition.

'Hi, yes, we have "been everywhere man," it seems. Ben, is with the children in Smiths, to choose books, with the book tokens you generously gave them. We're heading for Costa in Union Street. Could meet there at four o'clock? There's a five twenty- seven bus to the harbour.' Pause. 'What's that?...

'Yes, Bens bought four pints of milk. There's more coming with the online shop, due at the slipway for six.' Erica complimented Felicity, on her organizing skills and how lucky Ben was. Felicity, not wishing to cause division said that she thought Ben was representative of husbands and men in general, with regard, to domestic priorities. Basically, a challenge for either wife or mother to get them organized.

Felicity, was stood outside WH Smith to pick up a signal, and finished the call when Ben, and the children walked out. There was a consensus among the children that their mother might censor any book that lacked educational merit and Ben, their father was allowed to advise and assist instead. It did give Felicity opportunity to make a call to Erica and arrange where they would meet up before they returned to Princess Katrina.

'What did you choose Caroline?

'Ten Girls who changed the World.'

'That's up your street.'

'Patrick's bought a book on British Paddle Steamers,' said Justin.

'I detect a fatherly interest in that choice Justin. And what did you buy then?'

'Sea Fishing for beginners. But Mum. I'm not really a beginner. There may be on one or two things I've missed.'

'Very sensible Justin. It's good to hone up on skills. You might start catching bigger fish than Danny.'

'That wasn't the reason I bought the book Mum.' Felicity addressed the issue in hand.

'Look Grannies said she'll meet us at Costa's for four. Then you'll be able to show her the books you've bought. Are you happy with your book choice Patrick?

'Yes, of course. They keep asking me about paddle steamers at school. I need to become more of an expert.'

'That sounds like educational to me.'

'So, you approve.'

'Of course. I'm sure your father does.'

'He can search out the competition, maybe?' Ben joined in.

'Princes Katrina is too individual to have competition.'

'There speaks a proud man. But I agree.'

'Really?'

'You say that as if you don't get agreement from me?'

'Do we have to have a squabble in the high street?' asked Caroline, who took on the role of responsible adult, at times, when she felt her parents were getting a bit tetchy with one another.

'You're quite right Caroline.' They walked away from the stationers towards Costa and since it was near to four o'clock went in and found a table by the door. It was Justin's idea, to sit near to the door, who was perhaps the keenest to meet up with granny, whom he knew would take a keen interest in his book purchase. The other two joined their father who went to order.

'Can Danny come aboard again?' Justin asked'

'I don't see why not. While we're at the mooring. He'll need to wear a lifejacket.'

'Danny can swim.'

'We had a near miss with Freddie when he went overboard. Your father recently had inflatable lifeboats fitted which saved the day. It's not just about being able to swim Justin. When the water's cold you can quickly get hyperthermia.' Justin was studying the lit display above the Costa Counter advertising hot Kit Kat Chocolate.

'Can I change my Red Berry Fruit for that?' Justin pointed toward the Kit Kat chocolate display.

'You'd better be quick your father's about to order.' Justin left his window chair and hurried across to where Ben, Caroline and Patrick were queuing to be served at the Costa counter. Window space near to Felicity accommodated the shopping trolley and several hessian bags full of groceries and other necessaries.

The hessian "canvas," type shopping bags reminded Felicity of how Robbie spoke about when he lifted a trap door inside the fo'c'sl'e which led to a former paint and canvas locker, and discovered ten bolts of duck canvas (39 yards length) and two bolts of light underlay hatch canvases. Covered, out of sight by heavy duty treated canvas. Mooring rope was visible at the outer edges, which suggested that the canvas covered further rope coils. Robbie's curiosity revealed the find when he drew the canvas away.

'Guess the new rope around the canvases kind of helped preserve it,' he said to Ben and Felicity later when he was on the wheel. Felicity remembered thinking of how durable duck canvas was and wondered what use it could be put to? There were several winter months ahead and she was reminded of how Ben said that when his holdall developed holes from wear and tear, he cut it apart; measured out duck canvas replacement patterns; stitched them together. Next, stitched light cord with extra width at each end to neatly attach, with stitching, to the holdall's sides. Felicity considered that Supermarkets advertised on carrier bags. Why couldn't Princess Katrina cruises be advertised on the side of a canvas holdall? Immersed, in her thoughts she didn't notice Erica walk through the door.

'Felicity, you have been busy shopping. I hope you found my shopping trolley useful?

'I did Erica. You've arrived just in time. I desperately need some responsible adult support. My husband might as well be another child in these runs ashore.

Chapter 56

Ben, rowed back with the children. Patrick in the bow, with Caroline and Justin in the stern. Two carrier shopping bags fitted under the centre thwart. Felicity had explained to Erica her plans to sew canvas decorative bags while they walked from the slipway, across to the Yacht Chandlers.

Erica, said that she had large dress cutting scissors which she reckoned would cut duck canvas. It being a lighter weight, than conventional canvas. Jamie, was serving front of house and supplied Felicity with four sewing palms, needles and white-waxed thread, which would be easier to work and give a professional appearance. Erica, paid for the thread, which cost forty pounds per one pound weight.

'It can be my Christmas present to you and Ben,' she said.

'It'll be something to occupy me with until the Spring arrives. We can lay a workshop out in the restaurant on trestle tables, Felicity. I'll cut the canvas out from patterns. You'll need some cord to make the handles. There were drum rows of cord and light rope down the far side of the Chandlers. In the end they selected two hanks of white nylon braided rope which were at a twenty per cent discount. Erica, was taking the project in hand.

'You'll need words or decoration on the side.'

'Yes. We can photo print on to canvas. Maybe someone local would be able to help? Don't see it as a problem. We'd better get back I can hear, the sound of an outboard motor. Ben's, on his way back.'

It was dark when they arrived at the slipway. Harbour light reflection danced across water, near to the pier. It was close to high tide, which made the dinghy launch easier. When Ben returned with the larger ship to shore dinghy, he was able to tie up at the top of the slipway. He spotted a carrier with a profile of a yacht under sail with Yacht Chandler printed above, which Erica was carrying.

'What have you been buying then, in my absence? He asked jokingly.

'We're going to put some of that canvas that Robbie discovered to good use and sew up some holdalls,' replied Felicity.

'Or shoppers – haven't decided. We're only at the design stage,' said Erica.

'Taken my idea, have you?'

'They'll need to be more commercially viable than your attempt,' said Felicity.

'I don't doubt that. Mother was always a dab hand at re-tailoring clothes to make them fit.'

'The school jackets were quality cloth and they fitted well. After adjustments had been made, it was better than you growing into a blazer, like some did.'

'Not a criticism. Just a recall from earlier times.' Ben, held the hooked end of the boat hook and proffered the wooden handle.

'Take a hold as you step aboard. It'll steady you. Leave the shopping trolley and bags for me to load.' Once aboard Felicity and Erica sat on opposite side thwarts forward from the outboard, while Ben hopped ashore and with a round turn and two half hitches, secured the painter to a ring bolt, with a round turn and two half hitches. Felicity, now on board, was able to grip the wall edge, with the boat hook to keep the dinghy alongside. Ben, able to step from slipway to boat and stow bags and trolley.

'What have you done with the children?' Asked Felicity.

'Put them in chains, in the bilges? No, they're in the restaurant watching – Home Alone 2 – Lost in New York. Caroline, of course asked "will they be making a film called – Home Alone – Lost on a paddle steamer. Now, I thought she was keener on life aboard, with Abigail having slept aboard last week?'

'She was just winding you up Ben,'

'Never mind. Children are there to keep, you on your toes. I should know,' said Erica.

Ben levered the boat away from the side of the slipway. A short ignition whir led to the outboard roaring into life. Any further conversation made difficult without shouting.

After the children were settled in the restaurant, in pyjamas and dressing gowns to watch a film with Erica, Ben, and Felicity went to the wheelhouse to be alone. Prior to re-furbishing of cabin space, the wheelhouse had been a part bedroom and part sitting room. A kind of hideaway for the two of them. Felicity commandeered the chart room as an office, when they were on the moorings. It offered sanctuary, from the busyness of the restaurant and accommodation, with a wide sweep of view across the harbour from the wheelhouse.

'That trial run to Elberry Cove went really well,' she said to Ben, who was sat on a stool in the wheelhouse having a flick through Patrick's book of British Paddle Steamers which he'd loaned him for the evening. Felicity placed a mug of cocoa on the raised collapsable table that Robbie had made and drew a stool closer to sit next to Ben. A fan heater that was stood on the wheelman's plinth directed a warm blast of air toward where they were sat.

'I've prepared an itinerary for next year.'

'Let's hear it,' said Ben who closed the book and picked up the cocoa mug.

'I want a bit more enthusiasm from your quarter. ' Ben, unlike Felicity did not find a shopping expedition energizing, but she was determined to get his thoughts and agreement on next year's early work rota around Princess Katrina.

'January 25th. To be confirmed a 1400 interview with Devon Radio.'

'Really?'

'Yes. I contacted Devon Radio hoping for an interview and chat about my children's book.'

'Where does Katrina fit into that?'

'Adrian, the programme editor had seen the photo on the Herald and Express and said he wants to incorporate an interview about my book with one about Princess Katrina and our life aboard. It's free advertising Ben. Radio advertising can be expensive.'

'Okay, I get that.'

'So, you're okay with it?'

'Looks like it comes with the territory. Not sure I could cope with a television appearance.'

'There's an idea. No, we can get some information about the cruise dates out over the radio. I can see my book not getting much of a mention. It's not until 25th January. A follow up from the Elberry Cove run and we could have another on 15th March incorporating a beach barbecue.'

'That would mean ferrying everyone to the beach.'

'We could do that. It would likely be yacht club members and we've got interest from the Paddle Steamers Preservation Society.'

'Will they want to barbecue?'

'Doesn't matter. We can replicate a meal aboard for those who want to stay aboard.'

'How much?'

I've costed it out and to cover fuel, food, and crew we'd need to charge thirty pounds and get bookings in the region of fifty minimum. We could plug the barbecue cruise at the radio interview and run an advertising campaign. I'll set it up on the website. Get some posters out and advertise straight after Christmas.'

'And what about the summer season?'

'There can be a restricted ferry service to Paignton and Brixham, during the week and a Sunday cruise to Dartmouth. A daily service risks a cost, over-run.'

'In bad weather conditions you have to factor in that numbers will be down.'

'There's plenty of titivating to paint work and deck seating to be installed on the fore and after deck. Otherwise. we're up to speed on the engine room side. That was the main concern. We're qualified to carry passengers during the months of March to September,' said Ben.

I have every confidence that my husband can get the deck side sorted by March.

'Lets's drink to a successful summer season of cruises aboard Princess Katrina,' then said Felicity.

They clinked cocoa mugs together to toast this. On noticing that the wheelhouse clock was at a quarter to nine Felicity exclaimed

'Look at the time, They need to be in bed.' Felicity hurried through the bridge door and down the companionway.

Ben switched the heater and overhead light off before he walked out on to the bridge. Berry Head light house flashed across the bay. National flags on poles along the pier no longer identifiable by their colours and design.

Ben turned to look back into the wheelhouse, which should have been in near total darkness. He saw on the wheelman's plinth, a white/ blue luminescent cloud like shape, that formed into a misty figure of a man in a sou' wester and long smock. Hands that formed from arms, could be seen to hold the spoke hands of the wheel. A misty, bearded head turned and Ben was sure there was a smile directed, to where he was stood on the bridge. The ghost-like head appeared to move back with ghostly eyes directed toward the compass in front. Ben transfixed, watched as this phantom cloud-like figure, then began to disperse, just like a light wave of a cloud in the sky might. It was dark again in the wheelhouse.

the end

Other Books by Sam Grant

Please check out these other publications by Sam Grant.
Follow blogs, poems and stories at
Samgrantpublications.wordpress.com
Sam Grant, Author – Facebook.

Atlantic Hijack (978-1-78222-291-0)
Action, mystery. Sea adventure in the South Atlantic
A secure orderly passage aboard a cargo liner is Ripped apart by a brutal terrorist attack. Author Sam Grant brings his professional seafaring experience to Bear in this thriller that sounds all too familiar from Our evening news bulletins.

Apprentice Mike Peters is finding his feet amongst a cast of nautical characters as the Albany Princess voyages to Montevideo. But the ship's personnel are not all that they make themselves out to be as revealed during a rapidly unravelling hijack in the South Atlantic.

River Escape (978-1-68222-574-4)
Sequel to *Atlantic Hijack.*
Action, mystery,
Venezuela: An oil terminal in the River Orinoco, Venezuela. Following on from a military coup. Mike's pressured efforts to prepare the tanker for the load of boiler oil – compromised by a refinery postponement.

An influential young woman, boards who starts calling, the shots?

Hidden identity of a rescued yachtsman and two female companions further compromises the ship's safety ...

Chilling Encounter by Sam Grant (978-1-78222-685-7)
Destination Lagos, Nigeria.
Refrigerated liner Albany Contessa on voyage – a part cargo of gold ingots, hidden within machinery cases, aboard.

Mike is the newly appointed Staff Captain.

A Coaster rescue endangers loves aboard and leads into a further attack with shooting, and need for Foreign Office intervention to avoid international conflict.

The latest in the Sam Grant series of adventures at sea, which include *Atlantic Hijack* and *River Escape.*

Dancing on the Beach (978-1-78222-431-0)
Romantic thriller – Second Edition 2023
Phillip Norton obtains summer work as a deckchair attendant in Batcombe. Previously he works at a bank in the City.

Part of Phil's duties are to deliver dairy cool boxes to the Sea View Hotel via the cliff railway. Soon he is into a heady romance with the receptionist.

But with cruise liners anchored off Batcombe Bay the Sea View not only hosts holidaymakers, but also has connections with a more sinister trade...

Persuasion's Price (978-1-78222-687-1)
Mystery thriller
A quiet market town in England is shattered by an explosive mix of gang rivalry and shady deals.

A family is torn apart and, with the involvement of the secret services, events take an unexpected and sinister turn.

Persuasion's Price
The Play (978-1-78222-870-7)
Play, in ten acts. Includes full script and stage instructions ready for rehearsal.
Drama group requires curtained stage.
Back stage management has six-scene preparation.
Cast of thirty-two, with possible, actor duplication for smaller parts.
Ninety minutes run time, plus interval.

Galactic Mission (978-1 78222-512-6)
Science fiction
It is 2110. In an advanced technological world of holograms transmitted by mobile phones; food made by a Maxi Maker, drone trays, clones and automata concierges, QUADRANT is the world government.

But the world is not at ease and relationships are put under strain.

James Walters is a sales manager for an international conglomerate, based in the UK. One day he encounters Adriana – "The Empress Adriana" – from the Galactic Command Force ...oh, and ruler of planet Earth and all Planets, surrounding the sun.

Inspiring sources thwart planetary conflict

Galactic Mission Part Two (978-1-78222-773-1

Science fiction, sequel to Galactic Mission

In this classic sci-fi adventure, the main characters from Galactic Mission, including the Empress Adriana, are working to divert comets away from Earth by firing a missile from Mars.

Adriana, has decided to stay in human form, but seeks a closer relation-ship with James, who prefers Lara. He backs away. Adriana is restricted in power. Although Captain Dryson and Alfredo – two android machines – carry out her instructions.

After the comets are directed away from earth, Galactic Force returns with Antar-XP200, and two new androids, to replace Adriana, on Mars. Adriana regains full power and a chosen group leaves for earth by spaceship with the intention of gaining control over Quadrant, who are returning, now that earth has been saved.

Short Story, Verse, Commentary

Colin H Coles (978-1-78992-000-2)

Pink blossom, daubed an avenue of cherry trees, caught in still air;

Near silence save for a buzz of spring bees. This, yes, I remember this From that visit to Broadhurst Abbey. It all began with that good feeling of being alive to nature's resplendent new life. I later promised brother Patrick, not to divulge my experiences at the Abbey, but...

Venue for a Delegation

He ran back along the wooden deck, in open necked shirt, best go ashore jeans and polished brown shoes...

'Captain, Captain,' he called out...

'What is it Bosun?'

'They're not coming back.'

'Do you want to stay then?'

'No Captain but they won't leave the bar!'

'Well, you'd better get on board then.'

Winter in New Jersey

Gentle waves, trickle tumble, tease dry sand....

Wind, tidal flow, fearsome rise and fall, contrasts, ray rippled sun dance, cross quiet scene.

Waves – Verse

Entertaining and horizon-expanding short Stories, poems, and observations.

Further poetry and short story publications by Sam Grant

Poems with themed notes (978-1-78222-464-8)
Love Starved by Electronics is a sonnet selected for a 'Sonnets for Shakespeare' anthology.
In *Riding Through Time* ghostly horsemen appear to ride down the ages.
Captured into their Realm – a meeting with an alien depicted in verse.
Eye of the Storm; The Time Makers Kingdom; Thankful Thoughts and *Spirit of Spring*. These are a few of the poems in this varied anthology.
Notes have been prepared and included by Sam Grant to give background information and set the poems in context.

Mists of Time (978-1-78222-708-3)
From epic poem to scary short story, *Mists of Time* entertains and enlightens. In the title poem, author Sam Grant takes us on a journey. Perhaps his journey, down a leafy lane to a farm in summer, off to sea and beyond.
Secret Cave is a short story informed by a love of sail boat sailing, a reflection from the author's young life, before the author embarked on a career in the Merchant Service.
Part One – Poems both in traditional and modern form.
Dramatic, but also light-hearted topics explored.
Part Two – Short stories.
Individual cameo chapters.

Sam Grant, Author

URL *amazon.com/author/grantsam*

samgrantpublications.wordpress.com

Books are available from good bookshops. Please give ISBN. And variously online from Amazon, Waterstones, Barnes & Noble.